Whispers in the Night

Bob Haider

Published by Bob Haider, 2024.

This is a work of fiction. Similarities to real people, places, or events are entirely coincidental.

WHISPERS IN THE NIGHT

First edition. July 21, 2024.

Copyright © 2024 Bob Haider.

ISBN: 979-8227404404

Written by Bob Haider.

To my dear friend, Ed Artl

Prologue

A tow truck moved slowly along a dark country road as the temperature dipped into the low twenties while wind gusts blew a menacing snow sideways across the road. Searching for a farmhouse amidst the darkness the driver turned on the bright lights in an effort to enhance his visibility, but when a flood of large snowflakes zoomed into the windshield, he quickly flicked the bright beams off.

Another man sat in the passenger's seat with a flashlight casting a narrow beam over a road map on his lap. In an attempt to get his bearings, he rolled down the window and aimed his flashlight into the darkness. As the snow whipped against his face, he squinted into the dark countryside, but absent the aid of city streetlights, the low powered beam of his flashlight proved futile. He shivered as he quickly rolled up the window in the poorly heated truck.

It had begun snowing at five o'clock in the morning. Four inches of snow had been predicted but it was now 4:30 in the afternoon and the white stuff had been falling unabated. A January snowstorm in Chicago is certainly not unique but before the wee hours of the next morning arrived more than 23 inches were destined to fall on this dreary day. It would be the largest single snowfall in Chicago history.

The only reason the tow truck was able to move through the day's accumulation was because it was fitted with a snow plow.

"Why the hell did we get a tow truck anyway, if we're not actually gonna tow the car when we get there?" asked the driver.

"I told you...to make it look like we're pickin' up a car."

"Oh," the driver nodded.

As his partner spotted a faint light, he yelled, "Turn right."

The driver eased into a right turn and they moved up a long driveway, the lighted windows of a farmhouse becoming brighter as they approached.

The man on the passenger's side peered out the window, and said, "Yeah, this is it. I can see the autos in a fenced in area. Let's go."

The driver pressed the breaks a bit too quickly and the tow truck skidded slightly to a stop. As the two men exited, a pair of snarling guard dogs slammed into the steel mesh fence barking ferociously while exposing their sharp white fangs.

"Damn! They scared the crap out of me!" yelled the driver.

"Don't worry; they can't get to us," said his partner. "They're penned in. Come on," he said, as they scaled the steps of the porch and knocked at the front door. The porch light flicked on, the door opened and an elderly man about sixty years old appeared.

"Evenin'," he greeted them, as he gazed over their shoulders at the tow truck. "My, it's an awful cold night to be out. Come on in and warm yourselves. My name's Ned Fillmore."

The two men nodded and entered.

Ned closed the door behind them and shouted toward the back of the house to his teenage son. "Billy? Put the dogs in the shed out back, would ya? Need to get them out of the way. A couple fellows are here to pick up a car."

"Okay, Dad," said Billy, as he threw on a coat on and exited through the kitchen's back door.

Ned turned to his two guests, and chuckled, "You certainly don't want any dogs snappin' at your heels while you're hookin' up an auto."

The two men nodded and noticed the large German-Shepherd lying on a throw rug in the living room beside the television set, and they could hear another dog barking from another room in the house.

Ned noticed their uneasiness. "Oh, we like dogs. One in back is in the bedroom, 'cause he's a bit excitable, but this one's more docile" said Ned, as he eyed the two men, and added, "I thought tow truck fellows always operated solo."

"Bad night," replied one of them curtly, his dark eyes emotionless.

"Oh, yeah, it would be good to have some company tonight in case something happens."

"Yeah," said the other without expression.

A woman entered the living room, and Ned introduced her. "This is my wife, Val. They're here to pick up a car," Ned informed her.

"You chose a heck of a night to come after it. Can I offer you some tea to warm your bones?"

"Well, if it's not any trouble."

"No trouble at all. It's already made," said Val, as she turned and headed for the kitchen.

When Billy reentered the kitchen, he stomped the snow from his boots and yelled, "Dogs are in the shed, Dad."

The two men eyed each other but now their expressions displayed a sickly smile and nodded silently. It was their signal to begin, as they reached inside their coats and pulled out silencer-laden semi-automatics.

The dog lying docilely beside the television was the first target.

Ned was their next victim.

The fate of Ned's wife and son quickly followed.

Chapter 1

October 2008, Washington, D.C.

The arc of the rising October sun cast a golden hue across Washington and bathed the massive Capitol Dome in morning sunshine. As Anthony Narducci walked through the Washington Mall, he paused momentarily alongside the Reflecting Pool, which had not yet been drained in preparation for the up-coming winter. He watched as a leaf fluttered lazily downward and joined the rainbow of autumnal color floating atop the tranquil pond. Hundreds of golden-brown, deep purples, and reddish orange hues mingled as autumn's leaves floated effortlessly atop the water—-pushed along by the tiny ripples created from a gentle morning breeze.

With the completion of his life-long assignment, Anthony flashed a crooked smile as he resumed his walk westward, a black satchel flung over his shoulder. The seventy-three-year-old moved with the aid of a cane necessitated by postponing a much-needed knee replacement. The cane helped to support his six-foot, one-inch, two-hundred-ten-pound frame and relieve the stress from his painful arthritic knee. Today both knees were especially painful.

The years had certainly taken their toll upon Anthony as evidenced by deep lines etched upon his weathered face. Time had robbed him of his once full mane of thick brown hair...now sparse and gray. His once keen and lively brown eyes looked tired as they sat deep within their sockets and reflected a demanding and stressful life.

As Anthony approached the far edge of the Reflecting Pool, he turned north toward the Vietnam Memorial. This was Anthony's first visit to the National Mall of Washington, D.C., and he had come here for one reason only—-to visit the Wall.

When he arrived at the Memorial, he stopped to peruse the book that provided him with the name he sought. When he spotted it, he made a mental note of the panel referenced upon which the name appeared.

As Anthony turned, he was immediately struck by the enormity of the Memorial. Two walls, each 246 feet in length, meeting at an angle in the middle. Fully seventy-two separate panels on each wall of shiny black granite that stretched out before his eyes and overwhelmed him.

Upon each panel were neatly etched the engravings...the names...58,209 names in total. That was an increase of fifty names since the Wall was completed in 1993. Divided into Eastern and Western panels the list of names started and ended at the vertex of the Memorial beginning with the year 1959 and arranged chronologically through 1975.

Like most Americans, Anthony heard many times the number of Americans killed in that horrible, senseless war, but he had no sense of the reality of that many deaths. It was an abstract number...until now.

"My God," he muttered in a muted whisper.

Despite the early hour, Anthony found he was not alone, as a half dozen people were stationed at various stages along the wall. They all moved slowly and respectfully as they visited the Memorial or were motionless in quiet reverence, as they stood before one of the panels that bore a familiar name.

As Anthony proceeded slowly down the gently sloping pathway, he felt as if he were entering the hushed silence of an outdoor mausoleum. One woman knelt before a panel as she paid her respects, and, as Anthony passed her, he could hear her moans of sorrow and saw tears running down her face. The passage of so many years had not diminished her grief while poised beside the wall.

Anthony walked past a young man who appeared to be in his early twenties. He stood silently, head bowed, before the lettering of names. Anthony surmised he was paying his respects to his grandfather perhaps.

Anthony moved to the vertex of the Memorial from which all names proceeded and stood in front of the panel he sought...01E. He perused the list of names by starting at the top and scanning downward to the fourth line until he spotted the one he was here to see...the third name from the left.

Anthony set his cane against the wall, and then slowly knelt on one knee, grimacing from the painful arthritis. Anthony reached out and brushed his right hand across the letters that stood half an inch high. When he did so, he saw the reflection of his own face staring back at him in the shiny black granite, as his features mingled with the lettering of the familiar name. He quickly raised his hand to his face to hide the moisture forming in his eyes and bowed his head in prayer.

Anthony whispered a short prayer to pay his respects. He couldn't remain on one knee long as he made the sign of the cross, grabbed his cane and pushed himself up. He checked his watch and saw it was a quarter past seven. By this evening, he would be on a non-stop flight to Rome where he planned to rest, relax and rejuvenate himself in the country of his ancestors.

Anthony turned toward the east and gazed at the massive dome of the U.S. Capitol glittering in the morning sunshine. While the flag atop the dome fluttered in an ever-increasing morning breeze, Anthony inhaled deeply and filled his lungs with the fresh crispness of autumnal air.

Anthony looked back at the thousands of names etched into the smoothly polished black granite, and, as if speaking to all of them at once, he whispered through his emotion. "They played parlor games with America's youth...except unlike when any of us were kids playing army man in the backyard you didn't come home for dinner one night."

Anthony swallowed hard to force back the emotional lump rising within him.

The mist returned to his eyes as he focused upon the name he had come to visit, and he spoke the young man's name in a throaty whisper.

He leaned his back against the wall and once again placed his cane against the black granite. He then pulled the dark satchel from his shoulder, opened it and removed a small tape recorder. He popped in a blank cassette. With his back still to the wall, he gingerly slid down against it until he was seated upon the pavement, his back resting against some of that panel's list of names.

Anthony flicked the button on the recorder, and, as he reflected upon the past fifty years of his life, he brought the microphone to his mouth...

Chapter 2

For me it all began in 1955 on the campus of William and Mary in Williamsburg, Virginia. After all these years I still remember that day very clearly. It was spring and the Williamsburg campus was alive with students and color. A variety of flowers were in full bloom and their sweet aroma mingled with the scent of freshly mowed grass while immaculately trimmed hedges around the contours of the campus displayed their lush greenery.

I was in the last semester of my senior year and the past autumn I'd sent out over fifty resumes in pursuit of prospective employment, and with just a couple of months remaining before graduation, I didn't know what I'd be doing yet.

Unlike so many others who were soon-to-be graduates hoping for just one job offer, my problem was quite the opposite. I interviewed with more than a dozen company representatives who visited me at campus and I had received fourteen offers of employment. My dilemma was to pick the right opportunity, the one that interested me the most, and the one that would afford me a lucrative career. I took the process of choosing a career very seriously, because, if I chose incorrectly, I would surely regret it. Back then, employees stayed with companies in many instances for their entire career, and my collegiate counselor said that the first job a person takes often sets the course of their life forever. I didn't know then how right he was.

My first class of the day had just ended and I had an hour before my next one, so I was heading to the student union where I planned to bone up on some vocabulary for one of my foreign language classes. I was surprised when an unfamiliar man approached me with an extended hand.

"Hello, my name is Sam."

Hesitatingly, I shook the man's hand. He was tall and lanky, and, though he was wearing a suit and tie, an air of discipline and authority emanated from him, as if he would be more at home in a military uniform than civilian clothes. His hair, cut very short in a crew cut, served to strengthen that perception.

"I'm visiting the campus today to speak with a few select individuals about future employment," he said.

"Oh?" I replied, as I didn't know if the man was referring to me or if he was merely going to ask for directions.

"I understand you're a straight A student."

"You know me?"

"Anthony Abednego Narducci. Your parents died in an automobile accident when you were eight years old. You were their only child and you spent the remainder of your youth in foster homes. With the death of your parents, you withdrew within yourself, didn't participate in sports, but buried yourself in your studies."

I stood there speechless in awkward surprise and felt very uncomfortable with the man's knowledge of my past. It felt creepy to me.

"We keep tabs on the people we wish to interview," he smirked. "As for you, you're graduating this spring after receiving a full scholastic scholarship to William and Mary where you have maintained an A average."

"Well, I did have a couple of Bs in the mix."

The man rolled over my correction without reference. "I understand you speak Russian fluently."

"I'm also fluent in Spanish and Italian as well as conversant in several Asian languages—-Chinese, Japanese, and a few dialects of Southeast Asia."

Another smirk flashed across the man's face. "Well, not much call for those others," he said, seemingly unimpressed with my academic credentials, which seemed odd since he'd made a point of mentioning my prowess in languages.

"Is there some place we could talk privately?" he asked. "I'd like to hear about your interests...what you see yourself doing after your graduation."

"Yeah, okay. Sure. I was just heading over to the student union. It shouldn't be very crowded this time of day and we could get a table that's fairly private."

"Yes, that would be fine."

As we walked the remaining two blocks to the student union in silence, my discomfort began to dissipate. Instead, I found myself intrigued this man knew so much about me. Rather than taking any offense, I felt flattered and very curious, even anxious, to hear what he was going to say next. He had a definite air of secrecy about him, but that only served to whet and pique my curiosity further.

When we arrived at the student union, he purchased a coffee for each of us and we headed toward the back.

"Yeah, we'll be able to talk privately here all right," he said as we sat down. He paused for a few moments while each of us prepared our coffee the way we liked it.

"So, do you have any idea of what or whom I represent?" he asked with a self-assured grin.

I could play that game too, I thought, as I replied, "Well, with all you seem to know about me, with that short haircut of yours, and your air of secrecy, I'd say you're with the government, specifically Army Intelligence, and that you're here for recruiting purposes."

From his reaction, I surmised he was impressed by my response, as his self-assured grin quickly widened.

"Not bad, Kid. You're wrong, but you're not far off the mark. I'm here to see you about possible employment all right, but not about joining Army Intelligence, so let me get right to the point."

I nodded with appreciation.

"By way of background, in 1947 Congress passed and President Truman signed the National Security Act, which among other things created the Central Intelligence Agency."

Mention of the Central Intelligence Agency didn't stir any reaction in me. Nowadays people hear the CIA mentioned and they immediately think of a dark, secretive, intelligence operation. Some think of the CIA as an intelligence arm of the U.S. Government whose sometimes-illegal clandestine activities through the years were brought to light by congressional inquiry and oversight in the mid-seventies. But in 1955 I didn't flinch when this fellow Sam referred to the Central Intelligence Agency.

"There are many different Intelligence organizations within the U.S. Government and I won't go into them now, as it's irrelevant to our discussion at hand. Anyway, when Eisenhower was elected in '52, he appointed John Foster Dulles as his Secretary of State, and his brother, Allen Dulles, as the head of the Central Intelligence Agency."

I nodded a bit as he spoke simply to show I was paying attention.

"Allen Dulles received a very large budget in order to get the CIA better organized and more up to speed and while doing so Mr. Dulles has greatly expanded the CIA. Originally, we recruited World War II veterans," he stated, without mentioning that many of those recruits were German Nazis from the war.

"That source of manpower, however, has been depleted, and we are now very much in need of bright, intelligent and dedicated young men as we continue to expand. We have positions to fill, but we're very selective about whom we interview and even more discerning about whom we hire. We do our homework. That's why I knew about you in advance. You see we check potential candidates first, because, if they don't measure up, we don't bother contacting them, and they never know we were looking into their lives. You should feel very proud, Anthony, because you are one of those select individuals in whom we are interested."

"Thanks," I nodded, as I took a sip of my coffee. I'd gotten up late this morning and didn't have time to grab a cup before my first class and it sure tasted good. As I set my cup down, I eyed the man seated across from me. I pondered what he'd said so far, which wasn't much...just a meager history of the genesis of the CIA and that the Agency was interested in me. In what capacity I didn't have a clue, and that was hardly enough for me on which to base a decision of employment. Nevertheless, I was more than mildly intrigued.

"You've mentioned that you're interested in me, but you haven't said anything about what the job entails."

"Oh, you're getting ahead of me, Anthony," he chuckled, as he brought his coffee cup to his mouth and eyed me while he took a sip.

"We're interested, yes, but before any offer of employment is on the table, you would need to take an aptitude test among other things."

He must have seen the effrontery on my face, because he responded quickly.

"Oh, it's not to see if you're smart enough. We already know that. You certainly have the intellectual capacity for the job. The test I'm referring to will tell us where your interests lay and what you're good at. It's a real shame that the vast majority of people never learn that about themselves."

"I'm not sure I follow you."

"Most people never take an aptitude test to see in which area they would excel. So, in that sense, you'll be one of the lucky ones. You see no matter how intelligent you are, you're going to be better at some things than others, and we'll want to know what those things are."

"I see."

"If a job offer follows, we could then match you with the right job that suits you. No promises though, because the competition is fierce for these jobs. You see, we test many more individuals than we hire."

I reached for my cup and took another sip of coffee as I absorbed what he said. Feeling a little cocky at being approached by a representative from the Intelligence arm of the U.S. Government, I replied, "No promises for you either, because I've already received fourteen job offers that I'm considering."

I could see immediately my comment didn't set well with him, as a disapproving smirk flashed across Sam's face, and he responded with some cockiness of his own.

"Let me tell you something, Kid. With all the competition for these plum jobs, the odds will be against you, but on the off chance we do make you an offer, and you don't like the sound of the job description, you can always say no," he said.

As he stared at me, I could see he was challenging me...daring me to decline at that point...but I merely nodded in understanding.

Chapter 3

That summer of 1955 I took that aptitude test and I must have done quite well because I was offered a job with the CIA.

The test results revealed in what I excelled and where my interest lay as well—-foreign languages—-but I could have saved us both a lot of time had the CIA merely asked. That bureaucratic arrogance should have given me a clue about the intelligence arm of the U.S. government...about any arm of the U.S. government for that matter.

I went through six weeks of basic training, which was quite grueling for someone who hadn't participated much in sports growing up. Then I had an additional eight weeks of training in counterinsurgency, and all of the training included becoming proficient in the use of various firearms. About ten percent of us received medals for the various levels of marksmanship, sharpshooter and expert as we were graded from the standing, kneeling and prone positions. Though I had never fired a weapon previous to that training, I earned a medal as an expert.

Every agent went through the same training so that if anyone was assigned a job in the field, the Agency didn't have to delay deployment...we'd receive instructions yes but no need for additional training. It all served to demonstrate the CIA was very serious about their agents and consequently we took our assignments seriously.

Allen Dulles was the Director of the CIA when I joined the Agency. A self-assured man he could speak to the President even if Ike was teeing it up on the prestigious Augusta National Golf Course home of the famed Masters Golf Tournament. Though the necessity of a visit to Georgia to interrupt the Chief Executive's golf game never arose, the point is if Allen Dulles desired to speak to the President, Eisenhower would take the call.

In Washington D.C. a man's power and influence are measured by his access to the President.

That access began in 1952 when the then newly elected President nominated John Foster Dulles as his Secretary of State. Shortly thereafter, the President appointed Dulles' brother, Allen Dulles, as the head of the CIA, and the Dulles brothers quickly became the most powerful duo of siblings in the country. John Foster Dulles, with the President's approval, set foreign policy and Allen Dulles augmented that foreign policy by carrying out covert, clandestine operations. It didn't take the brothers long to wield their enormous influence throughout the corridors of power in Washington, D.C. and around the world.

In 1954, in a decision that would have far reaching effects, President Eisenhower with the advice and direction of the Dulles brothers decided the United States would replace France in Southeast Asia and thus began America's involvement in Vietnam.

In April of 1955, just months before I joined the Agency, President Eisenhower authorized the CIA's first attempt to assassinate a foreign leader. The subject was Red China's Chou En-lai. Though the plan did not succeed, Allen Dulles was not entirely disappointed because of one overriding factor—-the precedent had been set—-and he was confident that future such endeavors would be successful.

The CIA was now officially involved in setting foreign policy through assassination of foreign leaders.

Of course, the U.S. spy organization didn't dirty their hands. They used intermediaries so they would have deniability in clandestine operations being careful not to become directly involved.

Among others, Cuba loomed on the horizon and would prove to be another example of such activity, but for the moment a different American organization was more interested in the island nation...an organization much more sinister.

Chapter 4

Today people hear the term Mafia and instantly think of organized crime and perhaps take it for granted everyone was always aware of the far-reaching extent of its evil tentacles in America.

Not so.

Oh, people in the city neighborhoods knew there was a criminal organization operating in their particular community. But for decades throughout the 1930's, 40's and for most of the 1950's America's head of law enforcement, J. Edgar Hoover of the F.B.I., refused to acknowledge the existence of the Cosa Nostra as a criminal organization in the United States. He refused to acknowledge there was a secret, organized criminal society; refused to acknowledge there was a National Crime Syndicate operating in America.

That would change on November 14, 1957 which became a seminal day in the history of organized crime in America.

A meeting was planned at the home of New York crime boss Joseph Barbara 200 miles northwest of New York City in Apalachin, New York which lies on the banks if the Susquehanna River. The crime bosses across America gathered on Barbara's 53-acre estate. A nation-wide crime syndicate that reached into nearly every facet of American life—-representing more than 25 cities—-the bosses of whom assembled to discuss several topics. The agenda included the garment industry, loan sharking, narcotics dealing, gambling, prostitution and casinos—-all of it controlled by Lucky Luciano and the Commission of mobsters he created.

The Commission, composed of the bosses, settled disputes among members within the crime family, and the main topic on the agenda for the Apalachin meeting was the replacement of Luciano as the boss of all bosses, since his deportation to Italy had occurred more than a decade earlier.

A conference of mobsters was not unique. Meetings had been called in previous years as well to discuss issues within the crime syndicate such as the Havana Conference in 1946 which among other things discussed a possible hit on mobster Bugsy Siegel.

What made this particular meeting in 1957 noteworthy was that local police noticed many expensive automobiles gathered in one place and began writing down license numbers. When they traced the autos to known criminals, the police raided the estate. Nearly sixty mobsters were arrested while more than forty others fled and got away.

The existence of a national crime syndicate in America was finally acknowledged.

Among those attending the meeting was Stefano Bonafacio, the Chicago operations boss with a cut in the Las Vegas casinos. He became noted as one of the cruelest mobsters in history due to gruesome tortures he ordered prior to the actual hit. It should be noted that Bonafacio did not do anything without the approval of his boss, Tony Accardo. Accardo operated behind the scenes being one of the smartest mobsters in history who possessed great instincts. He retired shortly before the Apalachin meeting and did not attend but continued to pull the strings in Chicago allowing Bonafacio to be out front and visible.

Carlo Marchetti was there as well. He controlled all of the Louisiana gambling operations by the late 1940's. He was also given a cut of the Las Vegas casinos in the 1950's as well. He operated as the crime boss of New Orleans and controlled the southwestern United States. He controlled the Latin American drug trade transported through Mexico and on into the U.S.A.

Salvatore D'Amato was also in attendance. He became the most powerful crime boss in Cuba who ran the narcotics and casino operations in Havana. He also controlled Florida and the southeastern seaboard of the United States for the importation of drugs from Europe and the Caribbean.

These men were among more than one hundred mobsters who attended the Apalachin conference and I was destined to learn much more about these mob bosses in the coming years.

During the late 1950's the American Mafia stood at the apex of their power, wealth and influence——until November 14, 1957 when their secret society was secret no more.

It is believed that the head of organized crime, Lucky Luciano had pictures as evidence of J. Edgar Hoover's homosexuality, and that's why Hoover, for more than three decades, wouldn't dare acknowledge the Mafia as an organization operating in America.

That was the power organized crime wielded at their apex when the highest law authority figure in America was relegated to nothing more than a pawn for their organization.

In fact, it was through this mob technique that Hoover learned to gather dossiers on politicians that served him very well in the future. Simply the inkling that Hoover might have personal information on various politicians got Hoover whatever he wanted and no American President dared defy him...or fire him.

Chapter 5

In 1959 on the day after New Year's, Salvatore D'Amato was at his Havana residence in Cuba. D'Amato had many business interests in Cuba which made him a very wealthy and powerful man, but he was soon to find his power was about to wane on that island.

The D'Amato criminal empire of prostitution, loan sharking, gambling, and drugs was not limited to the shores of Cuba. He controlled the entire southeast corridor of the United States from Florida, the Carolinas and even up into Virginia where the CIA headquarters were located.

D'Amato expanded and cast the tentacles of his powerful criminal empire into overseas interests as well. He had already expanded into several Latin American countries in concert with New Orleans crime boss Carlo Marchetti and together they were making contacts in Southeast Asia where America had established a presence in South Vietnam.

D'Amato's expansionist ideas were proving to be very lucrative both for himself and Carlo Marchetti. Though the New Orleans crime boss had teamed with the Florida mobster, Marchetti was nervous about his drug trade routes through Central America.

Both were suspicious of each other—-a crime syndicate trademark.

For the present, however, D'Amato was looking after his business interests in the wake of a growing revolution on the island of Cuba.

He was at his residence in Havana, seated in his study on January 2nd when one of his lieutenants approached him holding a telephone.

"Boss, Jimmy is on the line and he says it's real important he talk to you right away."

Salvatore grabbed the phone as he blew a puff of smoke from his Cuban cigar into the air that wafted upward, the gray smoke pausing as it hung aimlessly above his head.

"What's happening?"

"That revolutionary, Castro, he just took over!"

Unfazed by what he heard, and pulling another puff of smoke into his mouth, D'Amato asked, "Took over what exactly?"

"He took over the island, the country...the whole damn government boss!"

Now D'Amato's eyebrows upturned.

"He's nuts, boss! He announced he's diverting 50-60% of casino profits to Cuban welfare programs."

D'Amato's nostrils flared as he shot upright in his chair. His eyes narrowed into a laser-like stare of cold, dark loathing. The casinos in Havana were a source of huge sums of money to him.

"Those casinos are mine! Who does that bearded revolutionary think he is? He has no idea who he's messing with!" D'Amato snarled, as he slammed his fist against the table in hateful rage.

"You have to leave boss!"

"What?"

"You have to leave right now!"

"Why?"

"Castro is gathering up anyone and everyone he calls an undesirable. Don't even pack a bag. If you leave right now, you have a chance to get off the island but you can't delay. You've got to go now!"

Chapter 6

Castro was successful in seizing the reins of power in Cuba in part due to American assistance, but it didn't take the Eisenhower administration long to realize Fidel Castro had duped America in his revolutionary overthrow of the Batista regime. Castro had managed to infuriate both the U.S. Government and organized crime in one fell swoop.

A few months after Castro's takeover, John Foster Dulles resigned as Secretary of State on April, 15, 1959 because of a bout with cancer. He was awarded the Medal of Freedom and died shortly thereafter on May 24, 1959.

Allen Dulles wasted no time in filling the void from his brother's death as he advised President Eisenhower on what needed to be done about Castro and Cuba.

It was under this backdrop in the summer of 1959 when I was in my fourth year with the CIA that my immediate supervisor asked me to accompany him to Langley, Virginia to brief Allen Dulles on the latest intelligence data. Normally, the information would be sent up the chain and a low-ranking employee such as me wouldn't brief the Director, but as I would soon learn there was a specific reason for me being there. Unbeknownst to me, there was an assignment for which I was being considered and the Director himself wanted to check me out so to speak.

As we were escorted into the Director's office and introduced, the Director arose from behind his desk. I was surprised to see he was much shorter than the mythical stature those of us in the Agency had visualized him to be. He greeted us, shook our hands and gestured for each of us to take a seat and he sat back into his high backed, black leather chair.

"I understand you have some information," the Director came right to the point looking directly at me with his beady eyes.

"Yes," I nodded nervously, as I pulled some papers from my briefcase. "We have reliable data of intercepted communications that the government of Cuba is making overtures to the Soviet Union for economic, political, and military aid," I informed him, as I felt my voice crack nervously at being in the presence of the Director for the first time.

"Let me see those," he said, as he grabbed the papers from my grasp.

The Director fingered his thin Errol Flynn-like mustache as his eyes narrowed in on the intelligence data.

As he leafed through the briefing, he began to nod. He looked up at me with his steely stare. "Are you sure?"

"Positive," I replied with emphatic confidence while praying to God I was indeed correct.

"What makes you so certain," Dulles asked skeptically?

"I'm fluent in both Russian and Spanish among other languages, and I know very well what the original cables said after we decoded them. I know their meaning," I replied confidently.

The Director turned his glance toward my supervisor. "I'll have to brief the President," he said, as he arose, which gave me the distinct impression he was going directly to the Oval Office and had immediate access to the President.

The Director looked right into my eyes, and said, "Anthony Narducci," saying my name out loud. "I remember now. You're one of the fellows we recruited directly out of college."

"Yes, Sir...William and Mary," I answered, flattered the Director knew that and I had a serious case of hero worship at that moment.

Sometime later I was brought back to reality when I learned the Director routinely received advance information on every individual who came to his office—-he made it a rule to always be briefed on the briefer.

"Ah, Williamsburg," the Director nodded.

"Yes, Sir," I acknowledged.

"So, how long have you been with us?" he asked, though he already knew the answer.

"Four years, Sir."

"Time flies when you're serving your country. Make no mistake, Narducci. Yours is one of those rare jobs in which a person can actually serve his country," he said, as he glanced back at the report and nodded his approval of my assessment of the situation in Cuba.

"Good work, Narducci."

"Thank you, Sir," I replied in appreciation and great pride.

"If you learn anything else, I want to know about it immediately...no matter what time of day...and I'm not saying that as a mere figure of speech. I want to know!"

"I understand, Sir."

"Very well," he nodded repeatedly and added, "Be ready at a moment's notice to do some field work, Narducci."

"I'm always ready, Sir."

Dulles liked that response, as he nodded approvingly.

"Where would you like me to go, Sir?"

"That you won't know until the time comes...if the time ever comes at all," he answered in a voice that sounded irritated at my probing.

"Yes, Sir," I said, as I purposely kept my responses brief.

Chapter 7

In the summer of 1959 prior to the presidential primaries of 1960, Chicago mobster Stefano Bonafacio had a room booked at a Kansas City, Missouri hotel.

When the mobster heard a knock at the door, he glanced at his watch; his appointment was exactly thirty minutes early. Bonafacio smirked as he took a drag on his Cuban cigar and blew the smoke upward over his head. Bonafacio knew his underlings would answer the door, but he in another room in the suite would make his guest wait until the appointed time of their meet.

Bonafacio held the Cuban tightly between his teeth as he grabbed a newspaper, walked into the bathroom and sat down on the toilet.

The man was patted down in the doorway and when the underlings were satisfied, he was unarmed they directed him into a chair. This was a very wealthy man who represented one of the 1960 presidential candidates. He was accustomed to calling the shots in his world of money and power, but he would sit patiently until the Chicago mobster was ready to see him, because he knew the drill. He knew how mobsters operated, and he knew many of their idiosyncrasies from having dealt with them years ago in garnering his wealth.

Fully forty-five minutes after he arrived, Bonafacio exited the bathroom and entered the adjoining room still wearing his gray fedora in the hotel and greeted his old colleague.

"So, how's the bootlegging business these days?" the mobster chuckled.

The man representing the Kennedy campaign laughed as well. "I wouldn't have any idea how that business is doing nowadays."

"Once a crook, always a crook," Bonafacio retorted.

"You won't hear any denial from me on that score," the man smiled.

"So, what'll you have?" Bonafacio asked, as he approached the wet bar.

"Scotch...neat," he replied.

As Bonafacio prepared their drinks, he said, "I prefer bourbon; I heard once that democrats drink bourbon, so I'm surprised with your choice," he scoffed.

"Sometimes you have to play both sides to win," the man laughed though he was quite serious.

As Bonafacio turned and handed a glass to his former acquaintance in crime, he toasted, "Here's to a Democratic victory in 1960."

They clanked their glasses, swigged back a gulp, and the man said, "To that end is precisely why I wanted to meet with you."

Bonafacio smiled knowingly. "Yes, well, I imagined you wanted some kind of favor or you wouldn't have asked to see me," Bonafacio got quickly to the point of the requested visit.

"Not exactly," he said. "A favor is something that is granted gratis...that is until such time as another favor can be granted in return."

"So, if not a favor, what did you want to see me about?" Bonafacio asked.

"I always liked your style Stefano. You always got right to the point," he complimented him.

"Yeah, I'm a busy man," he responded seriously with a bit of irritation, though his casualness in making his guest wait was noted.

"I appreciate that so I'll get right to the point as well. "I wanted to see you about a job, a task if you will. It's not a favor; I'm willing to pay if it's performed properly."

"I'm listening," said Bonafacio, as he took a sip of his scotch.

"The official announcement for his presidential candidacy will be in January as is the custom for presidential candidates."

Bonafacio listened but made no indication either through his eyes or his body language that he was impressed.

"The first democratic primary is March 8th in New Hampshire. We'll win that. We have an enormous ground campaign of volunteers and we've got the money."

"So, what do you need me for?" Bonafacio asked.

"In that state we won't need you but it's my responsibility to look ahead, to see if there is a place where we can use your help. There will be other primaries on the road to the nomination. Wisconsin on April 5th, Illinois April 12th, Massachusetts and Pennsylvania both on April 26th and Indiana May 3rd. We're in good shape in all of them with our party's bosses along with the governors, senators and representatives."

"Yeah...so..." Bonafacio remarked.

"On May 10th it looks promising in Nebraska but we may have a problem with West Virginia on the same day. West Virginia is heavily anti-Catholic," he explained.

"So?"

"We're Catholic."

"Humph," Bonafacio scoffed, "so am I. What about it?"

"The party bosses in West Virginia are lining up with protestant Humphrey."

"They like Hubert?" Bonafacio asked with some surprise.

"Yeah, and that's where you come in."

"How's that exactly?" Bonafacio inquired.

"We can't afford to lose any of the primaries. No one is going to win enough delegates in the primaries alone to win on the first ballot, but a loss in the primaries would show vulnerability and we could then lose when the convention votes. I want your help with the West Virginia unions, and like I said, it wouldn't be a favor."

"And if we help and your candidate loses anyway?"

"We can negotiate a price and we can structure your fee so that you get more if we win the primary...a lot more."

Bonafacio smirked. "Is that your way of saying you don't' trust me?"

"No, that's my way of saying I don't trust anyone," Joe laughed.

Stefano nodded with the beginnings of a smile.

"It also means you have a stake in the outcome...an incentive so to speak. The better the candidate does, the better you do."

"Or vice versa," Bonafacio mused.

"We do have some time but the reason I contacted you now about this is that these matters do take time to organize."

"Hmm, yeah," Bonafacio agreed.

"But you get the unions to back him and he wins...,"

Bonafacio nodded. "Yeah, let me think about that. I'll get back to you. Ten days all right with you?" he asked.

"That would be fine," he smiled, as he extended his hand.

Whether the candidate was ever told about this meeting is unknown. What is known is that Senator Kennedy faced the religious issue head on, when he said, "I refuse to believe that I was denied the right to be president on the day I was baptized."

He won the union vote decisively and he won the primary overwhelmingly by winning 60.8 percent of the vote to Humphrey's 39.2 percent.

Oh, and by the way, despite how 'the job' was explained, Bonifacio made it clear—-it was considered a favor, which meant it would be called in at some point in the future.

Chapter 8

The fifties were a time of great paranoia...paranoia that verged on hysteria. When I came on board, the country was not far removed from the Red Scare of the McCarthy era, and those accusations aimed at people within the State Department that they spied for the Red Menace lingered long after the United States Senate Censured Senator Joe McCarthy.

For additional understanding and insight, one need only look at America's Interstate Highway system. It was not constructed for citizens to travel freely and enjoy the breathtaking panoramic beauty of America, though that certainly was an ancillary benefit. The Interstates were actually built as a means to evacuate American cities—-in case of a nuclear attack.

By the summer of '59, Communist paranoia was firmly entrenched within the Washington establishment and the American psyche as well. Call someone a communist and it was the worst thing you could ever say about them. But there was a dichotomy. The '50's were also a time in which an arrogant America believed it could do whatever it wanted to do—-whenever it wished to do it. With John Foster Dulles now deceased, the President relied on the expertise of Allen Dulles all the more.

"America cannot afford nor can we allow a Communist country to exist ninety miles from our shores, Mr. President. Executive Action must be initiated against the Marxist leader to remove him from power," Dulles advised the Commander in Chief.

Ike hesitated.

Dulles had expected President Eisenhower to be uncertain about such a policy and he was fully prepared to explain.

"Further action against Castro would occur on two simultaneous fronts. First, an invasion by Cuban exiles will be launched in which no Americans would be involved. The exiles will be fully trained but at secret bases. Only after the exiles had landed would America lend air cover which could be justified as American support for Cuban freedom fighters against a repressive and hated Communist dictator," he explained, as the President listened.

"Second, in an even more clandestine operation, the mob would be enlisted against the Cuban dictator. With the millions of dollars lost when Castro shut down their casinos and their other illicit businesses in Cuba, the mob has a great motive for wanting Castro dead. And again, Mr. President, no government involvement," Dulles quickly added.

If Eisenhower authorized the operation, Dulles knew he'd be making a deal with the devil but he was aware there was precedent. The players were different but America had collaborated with the mafia during World War II against Nazi Germany...and that was merely fifteen years prior. Still, the President hesitated. Castro was not Hitler.

"Our hands would not be dirtied, Mr. President, and no one ever need know of America's participation. The United States and everyone within the government would have plausible deniability," said Dulles.

Allen Dulles won out and persuaded the Commander in Chief to act against Castro.

President Eisenhower in the second term of his administration and less than a year and a half before the election of 1960 when a new administration would come to power in Washington authorized the overthrow of the Castro regime in Cuba. Assassination of the Cuban leader was at the top of the list.

Almost since its inception America has been preoccupied with the Caribbean Island of Cuba, but if the United States has suffered because of the close proximity of Cuba to our shores, one would be hard pressed to cite examples of any injury to our national prestige. With the hindsight of history, contracting for a hit on Castro is quite laughable since that gray bearded old coot outlived a string of presidents. But in 1959 combined with the paranoia of the times, the obsession over Cuba won out.

Chapter 9

Shortly after briefing the Director, I was assigned to the CIA station outside Miami, Florida. I was to interface with the Cuban exiles our government was training to overthrow the Castro regime. I could tell you I was there to assist in training so my assignment would sound more glamorous and that it would be in the nation's best interest, but in actuality I was there for one reason only—-I spoke fluent Spanish. Not many Agency employees did and we needed to keep the operation...Operation Mongoose which was the code name for the Cuban invasion...within the agency. I was to act as a translator so the Cubans would understand exactly what we wanted them to do...so much for a glamorous assignment.

Florida was not a pleasurable experience for me. The CIA didn't have the best of facilities for these guys in the camps outside Miami. Most were unshaven and hadn't bathed in God knows how long. On top of that, in the heat and humidity of a Florida summer you couldn't walk fifty yards without becoming drenched in your own sweat. I'll let you imagine how pungent the air was in an enclosed tent with those guys.

Ian Fleming's James Bond spy novels were popular in 1959 and in the spy series Bond could do the impossible. Real life wasn't that way and I would soon learn the CIA often couldn't even do the basics. History would bear that out. After decades of supposedly gaining experience in gathering intelligence, the CIA would be caught completely unaware again and again. The uprising in Iran when the Shah was overthrown and hostages were taken in 1979 caught the CIA totally off guard. Nor did the Agency know of the uprisings in Poland, Lithuania, and Czechoslovakia when those Eastern Bloc countries broke from the Soviet Union and the granddaddy of them all—-the collapse of the Berlin Wall—-i.e. the demise of the Soviet Union—-caught the CIA by complete surprise.

The Agency didn't have a clue any of those events were coming and that's just a smidgeon of what we didn't know.

I don't think people today fully appreciate the utter magnitude of the CIA's incompetence. The Soviet Union was the motivation behind the creation of the CIA. The Soviet Union was the very reason for the Agency's existence. When you understand that gathering intelligence on the Soviet Union was the CIA's top priority during the Cold War, you can begin to grasp how poorly the CIA functioned when their meager intelligence gathering apparatus couldn't even detect an event as momentous as the downfall of the Soviet Union itself. Oh, we knew their economy wasn't doing well, but that was the extent of our expertise. We didn't have a clue the Soviet Union was about to implode.

Is it any wonder why in later years the CIA became synonymous with incompetence?

Many years later, the phrase, 'it's a slam dunk, Mr. President,' would forever be changed in the American lexicon from an ironclad fact—-to a phrase synonymous with mistakes, incompetence and misinformation.

As for the mob, they would be in bed with the CIA for years as the Agency attempted to work hand in glove with the mob to bring down Castro, but that wasn't exactly unique. The OSS, the forerunner of the CIA, used the mob during World War II. Who could blame the government for enlisting the assistance of the mob? Is there anyone who wouldn't have approved of an assassination of Hitler to end his madness and stop the carnage of World War II?

That type of black and white choice is easy...assassinate Hitler; kill the monster. The problem arises when the government starts choosing subjective targets...gray targets as we call them. I thought Castro was one of those gray targets.

As it turned out, through all the decades that Castro was in power, he was nothing but lint.

It really makes one scratch his head and wonder what all the fuss was about. Anyway, the mob was involved all right, but not in the way a lot of people think. And you'll understand what I mean by that later.

Chapter 10

Through my immediate supervisor, word was sent that I was wanted on another assignment. The CIA did not discuss upcoming assignments with its agents in enclosed rooms—-wary of bugs planted either by the Soviets or by Hoover's FBI. Yeah, Hoover was always trying to dig up dirt on anyone and any organization. Maintaining dossiers on Americans from every walk of life kept Hoover in power and other governmental agencies were not immune. The CIA neither trusted nor cooperated with Hoover's FBI and vice versa. Over time, that spirit of non-cooperation became embedded within the intelligence agencies, and the consequences of that non-cooperation would have disastrous effects years later on 9/11.

I got a respite from the drudgery of the camps as I was sent to Miami for a week of meetings. After one of those meetings concluded one day, my immediate supervisor approached me and simply said, "Let's take a walk."

We headed outside onto the sidewalk and walked south. Across the street on our left, the large sprawl of South Beach stretched out to meet the Atlantic. It was a clear day and the sun reflected off the rippling water and flickered in millions of tiny sparkles.

As we passed the News Café on our right and continued south, my supervisor came to the point.

"Pack a bag, Narducci. You're going to Hollywood."

When you work for the CIA, you don't get to choose where you're going or on what assignment you'll be employed. You go where you're told to go. In that sense it's just like the Army. You get your orders and you go, but I have to say it wasn't any hardship for me. I was so thrilled to hear I was getting out of the sweatbox of Florida that I let out a whoop I'm sure could be heard for blocks.

"Hey! Take it easy, relax. It'll only be for a couple of days and then you're to report back here and resume your duties as a translator."

I didn't care. I was ecstatic because I could get out of Florida if only for a couple of days. How anyone can spend a summer in the sweltering humidity of Florida by choice I'll never understand—-even if not by choice. That humidity is enough to make a person go AWOL.

My supervisor handed me a small envelope, and said, "Here's a round-trip plane ticket to Los Angeles. You're to see a man. There won't be anything in writing. There won't be any record of your verbal discussion. If you divulge what is discussed..."

"That won't ever happen," I emphatically interjected.

My supervisor kept right on talking. "Everything will be denied and you'll be finished as a CIA employee, plus you'll go to jail for a very long time for breaking the non-disclosure agreement."

I guess because of my young age and the fact that I'd never been in the field he felt obliged to explain such things to me.

When I learned the nature of my assignment and the man with whom I would meet, I was stunned. It wasn't like I was removed from the situation and reading about it in a newspaper article or watching a movie and knowing I could get up at any time and leave the theatre. Yeah, it was like an out of body experience. I was going to be in the middle of it, very much involved, and with no option of leaving. Looking back with the aid of hindsight, it was then that I began to become disenchanted with the CIA...hell...with the entire apparatus of the U.S. intelligence community.

There was a surreal atmosphere that existed within the CIA at that time. It was like the Agency was playing a parlor game and the entire world was a giant game board—-a video game in modern parlance—-while the CIA and the U.S. government arrogantly thought they controlled every aspect of the game. They made the rules as they went along, and then broke those rules whenever it suited them. It was a Machiavellian enterprise through and through. Cheat, lie, steal and commit murder...whatever the State thought necessary to protect and defend a free and independent America was fair game. It was never an issue whether the American State was ever wrong because there was never any concern there would ever be any consequences for what any of us might do. Break the law...it didn't matter...we were the CIA. We were protecting America.

Because arrogance carries a firm belief of the incapability of ever making a mistake, arrogance is an extremely corrosive, dangerous quality in those who wield power. After all, the State is merely individuals, people who are in a position to wield power.

In discussions with other CIA operatives, I learned a lot about other illegal operations that were being planned as well.

Surprised that we talked amongst ourselves? It's one of the great myths about the CIA that agents never talk. Well, to be very clear, we don't talk to outsiders, but you get a group of us CIA agents together, and we'll chatter more than a bunch of frat boys bragging about their latest conquests on sorority row. Internally, we all knew what was going on.

Chapter 11

That afternoon I flew to Los Angeles and checked into a hotel. My instructions were to simply go to the Brown Derby where the meet was scheduled, tell the maître d' my name and a man would meet me there. I was not furnished his name.

The next day well before the designated time, I headed to the Brown Derby. I didn't want to be late for my first field assignment so I arrived thirty minutes ahead of the appointment.

Originally, Hollywood Director Cecil B. DeMille conceived The Brown Derby with its domed roof and it soon became a gathering place for Hollywood movie stars. The Brown Derby was in its heyday in the '40's and '50's and that domed roof actually served a practical function. Water was pumped up to the top of the dome and then gravity took over, the water ran down the sides into a moat below, then recycled to the top again. The purpose was to cool the building and thus the occupants inside. It worked. The Brown Derby became one of the first air-conditioned buildings in the country...or should I say water conditioned. Anyway, that's why so many Hollywood types frequented the place in the 40's and 50's. The Brown Derby was where the cool people gathered to stay cool in the California heat.

When I entered, I immediately noticed the ornate oval bar in the center of the restaurant. The bar had been featured in a scene from the 1945 film, *Mildred Pierce,* starring Joan Crawford. That was the movie for which she won the Best Actress Oscar. I never cared for her as an actress but here I was where they made the movie.

I gave the maitre d' my name as planned and he immediately escorted me to a private booth where burgundy velvet curtains hung and could be swung closed for additional privacy. I left them open as I sat down and waited for my appointment to arrive.

About twenty minutes after the appointed time, a man casually walked in and took a seat opposite me. He didn't look hurried and I got the distinct impression he wanted to be fashionably late so that I understood who was calling the shots at this meeting.

He wore sunglasses which he didn't bother to remove. Attired in a light gray suit tailored perfectly to the contours of his physique and he wore a pale blue shirt accented with a lavender tie. I learned later the sunglasses went hand in hand with his persona. He thought of himself as a Hollywood type. He was the one who arranged entertainment at the mob-controlled casinos in Vegas, and before that in Havana when the mob controlled the casino shows in Cuba, so he spent a lot of his time in Hollywood. He spoke with the entertainers and their agents and arranged dates and contracts for the Vegas shows. Since he considered himself a Hollywood type, he even invested some of his own money in the movies...if you can ever really refer to a mobster's money as his own money. I never heard whether his investment in the movie business paid off for him, but he enjoyed spending time in Hollywood where he met and mingled with movie stars and entertainers.

When it came to the mob bosses, he was a kind of freelance fellow. He worked for the big four bosses out of New York, Miami, New Orleans and Chicago. Since the various mob families weren't warring, it wasn't a problem for him to be affiliated with all of them.

He reached into his coat and pulled out a gold cigarette case, removed a cigarette and lit it. He was smooth alright. It must have been due in part to all that time he spent with celebrities. He kind of acted that way—-like he was somebody.

He sat and eyed me in silence for a considerable time. He didn't actually glare at me or look upon me with suspicion. He merely looked at me with a blank stare, which made me feel very uncomfortable though I tried not to show it.

"So, who the fuck are you?" he began the conversation immediately attempting to intimidate me and put me on the defensive, but I didn't let it bother me.

"Anthony Narducci," I answered flatly.

A smile flashed across his face, as he said, "Oh, Narducci. Well, that explains it...why they sent such a young punk as the messenger."

"And you are?"

His smile quickly vanished and transformed into an ugly snarl.

"You're pretty green, aren't you, Kid?"

I eyed him but didn't answer.

"Let me explain something to you. You don't ever ask someone in my line of work for his name. If I want you to know who I am, I'll tell you. Those who ask us our names make us very suspicious," he said, and in so doing explained one of the many Mafia codes to me.

In my briefing in Florida, I was informed the man I would meet was a made-man in the lingo of the Mafia. That meant to a large extent he was protected by higher ups within the Mafia, which didn't necessarily translate into a long life, as they could easily change their minds if given a reason, or if even the suspicion of a reason arose.

Not everyone who is killed by the Mafia is someone who has done something overtly unforgivable. Many hits are carried out because the bosses are nervous about someone whether they have reason to be or not...like someone who knows too much. If the bosses get nervous about someone, you can bet that guy will likely be the target of a hit.

Paranoia runs very deep in the Mafia and with good reason. Paranoia keeps them alive...at least for a time anyway.

The man who I would later learn was Johnny Pistelli didn't seem to stay angry at me very long though, as his snarl quickly evaporated, and he asked, "How old are you, Kid?"

I didn't want to get into exchanging banter with him about me, or my age, so I reached out, grabbed the velvet curtain and emphatically swung it closed.

As I eyed him now in silence, he stared right back at me with a steady grin on his face. I took the initiative and immediately steered the conversation to the point of the meeting while speaking quietly so as not to be overheard beyond the curtains.

"The U.S. government wants Castro dead," I said in a whisper.

"Whoa, that's blunt and to the point," he laughed loudly.

I was a bit taken aback but I continued on as if I hadn't been, and said, "We believe that there are those who share the same desire."

That took the grin off his face. "Damn straight!" he said with angry assurance and the sound of hate in his voice.

"We want to know if you could recommend someone for the job."

His countenance reflected the gravity of what I said. "You do get straight to the point, don't you, Kid? You don't beat around the bush. I'll say that for you." Then his grin returned, "I like your style, Kid."

I refrained from saying anything more, preferring to let him think about what I'd already said, as I waited patiently for an answer.

"I'll need to know how much you're offering, that is, if I might know someone who may be interested."

"$150K per person for as many people as you deem are needed...within reason."

He whistled.

"That's $150,000 for each man...if you feel you'll need more than one man for the job. We're leaving that up to you. Of course, the fee is payable upon results."

"The fee would be payable up front," he snarled.

"That's not up to me," I stated.

"Just telling you the way it is, and by the way, 150 is about fifteen times the going rate, Kid. You know what you're doing?"

The amount of money that America offered for a job was part of the obscenity of the American Government's psyche. Why pay ten thousand, when you can offer $150,000? The belief is that it makes people believe you're serious about what you're requesting if you offer much more than the going rate, and, the theory being is it lends a sense of urgency to your request as well.

The fact is it has the detrimental tendency to make Americans look very foolish. Government officials would overpay time and time again through the years. In most recent memory offering 25 million dollars to any Afghanistan for capturing or killing Osama bin laden. Offering such sums of money was more than obscene, however, because it showed how out of touch America was. In the case of bin laden, the $25 million was offered to people who would be lucky to earn a few bucks a day—-that is if they were able to make a living at all in that country.

"You guys must want Castro badly," he said.

"Yeah, well, like I said, we think other people want him just as badly as we do, if not more so."

For a time, he appeared to ponder the proposal without saying anything.

I pressed him. "Well? Anyone come to mind?"

He shot me a steely glare. He was not accustomed to being pressed by anyone, especially not a young inexperienced punk which is how he thought of me.

Slowly, he began to nod, the grin reappearing on his face. "Like I said, I like your style, Kid. I'll tell you what. I might know someone, but I can't give you an answer today, and I'm not going to give you any names."

I nodded that I understood.

"I'll run your proposal by some people I know. How's about I meet you back here one week from today, same time?"

I thought about my two days in Hollywood being extended to a week before I had to go back to the sweltering heat of Florida. I could tell my supervisor that the guy I spoke with told me to sit tight and that he'd get in touch with me...that I was told it could be a day, a week, or longer before I heard from him.

I quickly answered trying to hide my enthusiasm. "Yeah, a week from today, I think that would be fine."

For the life of me, I have no idea why I was selected for an assignment as sensitive as this, especially since I had no experience in the field. I certainly didn't need my fluency in languages to carry out this assignment, though I could have spoken Sicilian if the man I met had wanted to play it extra safe. Maybe it was because Allen Dulles took a liking to me from that one briefing...perhaps. Though another reason could have been that I was young and expendable in case something went wrong, and no one with any experience to speak of would be sacrificed.

It was more likely however that Johnny Pistelli was right. Maybe the reason I was selected to carry out this assignment instead of someone more experienced was because of a very simple and basic explanation—-because my last name ended in a vowel.

Chapter 12

Back in my Hollywood hotel room that evening I waited after phoning the number on the card that the maitre d' handed me on my way out of The Brown Derby. He'd told me there'd be no charge as it was compliments of the man from my business meeting.

It was only thirty minutes after I made the call that I heard a knock. When I opened the door, smiling at me from the hallway in a tight-fitting white dress was a platinum blonde. She was absolutely luscious, the cleavage of her full breasts protruding above the cut of her dress.

"Hi. I'm Christie," she smiled sweetly. "You called?"

I must have stammered like a teenager. "Yeah, yeah, come on in," I said trying not to drool on myself.

As she stepped inside, she glanced around the room and as she did so I noticed that she was carrying a small black overnight bag.

"This is my first time at this particular hotel. It's nice," she said, with a smile of approval, as she placed her overnight bag on the bed and sauntered up to me. She didn't waste any time, as she put her arms seductively around my neck and smiled softly flashing her pearly white teeth.

I looked into her blue eyes and wanted her more than anyone I'd ever seen in my life, as I felt the warmth in my groin beginning to rise. She moved her mouth to mine, and, as she kissed me, she emitted a breathy moan.

She pulled back and reached for her overnight bag.

"If you'll excuse me for just a moment, I'll slip into something that I think will be very much to your liking.

I swallowed hard and pointed to the bathroom. "You can change in there."

I watched her as she walked away, her hips sashaying ever so slightly with each step. My knees felt wobbly as I sat down on the edge of the bed and anxiously awaited her return. The seconds passed like minutes, as my manhood swelled in anticipation thinking about what awaited me.

When she opened the bathroom door and stepped back into the room, my mouth fell open in lustful anticipation. She stood as if posing for me, and I began a visual tour of her body. I started with her feet on which she wore white high heels. Sheer nylons adorned her shapely long legs, and, as I scanned higher up her slender figure, I saw that the nylons ended at a red garter belt and red panties. Continuing upward I saw her full breasts were partially covered with a sexy red brassiere and over it all a full-length sheer see-through red nightgown that she held open in the front affording me a lustful view.

I approached her as she moved toward me and pressed her body against mine and I gave her a long, deep kiss. She put her hands on my chest and pushed me gently and continued pushing, backing me up until I fell backwards onto the bed. She moved on top of me and reached for my belt, unfastened it, and opened my trousers. As she reached into my shorts and pulled my tool to the surface, I could feel the cool air greet it, which was soon replaced by the warmth of her breath, as she began working on me. Her tongue was absolutely magical.

That night, in my first encounter with a woman furnished by the mob, I began to realize that I could never envision myself settling for anyone less than a woman like her.

Women were just one of the tools the mob employed to draw you into their web.

Chapter 13

As a CIA agent with access to any number of criminal files, I soon learned a great deal about the ways of mobsters. For instance, a lot of folks think it's some kind of silly quirk that members of the mob have carried those goofy nicknames, but there's a very specific reason for that, though it's most certainly outdated now. It started back in the old days when mobsters believed, in their own psyche, that if the authorities didn't know their last name, they could remain hidden in anonymity. That's the reason that Johnny Pistelli at the Brown Derby got so agitated when I asked who he was. They're very guarded about giving out their names especially to someone they don't know. Even when speaking amongst themselves, they rarely refer to one another by name and sometimes speak in a kind of code for fear they are under surveillance and being bugged. That's the way it was when the man I met in Hollywood contacted his boss for a meeting in Las Vegas.

Pistelli placed a phone call from a public telephone shortly after exiting the restaurant. His contact had risen steadily in the mob over the years and was based in Chicago...Stefano Bonafacio. His arena of power was the Midwest...Chicago, St. Louis, Detroit and Milwaukee...though it also included Las Vegas. Among other things, the Chicago Outfit ran the skimming operation of the mob-controlled Vegas casinos, which had become a very lucrative business for organized crime through the years. And that explains why they were so angry and vowed vengeance against Castro when they lost their Havana casinos.

Most Americans have the mistaken impression the mob controlled all the Las Vegas casinos when the American crime syndicate was at its peak of power, but the truth is the syndicate never exceeded four casinos at any given time. Of course, that was back when there were fewer casinos but the number of casinos was never near what people thought they controlled.

When Stefano Bonafacio came on the line, Johnny Pistelli from the Brown Derby merely said, "Meeting, next, S."

"Got it," said Bonafacio and they both promptly hung up.

Meeting meant he needed to speak to Bonafacio about a matter of some urgency.

Next, meant the following evening in a city previously designated. In this case it was Las Vegas.

S was a pre-arranged code meaning the location in Las Vegas where the meeting would take place. In this case, it meant the Sands Hotel.

Thus, the man from the Brown Derby flew from L.A. and Bonafacio traveled from Chicago and they met in the casino's adjoining hotel. They didn't use each another's name and unless someone was very familiar with their voices no one would ever know who was talking to whom.

Rarely was the Chicago Boss without one of his many fedoras and like so many of his cohorts in the Mafioso, he smoked Cuban cigars. If you passed him on the street, he would appear as an elderly gentle type, but his placid appearance was quite far from the reality of his personality.

The Chicago mobster was known as one of the cruelest mobsters in history. Though Bonafacio always obtained approval from the Commission of bosses before any hit, once approval was granted, he had his men carry out the hit per his instructions. He often directed his henchmen to do it slowly, to torture the victim with knives, electrodes on genitals and blowtorches, while the guy hung helplessly and painfully from a meat hook embedded in the back of his ribs. Bonafacio instructed those who performed the gruesome task to take pictures in the various stages of their work...the pictures to be circulated later as a lesson to others.

When the men hired to perform the torture informed Bonafacio they were able to prolong the unfortunate victim's cruel torment by keeping him alive for forty-eight hours, the Chicago mobster chortled in laughter.

When the Bonafacio's bodyguard escorted Pistelli into the room, the Chicago boss was chewing on one of his Cuban cigars that he had not yet lit, and though indoors he continued to don one of his trademark fedoras.

"So, how's the movie business?" Bonafacio asked.

"Not as lucrative as I would like," Pistelli frowned.

The boss laughed heartily, "Invested in a couple of bombs, have you?"

"Hmm," he groaned without humor.

"Come, sit down and tell me what is so important."

Pistelli took a seat and proceeded to explain the details of how he had been contacted, that a meeting was requested and the request made of him at the meet by the CIA. "The guy's name is Narducci...Anthony Narducci."

"What did you tell him?"

"Only that I'd contact some people I know to see if there was any interest. I didn't mention any names and told him to sit tight for a week until I could get back to him. They're offering 150K for the hit...per man if we need more than one."

Bonafacio whistled. Then nodded approvingly, as he paused to light his cigar, puffed on it repeatedly, and drew a large waft of smoke into his mouth, which he blew out without inhaling. All the while his mind was processing the details of what he'd been told.

"It could be a setup," Bonafacio surmised, ever-suspicious in his dealings with anyone with whom he came in contact and especially wary of a proposal by the CIA.

"Yeah, I thought of that too, but rather than keeping this unusual request to myself I thought it best to run it by you."

"You did the right thing."

Pistelli nodded his acknowledgement of the compliment...something Bonafacio didn't dole out often.

"How do you know he was CIA?" Bonafacio inquired.

Bonafacio noticed Pistelli's eyes widen slightly with mild surprise.

"I don't know specifically. I didn't ask to see any I.D. but my contact before the meet informed me a government man wanted to have a meet to discuss a project. It didn't sound like something the FBI would be involved with and that's why I'm saying CIA."

"We'll need to tighten that up and find out exactly who is making this request."

"Yeah, I can do that," Pistelli nodded.

"You're sure you didn't mention anybody's name though?"

"Nobody," he replied without hesitation. I didn't even mention in what part of the country my contacts were located, so he doesn't have a clue who I might be discussing this with, or even where I was heading after that meet."

"Unless you were tailed," said Bonafacio so matter-of-factly that Pistelli could see he was merely stating the obvious and unworried, as he blew a large puff of smoke toward the ceiling.

"I wasn't followed," Pistelli said emphatically to alleviate any lingering doubt. "I was very careful."

"Good. I'll fly down to New Orleans to relay your message and I'll contact you with the outcome. Wait. No. On second thought, you come with me. They may have questions I can't answer about this guy. We'll leave day after tomorrow. Make some calls. Contact your informants to see what they can tell you about this fellow, Narducci."

Chapter 14

The Chicago crime boss and Pistelli flew to New Orleans and met with two of their colleagues in crime. Present was the host of the meeting, New Orleans crime boss Carlo Marchetti. His territory encompasses the entire southwest. Marchetti is a squat man with a round, ruddy face, and a protruding cleft chin. He has very little hair and he is also devoid of something else. He is totally humorless while he carries a constant scowl on his face, as if he were in a constant state of agitated anger.

Also in attendance, Florida crime boss Salvatore D'Amato who operates out of his home in Miami. D'Amato controls the drug trade in Miami, the Deep South, and on up the eastern seaboard to Maryland and into Virginia. He is a taller man of six feet, two inches and as the years pass, the pate of his head is now almost entirely hairless as well and he has recently developed a noticeable paunch. Since he was kicked out of Havana by Castro, his loathing for the Cuban dictator is unsurpassed by any other organized crime boss.

D'Amato and Marchetti work in tandem in obtaining and distributing illicit drugs though they were far from being friends or even partners. In addition to their sources in Latin and South America, the duo has recently tapped into another supply from Southeast Asia that has proven to be even more lucrative.

Though they both sell a good deal of the contraband in their home cities, the ruling families of organized crime decreed neither D'Amato or Marchetti were to have a monopoly in the drug business. The Commission ruled there was more than enough to go around for both of them and for all the rest of the big city bosses.

The Chicago boss, Bonafacio, is a very wealthy man who distributes the heroin and cocaine in his home city in addition to Detroit, Milwaukee, Kansas City and St. Louis.

This trio controls the drug trade in most of the United States, Central America and the Caribbean. They are three of the wealthiest, most powerful mobsters ever to operate in this country. Their take is enormous...minus a percentage to the ruling families of course. Even allowing for inflation, they make the Luciano criminal empire of the 40's look like peanuts.

They now met in a private room at a restaurant in the French Quarter of New Orleans. The organized crime triumvirate sat down to consider the question of a hit on Castro and while Johnny Pistelli joined them, he was there only to provide information from his meeting with the representative of the CIA and to furnish background information on his young contact.

These high-ranking mobsters are not the stereotypical dumb gangsters who stuff plate after plate of Italian pasta into their faces while slurping gallons of wine and loosening their belts around ever-expanding bellies. No. This triumvirate is much different than what Americans visualized when thoughts of the American Mafia enter their mind.

These men are quiet, reserved, and, as much as possible attempt to remain in the background of the American consciousness, though Bonafacio is flashier and louder than the other two and he needs to be reeled in from time to time. But unlike so many of their counterparts, past and present, it's their minds that set them apart from so many others in the field of criminal endeavor. They are intelligent, shrewd, cunning and devious, and, yes, they can also be sadistically cruel. They have indeed learned a great deal from studying the ways of the criminal bosses who preceded them. While they avoid many of the mistakes committed by their predecessors, they cull the best aspects of how those former bosses ran the business of organized crime.

One of the things they emulate from the old guard is refraining from addressing each other by name. The practice was certainly old fashioned and out of date, but there was no downside in doing so. Thus, when they met this evening, they didn't speak each other's names. Though Marchetti owned the restaurant where their meet was scheduled and they could speak freely, they took no chances.

"You really eat this gumbo, shit?" Bonafacio asked, as he tossed his eating utensil disgustedly onto the table.

"I've been in New Orleans for a long time now. I like Cajun," Marchetti replied with a snarl and immediately changed the subject. "So, what do we know about this kid...what's his name?"

"The spook's name is Narducci, Anthony Abednego Narducci," Pistelli answered, as the mobsters had no qualms about speaking the names of those who were outside their circle.

"Abednego...what the hell kind of name is that?" Bonafacio laughed.

Pistelli shrugged, "Maybe a family name on his mother's side."

"It's a Biblical name, I believe," Bonafacio offered.

"Forget the middle name!" Marchetti yelled. "It's his last name that's important! Is Narducci a fictitious name or does he appear to be one of us?"

"Actually, it could be yes to both questions," Pistelli answered.

"We could put out some feelers in Washington," D'Amato offered.

"My contacts confirmed for me he is CIA. Been with them since 1955."

"55? How old is he?" D'Amato asked.

"Just a kid really...still in his twenties."

"Oh, for Chrissake!" shouted Marchetti.

"They probably didn't want to waste a seasoned resource...in case we put a bullet in his brain," Bonafacio commented.

"Maybe so, but we can find out soon enough if this kid is on the level," D'Amato suggested, and continued, "The fellow Narducci shouldn't be the focus of our discussion. It's the subject matter that'll be difficult for us to confirm as a legitimate project. The CIA is not gonna run around talking about hiring gunmen to snuff that bearded son of a bitch, especially in the early stage when they've just recently approached us about it," he said, as he pulled out one of his thick cigars, bit off the end and spit it into his plate as he began the process of lighting the other end.

"Yeah, we confirmed the kid is who he says he is, but I doubt that anybody will have heard anything about this proposed hit on that fuckin' communist, not yet anyway," Bonafacio surmised.

"Yeah, that might take us some time to see if the CIA is legit about this venture or if they're just trying to set us up," said Marchetti with a scowl. "I don't trust those bastards one bit."

"Nobody does," Bonafacio laughed.

"Supposedly all this came straight from Dulles," said Pistelli.

"If this proposal is on the level, it would have to have come from him," noted Marchetti.

The others around the table nodded in agreement.

"Is that slug Dulles still bonking a different broad every couple of days?" D'Amato asked, as he puffed on his cigar.

"Who cares?" Pistelli offered. Though he was out of his element with the power and wealth in this room, he was trying to fit in.

"Women, they're like shoes. You've gotta toss them out and get some new ones every now and then," Bonafacio chuckled. "Always get a new pair of them at the same time," Bonafacio laughed heartily, as he always preferred two women simultaneously.

As their laughter ebbed, Marchetti snarled, "One thing's for sure. That fucking beard has cost us tens of millions of dollars!"

"Which will become hundreds of millions if we don't do something about it real soon," said D'Amato.

"The spooks know that. They also know if our guys get caught that it would all come back to us," said Marchetti, as he mockingly moved his hands together in a gesture as if he were washing them.

"Yeah," D'Amato agreed, "the Pontius Pilate CIA, how many times have they actually dirtied themselves on some foreign assassination only to appear not to have a hand in it?"

"And that's why we cannot put ourselves in a position of trusting anything they do," Bonafacio commented.

"Yeah," D'Amato agreed. "The spooks could employ deniability. That's why they want to use us. We'd get blamed, and who wouldn't believe we were behind a hit on Castro with the monetary motive we have for wanting him dead."

"Hell, even if we weren't successful, the spooks might double-cross us, turn on us anyway, and hand us over to the FBI for merely attempting a hit on Castro," Bonafacio offered. "Maybe it's all just a trap to put us all in jail. They can't get us on anything else so they get us on this."

"That might actually be right on the mark," D'Amato nodded demonstrably, "a complete setup from start to finish."

"I don't trust Dulles farther than I can spit," Marchetti snarled.

"And I don't trust him farther than I can shit," laughed Bonafacio.

"So, what are we saying? We don't want to do anything? We just let that two-bit Marxist Dictator get away with what he did to us?" D'Amato asked.

"No, no, no, we're not saying anything of the kind. Just because we're considering saying no to the CIA, doesn't mean we don't want to do Castro. Nobody wants that bearded fuck more than I do, but I may have a better idea," said Marchetti, who was the most cunning mobster of his day. He stroked his cleft chin while in deep thought as he considered an idea that had struck him.

"What are you thinking?" Bonafacio asked.

Marchetti hesitated, as he grappled momentarily on the implementation of his thoughts. When he was ready, he answered.

"What if we tell the spooks yes, but don't actually go through with it?" he suggested.

"How do you mean?" D'Amato asked.

"I mean we just go through the motions and pretend we're trying to hit the beard," Marchetti said.

"Pretend? What good would that do?" Bonafacio asked.

"Insurance," Marchetti clarified.

There was a pause in the room, as the other men in the meeting considered that word…insurance. Insurance was a favorite word in the vocabulary of a high echelon mobster as it generally inferred greater protection of their business interests. Insurance often involved a setup…a patsy who would take the fall. If it was performed properly, the patsy would be totally unaware that he was setup.

"Think about it," Marchetti explained. "The way I see it is a hit on Castro by the mob working in conjunction with an American Intelligence Agency is something the CIA would never want to get out to John Q. Public…I mean literally not ever…because if it did it would freak Americans out of their shoes."

The others nodded and muttered the word, "insurance."

"Bear in mind I'm suggesting we merely go through the motions. If we do that, we'd have something over them, something real serious over them, and we could use that for a long, long time."

Heads in the room were nodding.

"In addition to that, we'd also be protecting ourselves in case they are trying to set us up after all," said Marchetti.

"I like the sound of it," said D'Amato.

"I'm a bit confused," Bonafacio interjected. "Are you saying that we simply tell them yes to their proposal and then not go through with it?"

Marchetti nodded.

"Don't you think they'll get wise to that? I mean the fact we never actually put Castro in his grave will be a little obvious when he's cruising around Cuba from time to time in plain sight," said Bonafacio.

"Well, we'd have to work out the details, so the Agency thinks we're trying to do it. See, that's the key. We have to make it look like we're actually trying to kill the bastard," said D'Amato.

"We could use excuses! We could tell them we're trying to get Castro but as a Head of State he's surrounded by security and we can't get anyone close enough to put the hit on him," Bonafacio offered.

"We would eventually have to try," D'Amato noted.

We could send some guys in there, you know, people we don't need, patsies and sacrifice them," Marchetti explained.

"Yeah, yeah," Marchetti agreed. "Have our people inside Cuba hit them after they cross the border. Make sure the CIA sees it. They'll think we're on the level if they see our guys killed."

"Set a few guys up to take the fall," D'Amato nodded with a grin on his face. "I like it."

"Yeah, we've become pretty adept at setting people up," Marchetti added with a wide grin.

"We sure have! Remember that D.A. who was after me a few years back?" D'Amato asked. "We set him up beautifully with thousands of dollars going in and out of his bank accounts. Then we put the word out he was actually in bed with the mob. Instead of me, it was him who got indicted."

"Yeah, I remember," said Bonafacio. "He got put away but before he could serve more than a month of his time, your boys on the inside got him."

"Yeah, a jagged shank in his guts and he was history," Marchetti glowed as his ever-present scowl briefly moved into a satisfied smirk. "Well, that's what I'm proposing in a manner of speaking. We set some guys up and we simply do it in Cuba instead of here."

"Not bad," Bonafacio nodded.

"We could employ some of those Mexicans we use throughout the southwest in our drug trade. We setup some of those wetbacks as patsies when we employ them as decoys for the drug shipments from time to time. What the hell? We could sacrifice some of them in Cuba and never miss a beat," Marchetti boasted.

"Perhaps," said D'Amato, as he scratched his face obviously perplexed as he thought things through.

"What is it?" Marchetti asked.

"I think Cuban exiles would be better," he stated flatly.

"How do you mean?" Marchetti asked.

"Cubans have a vested interest in wanting Castro dead. Nobody would question it if a Cuban attempted to hit Castro. I've got my own Cuban connections. I could get some of them to enlist in such a project. Hell, they'd be lining up to put the hit on Castro. If Mexicans are used to carry it out, somebody might start asking questions. You know, like why would Mexicans be interested in whacking Castro?"

"Hmm, yeah, I see what you mean," nodded Marchetti.

"And the CIA is training Cubans now for an invasion," Bonafacio piped in. "We simply recruit some of them ourselves for this operation."

"And best of all, if any of them are killed or even if they're captured alive, they'll all be thought of as counterrevolutionaries by Castro's Cuba," D'Amato pointed out.

Johnny Pistelli, respectfully silent through most of the meeting, laughed loudly. "That's beautiful! The CIA is already training those guys anyway, so we simply recruit them and send them in thinking they're going to hit Castro and before they knew what hit them, they'd be dead on the jungle floor. Those Cubans would never know the difference. I've got to hand it to you—-this is developing into one helluva good plan."

Marchetti eyed the underling Pistelli sternly, and said without humor, "I'm glad you approve."

Feeling uncomfortable under the Marchetti stare Pistelli shifted uneasily in his chair.

D'Amato interjected a chuckle. "Those Cubans want Castro dead so badly they'd do anything to be a member of a hit squad to squash him."

"Yeah, and the fact that we actually send someone in to do it would be a good cover. The CIA will think we're cooperating," said Marchetti.

They all nodded in unison.

"We'll need to have other Cubans ready...not simply those in the invasion in case it doesn't go as planned," Bonafacio offered.

"I agree," said Marchetti.

"I can work on that," said D'Amato.

The mobsters at the table now paused to consider the scheme in the privacy of their own thoughts.

Marchetti now lit a cigar to enjoy with a brandy he had just ordered, but rather than being satisfied with the plan, a look of anger crossed his face.

"What is it?" Bonafacio asked.

"The problem is that the thorn would still be in our sides. All that we've discussed might be good in getting the CIA on the hook to us, but the fact is Castro would still be in power, and we're no better off than we are right now."

"I might be able to help in that regard," offered D'Amato. "You all have a cut in the Havana casinos but that was my operation and ever since Castro took over, I've been thinking long and hard about how to get my business back."

"What did you come up with?" Marchetti asked.

"What does a revolutionary need more than anything else?" D'Amato asked.

Bonafacio was stumped but Marchetti smirked, and offered, "Weapons...or the money to buy weapons."

"And if we just skip the money and I get him the weapons?" D'Amato postulated. "You think maybe I could trade weapons for getting my casinos back?"

"Hmm," Marchetti thought, as he considered the possibility. "And then the money would come back."

"I think the beard might be receptive to an offer of weapons in exchange for our casino interests...all kinds of weapons...and ammunition too," D'Amato suggested.

"It's possible," Marchetti nodded. "You've got nothin' to lose by inquiring."

"I'll see if we can get someone to approach him about a deal, but let's keep it a secret for now," D'Amato suggested.

"Secrets...between us...are you kidding?" Bonafacio laughed heartily.

Even Marchetti cracked a smile at that one, as he lifted his glass of wine, and as the others raised their glasses, he toasted, "That dirty-bearded, son of a bitch Castro doesn't know how lucky he is," said Marchetti, as they all toasted the development of their plan.

Chapter 15

In the summer of 1960 on separate occasions the iconic American entertainer, Frank Sinatra introduced an attractive brunette to the Chicago mobster, Bonafacio, and to presidential candidate, Senator John F. Kennedy. Both immediately began affairs with her.

Though Frank introduced the woman to both of them, he didn't receive any monetary reward for performing the introductions, so I suppose by definition he can't be referred to as a pimp. I'll leave it up to you to label him in whatever manner you feel is appropriate.

Kennedy was not aware, in the beginning at least, that she was also seeing the Chicago mobster. In actuality, it was absolutely unreal how many people were tied into the mob. This wasn't the old mob involved in prostitution, numbers, neighborhood dry cleaners and local restaurants. This wasn't even the later mob involved in casinos, cocaine, heroin and payoffs to local politicians.

By 1960 the modern mob had woven itself into every fabric of our society, so much so that it was now involved with the U.S. Intelligence Agency, presidential primary elections, and assassination attempts of a foreign leader in conjunction with U.S. government policy.

If a stoolie had blown the whistle on all of this, he wouldn't have to be snuffed by the mob. He'd just be locked away in some crazy farm, in some insane asylum. The American public would never believe him. No prosecutor would touch such a case, and, on the off chance that one would, no judge or jury would believe enough of it to convict him. It was too bizarre to be believable.

After winning his party's top spot at the nominating convention in Los Angeles, candidate Kennedy was briefed on the planned Cuban invasion as the national election campaign unfolded.

Briefings were not unusual for presidential candidates, though some received more detailed briefings than others did over the years.

Kennedy in fact was briefed more often than was Vice-President Richard Nixon.

Anyway, Kennedy was briefed and kept up to date on the Cuban situation. Kennedy was also informed the CIA approached the mob to put a hit on Castro and that the mob agreed. Whether anyone from the CIA informed candidate Kennedy of the price tag for the hit is unknown, but if they did, they wholly underestimated the fee and could never have foreseen or ever imagined the total cost of dealing with America's criminal syndicate.

Chapter 16

After Kennedy was elected and inaugurated in January of 1961, he met with Allen Dulles about the planned invasion of Cuba.

"I can personally assure you, Mr. President, of the plan's success. Cuban exiles have been trained and equipped at the secret bases in Florida that we established. They will land on the beaches of Cuba at a place called Bahia de Cochinos—-the Bay of Pigs."

The newly elected president listened intently but didn't ask many questions.

The premise, of course, was since the invasion would be accomplished with Cubans, America's hands would be absolutely clean, and then the Marines could go in later in a show of support for those who were throwing off a dictator's shackles in the cause of freedom.

The so-called secret bases in Florida where the Cuban exiles were trained and equipped were not done as covertly as the CIA thought because it seems everyone knew what was going to happen. Hell, even the *New York Times* ran a story on the front page regarding the upcoming invasion.

Of course, in order to maintain deniability, America couldn't very well have the invasion force disembarking from U.S. soil, so they shipped the exiles off to Guatemala and Nicaragua. They would depart for Cuba from there.

Did the CIA really think it could maintain deniability and that no one would really know what was going on?

The young president was also informed that CIA intelligence had gauged the Cuban people and the president was told with supreme confidence the Cuban people would welcome the invasion and would rise up in mass against the Marxist dictator.

What that assessment was based upon is subject to anyone's conjecture, because no one that I ever came in contact with in the

CIA believed that. It is most probable the briefer of the president simply made it up from his own over exaggerated optimism.

The American people were destined to hear something very similar more than forty years later during the Iraq War—-that the Iraqi people would welcome the Americans 'with flowers in the barrel of their guns'. Presidential advisors do exaggerate and embellish to further their point of view. That's all it is. Very few Chief Executives ever seem to ask the questions: What do you base that on? How do you know? What research did you do? Show it to me.

Is it any wonder why historians are so adamant about their subject of expertise? It's not that historians believe the colossal misnomer that has perpetuated itself over the centuries—-of history repeating itself.

No.

Historians encourage the reading of history not only for the knowledge to be gained but for the lessons to be learned there, but, quite frankly and regrettably, arrogance is not compatible with the learning of lessons.

Just because a governmental advisor says something—-whether to a president or anyone else—-doesn't make it so.

Kennedy was further informed that on the off chance anything did go wrong the Cuban exiles could flee to the mountains and begin a guerilla war.

What the President didn't know, nor evidently anyone else within the CIA despite the fact they were briefing the President on logistics, was the nature of the terrain where the Cuban exiles would be landing. In reality, the invasion force would have to wade through swamps to get to the mountains that were fully eighty miles away.

According to Sun Tzu who wrote the *Art of* War, which is studied by any serious commander of troops, it is an error of enormous proportions not to be familiar with the terrain of the country—-its mountains and its swamps.

To be ignorant of the basic geography of the area where you wanted to land troops was inexcusable and it was because of the Bay of Pigs operation that CIA became known mockingly as the Central Incompetent Agency.

Perhaps Allen Dulles was more interested in the spying and the espionage aspects of his job as CIA Director than in actually developing hard intelligence. In any event, Kennedy ultimately, gave his approval for the invasion to proceed that was developed under Eisenhower, which was scheduled for April 1961.

In the meantime, Kennedy continued his affair with the mobster's mistress and, after he learned of her simultaneous affair with the Chicago boss, he began to exchange messages back and forth through her about the assassination attempts against Castro. The messages were never written down. They were strictly verbal—-messages from the President of the United States to a Mafioso boss through their mistress-in-common, such as...

When will teams be deployed?

If they fail, are back-up teams ready to go?

Can they get close enough to the beard?

Hollywood would reject such a script calling it grossly unrealistic and unbelievable.

Chapter 17

As for me, I actually didn't know my connection with Mr. Hollywood at the Brown Derby had been successful until I heard through the grapevine the mobsters agreed to put a hit on Castro...or at least so they said.

When I reported back to Florida, the shit hit the fan when the Bay of Pigs invasion failed miserably in April, 1961.

Kennedy took full responsibility and quoted the old saying, 'Victory has a thousand fathers, but defeat is an orphan' as he acknowledged he was the responsible man of the administration. Amazingly, his popularity soared.

I guess there's some lesson there for politicians to stand up and admit their mistakes. Americans are a very forgiving people when their leaders take responsibility for their errors and don't attempt to duck and dodge behind political speak.

Though Kennedy was cool in public, privately he was absolutely livid. In a rage he vowed to break the CIA into a thousand pieces, and he really stuck it to Allen Dulles and Richard Bissell.

Bissell was the Chief of Covert Operations and the Bay of Pigs was his venture. Kennedy supposedly told both of those CIA honchos that in a parliamentary system of government it would be Kennedy as the leader of the country who would be gone, but in our system of government it was Dulles and Bissell who would have to go.

Those of us in the CIA were stunned when the news of the Dulles and Bissell firings rippled through the agency. The magnitude of those dismissals shook the very power structure of Washington. Allen Dulles was one helluva powerful man and before his brother, John Foster Dulles, died they had begun the process of expanding the largest spy organization the world had ever seen. They grew the CIA into behemoth proportions. The budget was not only enormous, it was secret. No one really knew the amount of money the CIA controlled. Thus, in actuality, the CIA didn't have a budget. They had a blank check with which to conduct clandestine operations...and they used it. God did they use it.

After the inauguration in January, 1961, however, it was the Kennedy brothers who surpassed the Dulles brothers as the most powerful duo of siblings in the nation's history simply because of the fact JFK occupied the Oval Office.

Someone who was in a position to know told me the person Kennedy was most angry with over the Bay of Pigs debacle. It was himself—-for not asking more questions, for trusting the CIA too much. Kennedy didn't make that mistake again.

Kennedy didn't place a lot of faith in the military either. His lack of confidence in the military dated back to his days of service in World War II. His perceptions of the military were formed when he saw up close and personal a bevy of incompetent officers during his time of service.

As it turned out there was also a beneficial side to Kennedy's skepticism regarding the CIA and the military. His skepticism would serve him well later in his administration during the Cuban Missile Crisis. He would oversee and take charge of that operation personally.

Anyway, I'm getting a bit ahead of myself.

Despite Kennedy's disgust with the CIA, he stepped up covert operations in Cuba and assassination attempts against Castro. This time, however, he placed his brother Bobby in charge of overseeing that Black Ops.

Since I had merely been a translator in Florida for the Cubans, I was one of the lucky ones. The shit that fell on so many others within the CIA never hit me because I was not one of the strategists.

After the Bay of Pigs fiasco, I was given another assignment, one in which I could use my expertise of Southeast Asian languages.

I was shipped off to South Vietnam.

Chapter 18

Meanwhile, the Kennedy administration was much more than a dichotomy for the mob. Organized crime was ecstatic over America's continuing and increasing commitment of troops to South Vietnam because the profits of the American Mafia were soaring from the drug trade. In fact, by the end of 1962 America's commitment in South Vietnam would rise to 11,500 military advisors. In the early 60's the mob's major concern was failure in Vietnam would allow a communist takeover of the South by North Vietnam and a likely repeat of what happened to organized crime when Castro had kicked the mob out of Cuba.

On the other hand, Attorney General Robert Kennedy was coming down hard on the mob. Not only was he jeopardizing the mob's access to millions of dollars of union funds by investigating Jimmy Hoffa, the Attorney General was also rough-handing the New Orleans crime boss Carlo Marchetti. In a very high-handed manner, the Attorney General ordered Marchetti deported. The mobster was unceremoniously picked up, flown south and merely dropped off in the middle of a Guatemalan jungle.

Marchetti survived none the worse for wear, made his way back into the U.S.A. but he was enraged and vowed hateful retribution against the Kennedys.

It is unknown whether the Attorney General was informed of the assistance the mob rendered in Jack Kennedy's West Virginia Primary victory in 1960...unknown if either of the Kennedy brothers ever knew...but from the actions of the President and the Attorney General one could draw the feasible conclusion they never learned of the mob's intervention on behalf of the then presidential candidate. It was a recipe for disaster.

Chapter 19

In hindsight, maybe being transferred to Vietnam after the Bay of Pigs was a punishment after all. I thought Florida was bad! My God, South Vietnam was like being in an oven set at four hundred degrees except it was accompanied by horrendous humidity. Just to give you some perspective, in Saigon the annual average humidity is 80.8 amidst an annual average temperature of 83 degrees! It was absolutely sweltering and there was no change of seasons. After you washed, a towel was useless. You could never get yourself dry. On top of that there was the rain. The rainy season literally runs for six months—-from May through November with an average monthly rainfall from 10 to 15 inches. When I was there, it seemed like it rained all the time, and when it did, it poured in sheets day and night.

The CIA had once again slated me as a translator, though I was under instructions to be prepared to participate in counterinsurgency operations which could come at any time. Working as a translator, however, was fine with me. I had no overwhelming desire to crawl on my belly through the bush with the insects and snakes of Vietnam in search of some far away hamlet that might be suspected of being controlled by the Viet Cong.

When I got off the plane in Saigon, I must have really looked out of place because an Army Private noticed me right away.

"You look like a lost puppy," he chuckled.

"That ain't the half of it," I replied. "I just got here from the States and I found out the hard way I can't sleep on planes."

"Damn! If you can't sleep on planes, you just lost about thirty hours of your life," he said, with a southern twang in his speech.

"No, I didn't lose those hours," I responded in exhaustion. "I experienced every single minute."

He laughed at my misfortune, but then said, "You know, you really don't look so good," as he grabbed by suitcase. "Come on. I've got a jeep. As soon as I drop off my supplies from the airport, I'm off duty and I'll drop you at your destination."

"While he picked up my bag with his left hand, he stuck out his right, and said, "The name's Davis, Jimmy Davis, Specialist Four."

"Anthony Narducci," I said, as I shook his hand.

"Where are you from?"

"Virginia."

"Oh, a fellow Southerner," he smiled, as if he were greeting someone from his own neighborhood. "I'm from Tennessee, Livingston, Tennessee."

I shrugged my shoulders and shook my head slightly as an indication I was unfamiliar with the town.

"Oh, I'm not surprised you've never heard of it. It's a small town," he explained, as he began to chuckle. "We only have two thousand residents. You certainly could miss it—-whether you were lookin' for it or not. In fact, a lot of folks who are lookin' for it can't find it. We're about a hundred miles or so northeast of Nashville and about a hundred and twenty miles northwest of Knoxville. So, it's pretty much in the middle of those two."

"Oh, okay. I know roughly where it's at then."

"You look like a hybrid—-someone between military and civilian," he commented, noting the obvious fact I was not in uniform.

"CIA," I responded since it wasn't supposed to be a secret.

"I figured that. There's a bunch of you guys around here, so you'll probably make friends right away. I assume you're staying at the compound?" he asked, as he led me toward his jeep.

I nodded.

"I'm surprised one of your CIA counterparts didn't send a car for you."

I shrugged. "I think it's a macho thing. They encourage us to stand on our own and fend for ourselves."

"Oh, I wonder if giving you a ride is appropriate then," he laughed.

"Yeah, it's okay," I said through my weary, blood-shot eyes.

"If you don't mind me askin', what's your mission?"

"Oh, I don't mind. It's not a mission cloaked in secrecy, nor is it very glamorous either. Just here as a translator."

"Maybe not glamorous, but you sure are needed."

"Oh?"

"Yeah, I'm one of the military advisors...a radioman. There are over 2,000 of us advisors here now. That's what they call us...advisors...but we do carry guns. I suppose you could call us non-combat troop advisors. Among other things I assist in training the South Vietnamese Army. We're attempting to bring their troop strength up to 270,000 or more, which isn't exactly a large army to say the least."

"A military advisor, you say. I think I know the drill. You won't fire upon anyone unless you're fired upon."

"Yeah, that's right," said Davis. "You could think of us as the troops stationed in Germany. They don't fight and we don't fight. Of course, when you come right down to it there's no war going on in Germany at this time. As for the South Vietnamese Army, some of them speak English and some of them translate for us, but it is slow going. I can't tell you how long it took me the other day just to explain to a group of recruits how to change frequencies on a radio," he said, shaking his head. "Yeah, you're needed all right."

"You said training among other things...what else do you do?"

"Minor things...routine patrols but no fighting, at least not so far anyway. I can't say I mind not seeing any combat, but I know a lot of guys who are really itching to get off on that."

"How do you mean?"

"Oh, guys who like the intrigue and the danger. It gets their adrenaline going."

"Yeah, I think I know the type," I commented knowingly.

It was that damn James Bond syndrome again. I learned later there were a lot of those types...CIA mostly. The CIA personnel were acting like they were still playing army man—-just like when they were kids—-and even though it was for real now, there was an atmosphere of make believe. They figured they could do anything they wanted to do, and they could never get hurt...never get wounded or killed. I actually think when those guys were confronted with a dangerous situation that their balls actually expanded.

This young Jim Davis was different though. He too was here because the Army had sent him, but I could see right away the power of carrying a gun didn't affect his ego. He was grounded. He had the close-cut military haircut, and he looked younger than me, but he certainly had the air of the military in him, which was borne out by the next thing he said.

"But we're here because we're needed, and so we'll do the best job we can to protect the freedom of these folks. It's the right thing to do, otherwise the North Vietnamese, the Viet Cong, will overrun them and the Communists will take over the country."

I nodded in acknowledgment of his commitment. It wouldn't be long before I learned that others...again CIA mostly...were into something else entirely which in many ways could be more dangerous than fighting the North Vietnamese. You'll hear more about that a bit later.

I rode with Jimmy as he dropped off the supplies he had picked up from the airport, and I asked, "How about a beer before you drop me to say thanks for the ride?"

"Think you can stay awake long enough to enjoy one?" he chuckled.

"Sure," I shrugged. "What's another hour when you haven't slept for the past thirty?"

Jimmy laughed robustly. "You just watch. One beer and it'll probably knock you on your ass. You'll fall asleep at the bar."

"I sure as hell hope so, but as much as I want to sleep, I'll bet I don't fall asleep," I responded, as Jimmy pulled his Jeep to a stop and parked.

"Come on, as payment for the ride, the first beer is on you," he said.

"No problem," I said, "and the second one is on me too," as we entered a nearby bar, took a seat at the counter and ordered a couple of bottles. I placed some bills on the bar, which the bartender grabbed and headed for the register to retrieve my change.

Jimmy raised his beer, and said, "Welcome to Saigon."

I clanked his bottle. "And thanks for the ride."

"So, how long have you been with the Agency?" he asked.

"Right at six years now. I joined the Company in the summer of 1955. How about you? How long have you been here?"

"I'm well into my second year stationed here."

"You like the duty?"

"Yeah, I can't complain."

A woman sauntered up to the bar and smiled at me as she sat down a couple of stools away.

"You know, I think this is having the opposite effect than you thought it might. I do believe I'm feeling a bit revitalized," I said, as I took a second gulp of my beer, and smiled back at the woman at the bar.

Jimmy noticed me looking at her and he grinned. "Just make sure you're careful."

"Oh, yeah, I always use protection."

Jimmy laughed robustly.

"What?" I asked.

He took a sip of his beer, and then leaned in toward me. "I mean be careful that it's not a shim."

"What's a shim?"

"That's a she, him...a shim. The Vietnamese are very petite. Some of the men dress up like women and Vietnamese men don't have the body hair, the heavy beard that us Americans do. They can more easily pass for a female. The locals call them shims."

I emitted a gasp as I glanced at the woman, or the man as the case may have been. I turned back toward Jimmy, and asked, "How are you supposed to be able to tell?"

"Oh, that's easy. You walk up to them, grab their crotch and if you feel something that shouldn't be there..."

"Oh, I don't know about doing that," I shook my head. "That could be a little freaky."

"You think that's freaky? Your only other option is to take one of them into a room, but then, once you get there, you risk...well, you know the risk," he laughed.

I slugged another gulp of my beer. "Yeah, I see what you mean," as I gazed at the person down the bar and then turned back toward Jimmy. "Well, you've been here for a while. Have you been to this bar before? Do you know who's who? Can you tell one from the other?"

Jimmy laughed. "I subscribe to the belief there are some things in life that a person has to learn for themselves."

"Oh, thanks a lot," I frowned, as I downed the last of my beer and signaled to the bartender for two more.

"It tastes good in this climate, doesn't it?" Jimmy commented.

"It sure does!"

"Yeah, the climate here is like a sauna all right and it never changes. There are no seasons here. Well, there's a monsoon season, but no changes in the weather other than that," he said, as he raised his second bottle of beer, and added. "So, get ready to get wet."

"God it's more humid here than Florida," I mentioned.

"Is that where you were stationed before you arrived in Saigon?"

"Hmm," I groaned, as I found myself continually glancing to my right and curious as to which gender the person was who was seated there. "I need to get myself a woman so I can get my mind off of this. You want to get one too?" I asked, hoping that he might want to keep me company in a strange sort of way. I suppose it was in case I made the wrong choice.

"Nah, I'll take a pass, but when you're finished, why don't you stop by. We'll talk," he said, as he told me where he'd be.

"Yeah, sure," I said.

"You do what you need to do, and I mean it, Anthony. Stop by later. We'll shoot the breeze. Besides, I'll be looking forward to hearing if you made the right choice," he said, as he nudged me with his elbow.

"Yeah, and I'll bet you'll laugh your ass off if I make the wrong choice."

His laughter told me he'd do exactly that.

"Even if you made the wrong choice, I doubt you'd admit to it," he chuckled.

After Jimmy furnished me with directions of where I could find him, he took off and my adrenaline surged, streaming through my veins as I looked toward the person seated on the stool.

Why I didn't collapse after that long of a flight I don't know, but I was horny as hell. I glanced again at the person seated just down the bar and found myself wondering. Maybe it was the danger involved in picking the wrong one, but I knew I had to try.

I moved down the bar and began a conversation and looked very closely at the person to see if I could tell if it was a man or indeed a female. It was an exercise in futility, but I had to find out, so we went upstairs.

When we stripped off our clothes, I let out a holler...a whoop of joy...that I had chosen correctly. I went right to it without any preliminaries at all and no small talk. In fact, I don't think I said two words to her. I think I was pretty rough with her because she groaned a couple of times and it wasn't the sound of seductive sex play. I guess it was just because I was in such a hurry and horny state. Anyway, it didn't last very long. I was finished in under a minute.

I left the bar and I did stop by to look up Jimmy. As I walked in one reason immediately came to me as to why Jimmy had declined to participate in a little whoring. He was lying up on his cot, his back propped up against the back wall. He was reading the Bible.

When he saw me, he immediately closed his Bible and set it down on his cot beside him and grinned at me.

"Was that all a put on?" I asked.

"Oh," he smiled widely, "so you made the right choice," he said, and added, "Congratulations."

"Come on, you were putting me on, right?"

"Only time will tell," his grin widened, "and of course we can always increase that bet if you're feeling confident."

Chapter 20

In the summer of '61 Jimmy and I had become good friends. Hanging out with him was like having a kid brother. You may not think that's such a big deal but since I was an only child it meant a lot to me. Besides that, we were both a long way from home and that often makes all the difference. Part of the reason we hung together as it turned out was because the group that I was translating for was the same group Jimmy was assisting in training with his radio work.

As soon as I reported for my translation assignment, the first thing I noticed about the South Vietnamese Army was how unbelievably little they were. I mean that literally. I think the group for which I was translating couldn't have had an average height above five feet, four inches. There were some taller ones around but not many. They had tiny noses and very small little hands, and, when I'd meet them and shake their hand, their little mitt was engulfed in my grip and I'm not that big of a guy. Their handshake was also very lifeless...not the firm grip and quick pump of an American handshake. Their handshake was...well...limp. Maybe it was an Asian cultural thing but their handshakes gave me the feeling they were embarrassed that Americans needed to be there for them. Looking back from the perspective of time, maybe it wasn't solely me. Maybe they were a little embarrassed at the need for any of us to be there.

After a full day of training and translating, Jimmy and I would stop at a bar for a drink to unwind. Since I was with the CIA, I could get Jimmy into any club and he appreciated that. Besides, things were a lot looser in Nam than they would be at a base back in the States. It wasn't so stringent and structured in Vietnam for the service guys who were stationed there. Oh, an enlisted man had to make some contacts, but after a guy did that, he could go just about anywhere.

Jimmy and I had a good time that summer shootin' the shit. I even got him onto the golf course enjoyed by the officers but neither one of us ever went back after that first time—-it was just too damn hot and humid to play golf. After we finished the eighteenth hole, I went into the clubhouse to take a piss. I guess it was just out of habit figuring I'd need to go after a round of golf especially after all of the water I drank. Anyway, nothing came out, not a drop. I heard once that when you can't take a piss in sweltering heat that's when you're dehydrated. I must have sweated off ten pounds that day and I am trim. When we sat down at a table, I still couldn't get enough water—-just kept drinking glass after glass with a bottle of beer in between each glass of water.

In South Vietnam, I got closer to Jimmy than anyone I ever knew in college. At William and Mary, I was simply too busy with my studies to socialize much, and I never bothered to join a fraternity, so I didn't have all that many friends and acquaintances. I was probably quite anal back in college—-well before that term of non-endearment became fashionable. Yeah, Jimmy was a good friend all right.

Most guys want to have a few buddies. You really needed to when you were that far from home. Like a lot of military people say who have been in combat...you're not so much fighting for yourself as you are for your buddies. Of course, we weren't in combat and it was doubtful we would be any time soon.

Jimmy and I talked about some of those macho types in the military who didn't want to make friends with anyone. It was some crap about not getting too close to someone if they had to go on a mission and didn't come back. The absurdity of that kind of thinking in the summer of '61 seemed outside reality.

I don't mean to imply there weren't any deaths at that point in the Vietnam conflict but there were very few. I believe the first official death in Vietnam was recorded in a friendly fire incident on June 8, 1956 when Sergeant Richard Fitzgibbon, Jr. was killed. As best I know the next death didn't occur until Captain Harry Cramer died in an explosion in October, 1957 and there was some talk about that being accidental. That, of course, didn't make him any less dead.

The first two names on the Vietnam Veterans Memorial are Major Dale Buis and Major Sergeant Charles Ovnand, who were killed by sniper fire in July, 1959. Now, in the summer of '61 two years later, there hadn't been any additional deaths of Americans since. So, I thought all this macho talk about being a loner and not befriending anyone was just so much bullshit.

One of the few things that concerned me in my friendship with Jimmy was the fact I had a college degree and Jimmy didn't. I didn't have a problem with it but I know that some guys are put off by that. I was just a little self-conscious about saying the wrong thing in the sense that I refrained from quoting literature and I steered clear of getting involved in any sort of in-depth philosophical discussion. It's not that I was a snob and thought myself superior. I just didn't want Jimmy to mistakenly think I thought that way.

Anyway, that degree of mine never did get in the way. Being that far away from home puts everyone more or less on an even playing field. I guess the field of battle always brings everyone involved closer than they might be under normal circumstances though the fighting hadn't started yet as far as we were concerned.

Chapter 21

It was in late December of '61 when Jimmy was out on a routine patrol that a fellow colleague in the CIA approached me in Saigon.

"Hey, Anthony, how are you doin'?"

I looked up and saw Pete Madison. Pete was a thin and fit person, which wasn't unusual in Vietnam. Nobody put on weight in that heat, and naturally the 'advisors' that the Army was sending over there were young men for the most part who were trim and fit.

Madison had a long nose beneath dark eyes and a crooked smile that conveyed a sense of arrogance, but it was those dark eyes of his that to my mind made him look like a con man. Since he was an older fellow, his hair was getting thin. I never asked him his age, but my guess is he was in his forties.

"I'm hot and wet! How do you think I'm doin'?" I answered him.

"You got a minute?"

I shrugged. "Yeah, I suppose."

"Let's take a walk. I want to talk to you in private about an opportunity I think you might be interested in considering."

I nodded and we headed down the street toward one of the local watering holes.

Pete Madison had been in South Vietnam for several years, how many exactly I'm not sure, but it was a long time. Consequently, he knew his way around. I met him shortly after I arrived. He was a pilot. He flew flights in and out of Vietnam on Air America, the CIA's airline. Yes, Allen Dulles had enough funds allocated to him from the U.S. Government for his own departmental airline.

I never asked him the purpose of the flights simply because I just wasn't that curious about it. Naturally, I assumed the cargo was supplies to beef up the South Vietnamese Army though I had suspicions of something else as well.

As we entered the bar, we passed a South Vietnamese woman who was seated on a stool at the bar waiting for some business, and Pete smiled at her as we passed by.

"Hey, sweetheart," Pete greeted her.

"Hi. You want me today?"

"Not right now, sweetheart. Perhaps later," Pete chuckled, as he led me to a table in the back where we sat down in a booth opposite each other.

He turned to me with a smirk on his face. "I had her last night."

"Oh?"

"You do partake, don't you Anthony?"

"Of course," I replied.

"Good. Maybe after we conclude our discussion, we can do the double team on her," he said, as he leaned out of the booth and smiled lustily towards her.

When he leaned back in and turned toward me, he asked, "You ever notice how tiny these Vietnamese people are?"

"Of course, it's hard to miss a feature like that."

"You notice their tiny little noses and little hands?"

"Who hasn't?"

"Well let me tell you those aren't the only things tiny on these women. If you partake of one of these women, you're gonna think you died and went to heaven."

"I told you I've already had the pleasure," I said, as I was beginning to get irritated with Pete. That wasn't unusual as it didn't take me long to get irritated in Pete's presence.

Pete ignored my correction, as he glanced at her again. "Yeah, she's got a nice little tight one alright, and she can do you great with her mouth too. She's got a great tongue. It never stops moving. I'll even let you have first choice—-tongue or snatch—-and whichever you want, I'll take the other."

"Sounds good to me," I replied nonchalantly.

There wasn't much to do in South Vietnam, and a guy can get really horny when he's just sitting around bored. The prostitutes were cheap, so when we finished our work for the day most of us banged the locals to pass the time.

"So, what'll you have to drink? I'm buyin.'"

"A cold beer for starters," I replied, glad to be getting a drink.

Pete raised an arm, "Two cold ones over here," he shouted toward the bartender across the room, and then he turned toward me. "You play much golf?"

I was surprised. He could have asked me that any time, so I was sure that wasn't what he wanted to talk to me about. We certainly didn't have to get a private booth in a bar down the street to talk about golf. I took the cool, nonchalant approach.

"I don't play. It's just not fun for me in this heat and humidity."

"Yeah," he nodded, "it can be rough out there."

The bartender set a couple of cold bottles of beer on the table and returned to the bar. Pete grabbed his bottle and raised it as if in a toast.

"Here's to a financially successful stay in Vietnam."

As our bottles clanked, I'm sure the look on my face was one that reflected some confusion at what he said. I didn't know what he was referring to and though I really wasn't much interested in what Pete Madison was scheming; I found myself asking nevertheless. "How do you mean?"

"Well, thereby we arrive at the reason I want to talk to you. Actually, it was someone else through an intermediary that suggested maybe we could talk," he explained mysteriously, as he looked around to be sure that no one was within earshot.

When he turned back toward me, what he said next sent a shiver down my spine in spite of the heat.

"The fellow you met at the Brown Derby said to say hello."

I was swallowing at the time and I almost choked on my beer.

"Evidently you made quite an impression upon him."

"You know him?"

"Me? No, not personally but I'm acquainted with a lot of his friends and I know a lot of other people who know him. I'm aware you met with him and, though I don't know for a fact specifically the subject of your conversation, I could make a pretty good guess as to what you talked about."

"No, you couldn't," I said, calling his bluff. I was confident he couldn't possibly be aware of anything so out of the ordinary.

Pete couldn't let a challenge like that pass. He just couldn't resist telling me what he surmised, and said point blank, "You talked about hitting the beard."

I was absolutely stunned!

I felt the blood rush out of my face and I don't doubt I turned as white as a sheet. Pete mentioned it so matter-of-factly. I was surprised to say the least, but like I said earlier, just about everyone within the CIA knew what was going on, but now someone had directly linked me to it.

"How'd you know that?" I asked him.

"Does it really matter?" he smirked.

I got very defensive and responded, "All I did was act as a messenger!" I nearly shouted across the table.

"Hey, I'm not judging you. Don't worry about it," Pete's smirk widened into a grin, as he took a swig of his beer, and continued. "I have certain contacts you might say, so I heard about the meet. Though I didn't hear the subject matter, no one had to explain it to me," he said, as his grin receded back into his arrogant smirk. "A CIA guy and a mobster meet and that's followed by a lot of talk through the agency the mob is going to hit Castro. Of course, you must know how we try not to use our own people for deniability reasons. It wasn't all that difficult to figure the CIA recruited the mob."

I pulled in a deep gulp of air. I hadn't thought before it would have been that obvious.

"Anyway, your Brown Derby man, Johnny Pistelli and his other contacts thought you might be interested in something."

I didn't say anything but I was perplexed as I looked at Pete, though I must admit that I was quite curious as to what he meant.

Pete smiled in his know-it-all sort of way, and said, "He got word to me through someone else that a proposition might be run past you. You see our business interests have grown and we need to expand. We need more people, people we can trust, people who have already proved themselves and can do a good job for us."

"I don't have a clue what you're talking about but if I were to guess I'd say it has something to do with drugs," I ventured. When his eyebrows upturned in astonishment, I added, "You're not the only one who hears rumors and can figure things out."

He gave me a nod of approval through that sickly smirk of his. "Well, I can see why a mobster was impressed with you, Narducci," he said, as his face eased into a complimentary smile. "Let me tell you, Anthony, you would not believe the money that's to be made from this operation. And it's so simple. We fly the stuff back via Air America. Since it's on our own airline, on our own flights, we never get checked," he chuckled in amusement. "Nobody looks at our shipments. We're the damn government, so why would anyone check our shipments?"

Oh, it's not that Allen Dulles established an entire airline to accommodate the mob and make it available to them. Hell, it was quite the contrary. In the mid '50's when America took over for the French in Vietnam it's very doubtful Dulles knew the mob used some of his agents for transport of the contraband. That's just the nature of corruption. In point of fact, by the early '60's if Dulles had learned of the mob's operation, and had wanted to put a stop to it—-that is before he was dismissed—-he couldn't have, because the mob would use their old standby—-insurance—-the CIA/mob connection to hit Castro.

Years later, when the Vietnam War escalated and the American casualty rates soared, I heard that drugs from Southeast Asia were actually smuggled into the United States by stuffing them into the body bags of dead U.S. servicemen, though that turned out to be a mere ruse to throw authorities off the main track. Nevertheless, it all sounded very disturbing and obscene to me.

"We make a stop in the Pacific to refuel," Pete continued, "but the contents don't ever get inspected. We fly the stuff into a lot of different countries—-Nicaragua, Panama, and Guatemala to name a few. We combine that with the South American drug trade that comes up from Colombia and Peru. Then the stuff is brought into the U.S. through Mexico for distribution. Usually, I only go as far as Latin America but every now and then I'll make one of the low-level flights across the Mexican border into good old U.S. of A. It's unbelievable what they have going here. The mob got into the Asian drug trade almost as soon as the French pulled out of South Vietnam and the U.S. came in. It's a damn gold mine, Anthony, and the mob is taking care of those who assist them in getting the stuff out. I don't know about you, but I got a little weary of constantly trying to stretch my salary over an entire year. You come into this and I'll tell you, you'll be set for life."

I took a swig of my beer. I was amazed. Though I was skeptical and found it difficult to believe everything Pete was saying at face value, he did make me think. I found myself reflecting upon my own financial situation. Pete was certainly right about that. CIA agents were pitifully under paid especially in light of the responsibility we carried. Maybe those involved in covert operations in the field made more...I don't really know...but, as a translator, I knew exactly what Pete was saying and it really hit home. 'But set for life'? Hard for me to believe.

"Anthony, you could make your entire year's salary in less than a month and you'll still be kicking down your government salary to boot. Being as young as you are, you probably never even considered this, but you'll have a mere pittance of a government pension when you retire. I can tell you at my age it starts to become really important to know a pension is going to be there for you when you need it, but it's also glaringly evident that a government pension is simply not enough to live on."

"Hmm," I mused as I thought about what he was saying but a pension didn't register with me as anything I ever thought about.

"And keep this in mind...all I'm earning on the side is absolutely tax free," he grinned, "and I'm putting it all away for when I need it someday down the road."

Money was another one of the tools the mob employed to draw you into their web...lots and lots of money.

While I was digesting all that Pete told me, I thought to ask, "Aren't you taking a big chance on telling me all this?"

That crooked, arrogant smile reappeared on Pete Madison's face, as he replied to my question. "Not at all, Kid. We always have insurance before we talk to someone," he said, as he reached beneath his shirt and pulled out a semiautomatic.

My eyes must have widened into saucers because Madison laughed heartily.

"I'm kidding. I'm kidding," he said through his laughter, as he returned the handgun inside his shirt. "In your case, you'll never talk about anything that's been said here, because if you do, then we spread the word you met with a mobster and enlisted his support to hit Castro. You think the CIA, the ones who sent you to Hollywood, will protect you?"

My eyes narrowed into beams of contempt as I stared at Pete Madison.

"You were expendable, Narducci. You were new, and you didn't have a lot of dollars invested in you yet. You think the U.S. government could ever let information such as a mob hit get out?"

Pete let me think about that for a while in silence, and when he broke that silence, he said, "You see, Narducci, whether you realize it or not, you're screwed for life."

Blackmail was the first word that came to my mind as I glared across the table at Pet Madison.

"You never should have accepted that assignment to meet with a gangster, because you're involved with the mob now whether you like it or not. They own you. You're so intelligent, so learned, and yet you fell for one of the oldest tricks in the book."

As Pete took a gulp of his beer, he stared back at me. I could see he was serious, and I began to feel uneasy and claustrophobic...like I was being backed into a corner with no escape route.

"Oh, don't get me wrong. You still have the option to say no...this time...but there will be another time when maybe you won't have the opportunity to decline. Believe me, that time will come, Anthony, because once you deal with the mob, the mob always deals with you."

I was listening in stunned silence and I knew that Pete was right.

"Of course, there's always the possibility they might put a hit on you...now that you know about the operation."

"Is that why you told me so much?"

Pete didn't answer. He just smirked at me.

I swigged the last of my beer and looked away trying to avoid eye contact. I didn't know what to say to him. My head was swimming. It seemed every time I turned around the things the U.S. Government was involved in and the people that they were involved with was getting crazier...assassination of foreign leaders, mob hits, drugs. I found myself thinking about my growing disillusionment with the CIA.

Pete could see I was uneasy about the whole matter, and he offered, "Tell you what, Anthony. It's not imperative I have an answer today. You think about it. Relax. Take a few days and mull it over. Payday is tomorrow. Take a good long look at that paltry amount of a month's pay and think about whether you want to exist on such a meager income for the rest of your life...with a few meager raises as the years pass. And then you think about the amount of money I told you could supplement that meager income. Just promise me one thing."

"What's that?" I asked without lifting my downward gaze.

"Promise me that you'll give it some serious thought."

I lifted my line of sight from staring at the table and looked into Pete's eyes. Without thinking about it, as if it were a reflex action, I found myself nodding, "Yeah, okay. I'll think about it."

I almost couldn't believe those words came out of my mouth but I felt I had to say that. I didn't think I had any other choice than to say I'd consider it at the very least.

"Good! Good!" He smiled widely, as he leaned out of the booth toward the bar. "Hey, we're lucky," he said, as he swung back toward me, and added, "She's not with another john. Maybe that's a good omen considering what we just discussed.

I looked at him blankly.

"So, what'll it be, Anthony?"

Distracted and still thinking about the proposal he had been put to me, I responded, "You said I could take a few days to think about it."

"No, no," he chuckled. "What's your pleasure...snatch or tongue?"

Chapter 22

In late December of 1961 I got a message to report to my case officer. As usual, it was pouring in Saigon and I was soaked by the time I traversed the one block to his office.

"You wanted to see me, Sir?"

He nodded. "Have a seat, Narducci," he said in a serious tone. I didn't find his serious tone unusual. My case officer in the CIA was always serious and completely devoid of any humor. As was his way he came to the point without any preliminary small talk.

"What I have is a bit sketchy, but I'll give you what I've got. Yesterday, some Viet Cong were interfering with some radio frequencies, so the 3rd RRU at Ton Son Nhut was contacted. They determined a jammer near Ben Hoa was on the same frequency, so an American took two companies of South Vietnamese troops towards Ben Hoa to locate and knock out the jammer. From what I understand this jamming of frequencies is something that occurs on a regular basis, and usually they would find a small group of Viet Cong and run them off. This time, however, it was different. There was reportedly a battalion size group waiting in ambush. The truck in which the American and the two companies were riding hit a road mine, and the men were thrown from the truck. They got into a firefight and all of the South Vietnamese were killed along with the lone American. The American was Jim Davis and I thought you'd want to know because I knew you were buddies."

My mouth fell open in disbelief. I felt like I'd been punched in the stomach and gotten the wind knocked out of me. It was as if in a microsecond Vietnam had suddenly become real.

"From what I understand he must have put up a good fight, because he had a carbine with six clips and expended all of his ammo."

I nodded weakly in appreciation that my superior had informed me, but I know I emitted a painful sigh as well.

My case officer said some other things, but I don't recall what it was, probably never even heard the rest of what he said. I felt engulfed in a foggy trance. He must have raised his voice because I remember he said, "That'll be all, Narducci."

When I left, I immediately went to the nearest bar and ordered several shots of hard liquor along with some beers to chase them down. Nothing in my life ever gave me as much pain in my gut as that day in Vietnam. Jimmy was a good guy. He was a friend...no airs...natural. I felt like I'd lost a brother I never had.

There had been numerous American casualties in Vietnam before Jimmy Davis was killed, but he was the first...at least at that time...to be labeled as a combat casualty and he was thus the first American soldier designated as killed in action in the Vietnam War.

Chapter 23

A couple of nights later, I was back in a bar when I felt a tap on my shoulder. When I turned around, it was Pete Madison.

"So, how are you doing, Anthony?"

I decided not to tell Pete about Jimmy though I don't know why. Maybe it was because deep down I knew there wouldn't be any empathy from Pete. He could be very standoffish at times and I early on got the impression he wasn't very sincere about anything. You know the type...people who ask how you're doing but don't really give a damn and do their best not to listen if you proceed to tell them. Anyway, I kept Jimmy's death to myself.

"Care for a drink?" I asked.

"Well, what do you think? I did walk into a bar," Pete grinned.

I signaled the bartender, as Pete took a seat beside me and ordered a beer.

Pete smirked. "Do I want a drink?" he repeated in sarcasm. "Why else do you think I'm here? I'm certainly not here to play miniature golf, although I may check out a hole or two in a few minutes, if you know what I mean," he said, as he poked me in the side with his elbow.

God, Pete was such an obnoxious asshole.

When the bartender served him, he took a long gulp of his beer. He then emitted a loud lingering belch. "Oh, that tasted good—-twice."

"So, what are you up to today?" I asked.

"Ah, nothin' much. I just came in for a drink and maybe hang out with one or two of my lady friends."

I nodded without saying anything.

"So...uh...you give any thought to that proposition we discussed?"

With Jimmy's death, my previous conversation with Pete had completely slipped my mind. In fact, it was so entirely out of my consciousness I hadn't thought of it since the day we spoke, but the prospect crept into my mind now. Maybe I wasn't thinking rationally to even consider such a proposition, although I don't think that's necessarily the case.

As I stated earlier, I'd already heard some things from various colleagues within the CIA that turned me off to the whole espionage thing—-assassination plots, enlisting the mafia in those plots, counterinsurgency, various covert operations, the involvement of organized crime in a presidential primary and even a President passing messages to a Mafia chieftain through his female liaison, but what rankled me most of all it was the way I was used by the CIA to make contact with the mob.

I hated to admit it to myself but Pete Madison had certainly been right about that though I would never tell him so. Agreeing to meet with a mobster on the subject of assassination would haunt me the rest of my life...the end of which might not be all that far down the road.

Anyway, it was because of those things that I began to consider Pete's proposal. With my growing cynicism about what America was doing and what they'd done to me; it would be a way for me to stick it up the government's ass.

Without considering the matter any further, I found myself turning toward Pete, and saying, "Yeah, okay. Why not? Like you said, I could certainly use the money."

Pete smiled that half-cocked grin of his and raised his glass. "Well, here's to a very lucrative partnership."

Chapter 24

And that's how my life in crime began, just as simple as a young bride saying, 'I do'.

I took a swig of my beer and turned back to Pete, and asked, "I guess my only question at this point is what I am supposed to do?"

Pete looked around the bar, and said, "Let's get a table in the back where we can talk about it without being overheard."

I left some money on the bar and nodded to the bartender, as I grabbed my drink and followed Pete. After we sat down, he got right to the point.

"We need people to box up the merchandise and load the planes, but it's got to be people who are in on it and thus will not ask any questions."

"You already have a few people doing that?" I asked.

"Sure. Like I told you before, we've been doing it right along, but we need more people so we can make bigger loads, and that'll be bigger payoffs to us," he smiled widely. "The stuff is already packaged, but we want to get it into government boxes so it'll look more official. Since you're CIA, you could help with that. The boxes don't have to say CIA, just U.S. Government...you know...as long as the boxes have something like an official look to them."

"But how do you get it off on the other end?"

Pete eyed me with a cold, dark stare for several seconds in silence.

His unrelenting stare made me very uncomfortable. I felt like if he'd had a knife in his pocket, he'd have pulled it out and stuck it in my eye then and there. I didn't know what I'd said to warrant such a loathsome stare, but I soon got my answer.

"Let me explain something to you, Narducci. Don't ask questions about things you don't need to know about. You worry about this side of the Pacific...nothing else. You ask a question like that again and the wrong person hears it, you're liable to get a bullet in the back of your head. Got it?"

"Yeah," I answered nervously.

"This is no game. This is big business...I mean big fuckin' business. People can go to prison for a long, long time for doing what we're doing, but that's not the worst of it. There's a lot of money at stake and the people who make that money guard their interest very jealously. Before anyone goes to prison, they might make sure that person doesn't talk...like dead in the ground doesn't talk with several bullets in his head. So, you'd better understand that very clearly before we go any farther. Got it?"

"Yeah, yeah, I got it," I answered with irritation.

"All right, shall we review the rules?" he asked.

I gestured for him to proceed.

"Rule number one. You're told to do something—-you do it. You don't ask questions. People who ask questions make the bosses very suspicious, and if they're suspicious of you, you might wind up dead."

I nodded in understanding but hoped Pete didn't glance at my chest for fear he would see it heaving as I felt my heart pounding.

"Rule number two," he continued. "No matter what the nature of the job is that's assigned to you, don't hesitate. People who hesitate in carrying out an assignment also make the bosses nervous. Hesitation makes them think your allegiance lies elsewhere. Thus, hesitation can also get you killed. You just do whatever it is you're told to do and do it unquestioningly and promptly."

I nodded again without speaking, and I felt myself getting a bit heady with a rush of adrenaline. Yeah, I can't explain why, but in just matter of moments the talk of danger had flipped me from being frightened to giving me a rush of excitement.

"Rule number three is don't ever talk about the business in which you're about to be involved and I mean to no one, not even with the whores in these bars. A lot of these whores are actually plants who work for the other side."

I'm sure the expression on my face revealed my surprise at what Pete had said.

"Yeah, a lot of these prostitutes have been placed here by the North Vietnamese to gain information while the women perform for the American servicemen," he explained. "And let me tell you, the cunts are cunning. Hey, I like that," he laughed. "The cunts are cunning...the cunning cunts."

I faked a smile but didn't laugh.

"And they're real coy about it too. They don't ask blatant questions like where are you headed and what will your troop strength be? No. They've been schooled better than to be that obvious. They smile seductively while they're in bed with you, and ask, if you go on a dangerous mission, you will come back to your favorite lady for sex? You'd be surprised how many chumps start talking about where they're heading, when they're going, and how dangerous it will be for them. The army still hasn't caught on that a lot of these whores are working for the enemy. The point is, the bosses have their hand into more than just drugs in Southeast Asia and prostitution also makes them a good buck. So, if you talk to any of them about what you're doing, you'll be dead, because eventually the bosses will hear about it. You see a lot of these whores work for the mob in addition to the North Vietnamese."

Again, he must have read my surprise.

"Oh, yeah, the mob isn't limited to drugs. You wouldn't believe what they control in Saigon and how many things they have their hands in but we're not going to get into that. Less is more in that case. If you don't know about it, you can't talk about it. Just remember to keep your mouth closed—-real tight."

"Okay," I replied, as I verbally acknowledged the rules. "I understand."

"Rule number four is a bit tricky. The mob doesn't like a snitch, even if it's someone who is telling them about another guy who is ripping off their operation. On the other hand, if you know of some rip off that's going on and don't' let it be known, the bosses will suspect you're in on it. That is, if they ever find out about it, and believe me, they eventually learn about everything when it comes to their business interests. They have ways of getting information. So, in a nutshell, don't you ever be a snitch."

"So, how do I handle a situation where I might know something is going on but not be a snitch?"

"You tell me and only me. No matter whom you meet along the way, no matter how much experience you gather doing this, even if you do this for the next two or three years, you tell me and me alone. I've built up some credibility with the higher ups in doing this for a while and I'll send it up the chain and it'll be handled."

"Okay, I got it."

"Rule number five is that if you ever get caught, you're to be a standup guy and not rat on anyone involved. Rats are killed. You keep your mouth shut! You do your time and you talk to no one, not cellmates or other inmates, because they are often informants that go right to the authorities with information they learn from other inmates."

I nodded. I'm sure the look on my face was very serious because this was pretty heavy stuff I was hearing.

"I think that's about it. I think I've covered all the preliminaries. If anymore comes to mind, I'll let you know. In the meantime, you sit tight. I'll be in touch to let you know about the logistics and specifics of what you'll be doing. Do you have any questions?"

"Uh, no," I answered quickly and without hesitation.

That seemed to impress Pete Madison because he smiled widely. "Good. Good. You're learning fast, Narducci. No questions asked and no hesitation."

Chapter 25

Ten months later, in October of 1962 the world held its breath as the two nuclear superpowers squared off over Cuba. The Soviets had placed nuclear missiles on the island just ninety miles off American shores. Cuba was so close that missiles launched from there would mean the government would have just a few minutes to detect the launch and react.

Everyone in the world was on alert.

Military and civilian advisors pressured Kennedy to invade Cuba to knock out the missiles before they became operational. The pressure on the president to order air strikes and to be followed by a full-scale invasion was intense in the early days of the thirteen-day crisis.

Kennedy thought all of his commanders should be issued a copy of Barbara Tuchmann's *The Guns of August*, published that same year. The book recounted how events spiraled out of control and erupted into World War I.

Kennedy wanted to avoid events escalating into a nuclear war. He ordered the cessation of assassination attempts against Castro, so that wouldn't conflict with his attempts to resolve the missile crisis. Whether those orders were immediately carried out is a matter of conjecture, but Kennedy resisted the hawks and was able to resolve the crisis without the necessity of using either the tactic of an air strike or an invasion, and the missiles were withdrawn.

I guess Cuba was a big deal after all...at least when it came to nuclear missiles being deployed there. That just goes to show you that this CIA analyst got it wrong on what Cuba meant to USA security.

In the eyes of the world, it was the Cuban Missile Crisis in which Kennedy became a statesman, as his popularity soared once again.

From that point forward, barring any unforeseen political disasters or economic collapse, it was generally agreed Kennedy would be untouchable when he ran for re-election two years hence in 1964. It is worth noting that the mob also agreed with that assessment.

The Mafia chieftains understood Kennedy would be unbeatable in the '64 national election. That perception of Kennedy's invincibility would have profound effects upon both the mob and the American political scene.

Chapter 26

Once I began working on the shipment of drugs, I didn't really know what was in the boxes. Oh, I knew it was drugs I just mean I didn't know if it was cocaine or heroin. Maybe it was both. You see I learned early on from my mentor, Pete Madison, not to ask any questions. I kept my mouth shut and the money I received for doing my job was more than I would ever have imagined.

I assisted in shipping drugs out of Vietnam for the full year of 1962, and I got to be pretty good at requisitioning some U.S. Government packaging. My cover was that I was assembling pamphlets regarding my duties as a translator. I said I was putting together a Vietnamese-to-English dictionary, and vice versa, of phrases and the like. Funny thing is no one ever called me on it. I guess they just assumed I had access to a printer and a publisher of some kind who could put it all together into something like a binder, a book. No one ever asked to see one of the non-existent pamphlets. They just took my word for it, so I got all the boxes and government stencils I could ever use.

I must say I became quite proficient at making everything look very official. I also assisted in loading the planes. The drugs were placed in the boxes and the boxes were labeled as U.S. Government Property. As far as I know, no one ever opened a single box for inspection. I don't know if the official looking boxes were ever needed on the other end when they were being unloaded because Pete never told me anything about that side of the operation.

In retrospect, I think the boxes were merely another form of insurance. They were used just in case the authorities ever boarded one of the planes to have a look see. The hope, of course, was that the boxes looked so official that no one would ever dare open them. And it worked. Yeah, the mob was really into that word—-insurance. They always looked for ways to protect their interests.

By the end of '62, we had recruited others to help in shipping the drugs, and I had even trained another person in the art of 'government packaging'. You see the South Vietnamese Army had also increased their troop strength, and with that came the need for more translators. It was explained to me not to get nervous. My job with the mob and my life were not in jeopardy simply because I was training someone else. I mean they weren't getting ready to eliminate me. The mob simply wanted another guy in place fully trained in my function as backup just in case some stray Viet Cong mortar shell took me out of commission. I went along with that explanation. Hell, what other choice would I have had but to go along with it?

It was just after Christmas of '62 when Pete Madison surprised the crap out of me. I was seated at the bar in one of the clubs when he approached me, and said, "Let's get a table in the back, Kid. I've got some news for you."

When we sat down, he came right to the point.

"You're goin' home."

"What?"

"Well, you're not going home to Virginia, but you are going back to the States—-Louisiana to be specific. You're heading to New Orleans where you'll be assigned other duties. It's like I told you once. You impressed the boys back home, and the bosses like what you've been doing here as well, so they're sending you back to the States.

I started to laugh. "Aren't you forgetting something? I'm with the CIA. The mob...uh...the bosses can't just send me back to the States."

Pete looked at me as if I was the dumbest hick he'd ever met. "After a year now, you still don't get it, do you, Narducci? For a college grad you're a dumb shit, aren't you?"

"What do you mean?" I asked without getting angry.

"You, better than most anyone else, know the connection the CIA has with the mob. You think for a second the mob can't get the CIA to send you anywhere in the world? Hell! If the mob wants you in New Orleans, then that's where Uncle Sam is damn well going to send you."

Again, I hated to admit to myself that Pete Madison was right but I had never actually sat down and really thought about how powerful the mob had become.

"Hell man," Pete continued, "the mob and the CIA are joined at the hip. The Agency can't afford to anger them for fear the American people will learn the CIA and the mob have been trying to hit Castro. And believe me! The mob would let it be known. They'd have nothing to lose except for a few would-be hit men roaming around Cuba they don't give two shits about anyway."

I nodded reluctantly

"Besides," Pete continued, as he gazed at me solemnly, "it could never be proved who the CIA talked to within the higher echelon of the mob."

"Yeah, it could," I interjected. "I talked to Johnny Pistelli and he could tell the authorities who he spoke..." I stopped in mid-sentence, as the full realization swam over me.

That familiar, obnoxious smirk returned to Pete Madison's face, as he eyed me, nodded and said, "Yeah, now you're starting to get the picture, aren't you Narducci?" he asked rhetorically, as he almost laughed at my precarious situation.

He continued. "Anyway, there's a CIA office in New Orleans and that's where you'll be reporting. What your assignment with the CIA is going to be, I haven't got a clue, nor do I give a shit, but you just report to that office for work, do your job and sit tight. Eventually, someone will contact you."

"Well, what about the operation here? Don't you need me to...?"

"Hey, you trained another in what you were doing, didn't you?"

"Yeah," I answered matter-of-factly.

"Then don't worry about the operation on this side of the Pacific...just thank your lucky stars you're getting out of this God-forsaken, mosquito infested country."

Chapter 27

Ever since the American crime syndicate arrived in Southeast Asia, they quickly made contacts and set up shop with Asian mobsters. The American crime syndicate did their homework. They learned the Vietnamese were making a mere pittance of what they could have garnered if they went worldwide. Of course, the Mafia didn't inform the Vietnamese of the vast potential open to Asians but did make a very lucrative offer. The American mobsters presented the Asians with a very profitable incentive for dealing with them—-exporting their drugs beyond the borders of Vietnam—-and thus making them much wealthier. When that offer came their way, the Vietnamese quickly agreed and proceeded to cultivate the poppy fields with added zest.

The Mafia went International long before it dawned on American corporate executives there was a lot of money to be made going global.

Those in charge of the operation were the smartest most cunning mobsters ever known and I was snared in their web. Pete Madison could have cited an additional rule number six to me—-make a pact with the devil and screw yourself for all time.

These guys really knew how to protect their illicit empire. They'd tip the Feds about a shipment of heroine, sacrificing the shipment through some bogus corridor so as to protect their actual drug route. That also served the purpose of making the Feds think they had more of an impact on the drug trade than they actually did. In reality, the Feds didn't make a dent in it.

Whatever the source of the drugs, whether originating in Asia or South America, the shipments would come up through Mexico. The drugs would be moved across the border usually on low-level flights...some of those flights were with the compliments of Air America.

As far as I know, these mobsters were the first to come up with the idea of sacrificing a drug shipment to protect the overall operation. It's unbelievable how much money they made in drug trafficking. In actuality there was so much money to be made that if the Feds somehow managed to capture nine out of every ten shipments the mob would still make money. It was that lucrative! Of course, if you tried to cheat these guys out of ten bucks, they'd kill you for it...though that has more to do with the act of cheating than the monetary amount.

The planes crossing the border would land in any number of places in the desert where the drugs would be unloaded and placed into the trunks of automobiles. The cars were outfitted with fake plates, fake registrations, and VIN numbers, and would then leave in one-hour intervals and drive up and across the country's interstate highways. It was always autos, not large semi-trailer trucks, because, though the semis would have been able to make bigger hauls, they would also draw more attention to themselves and would have to stop at weigh stations. The mob left nothing to chance.

Those who drove the automobiles didn't know what was in the trunk of their respective autos or even who hired them. All they had was a designated location of where to drop the car. The drivers were under strict orders to stay five miles per hour below the speed limit and to observe all the rules of the road. The bosses didn't want any of them stopped for a traffic ticket and risk the trunk being opened in a routine check. It was a piece of cake and the mob operated that way for years.

For the most part, there were no incidents, though there was this one time I heard about. One driver exceeded the speed limit in Louisiana and was stopped. The highway patrolman didn't open the trunk, but he did write the guy a speeding ticket. The mob kept tabs on such things through their contacts with local authorities. By the time the driver made his delivery in Ohio, the mob had already heard that the guy had received a speeding ticket. After he made his drop, several hoods picked him up and he was taken to a secluded spot...some old, long since abandoned farm, and the guy was staked down on the ground spread-eagled, his hands and ankles secured tightly by rope to stakes in the ground.

The story goes something like this...

One of the mobsters asked the poor sap, "Are those ropes too tight?"

The guy was so frightened he couldn't speak regardless of the fact he was gagged, and he stared at his abductors in wide-eyed terror.

Sometimes it's the fear of the unknown unaware of what's coming next that is so horrifying for victims of the mob's wrath.

The mobster squatted down and asked the question again. "Is that too tight?"

The victim nodded repeatedly in the affirmative.

"Just a second," he said. "I'll get something to loosen the rope a bit," as he arose and went to a shed. The mobster returned with an old, rusty hatchet, and proceeded to 'loosen' the bindings just below where the rope was tied to one of his hands.

Even beneath the gag, the victim's muffled screams of agony were loud and shrill, though there was no one around for miles to hear him.

"There! How's that, asshole? Let me loosen those other ropes too."

The mobster proceeded to 'loosen' the rope around his other hand at the wrist and then both feet at the ankles, as the victim's blood curdling screams continued unabated.

The mob bosses wanted the guy to suffer as a lesson to other drivers for whom they would present pictures for the penalty of exceeding the speed limit. Yeah, one of the hoods took pictures. It must have been a Bonafacio hit.

One of the mobsters looked at the victim's appendages still tied to the steaks in the ground, while the blood spurted from his wrists and ankles, and commented, "We could leave him here as is. He's gonna bleed out real soon."

Observing the gruesome scene, another of the mobsters laughed, as he replied, "He certainly wouldn't get very far on those stumps before he bled to death."

"Ah, we'd better err on the side of caution, just in case," replied another amidst the ongoing agonizing howls of the victim.

"Yeah, I suppose you're right," said the other, who raised his hatchet, and was about to finish him off.

"Wait! I've got a better idea. I was here the other day, and I happen to know that piece of machinery over there still works," he motioned with a tilt of his head, as he departed quickly.

A few minutes later, the goon returned behind the wheel of a thrashing machine and he intentionally approached very slowly, tauntingly so, terrorizing the victim all the more seeing what was coming.

The mobsters never bothered to bury what was left of the guy or hide the bloody pulp that remained. They left the remnants of what had once been a human being for the bugs and the birds.

Yeah, the mob has always been into pain when they're sending a message. No doubt they distributed the pictures to future drivers. It was through such fear that mobsters ruled their kingdom of crime. For the most part, the fellows who carried out such gruesome killing assignments were psychopaths and sadists. They literally enjoyed what they did. I know for a fact many of the assassins taunted their victims—-laughing heartily as they inflicted excruciating pain—-while the victims longed for death that would bring a cessation to their torture. You see a man's fate at the hand of the mob is not always a quick, unexpected bullet to the back of the head but often times a very slow and drawn-out torturous death.

Chapter 28

At this juncture I believe it is timely and appropriate for me to recap the times from the perspective of a member of the intelligence community on the scene.

The sixties have been seen as a decade of great change within America and indeed they were. It was a decade of the great divide as the turbulent 60's broke free from the languid 50's—-a crack in time—-that starkly announced the separation of one generation from another when one set of issues changed America's direction.

Specifically, 1968 is the year cited as the pivotal days of change. Those who subscribe to 1968 as the crucial year point to several occurrences. They cite the police riot in Chicago's Grant Park during the '68 Democratic Convention when the Vietnam anti-war protests were in full swing; they point to the assassinations of Dr. Martin Luther King and Senator Robert F. Kennedy which tragically shattered the hopes of many of the younger generation; they note the sexual revolution when free sex was the order of the day; they further point to the younger generation questioning its government and vowed America would never again walk into the dark void of war with unquestioned obedience; and they conclude by mentioning both the generation gap and the credibility gap created by a distrust of what the government was telling its citizens about the Vietnam War—-pointing to the release of the Pentagon Papers in 1971 as bearing out their claims.

It is through this prism I viewed the 60's but I do not subscribe to the theory 1968 was the pivotal year. Living through that decade my view is the watershed year in America came five years prior.

1963 was less than ten years removed from McCarthyism, and, though the country was not paralyzed by the steel grip of the intense paranoia of the Red Scare of the '50's, it was nevertheless a time of deep concern about the Soviet Union and a time of staunch anti-communism. After all, in 1957 the Russians had beaten us into space with Sputnik, and the summer of '63 was less than one year removed from the Cuban Missile Crisis, which literally scared the shit out of the American people, as it did most citizens of the Soviet Union not to mention the citizens of the world.

When remembering 1963 one must take into account anti-Communist fervor throughout the country. Additionally, one must not overlook the importance of what occurred in 1959—-when Castro took power and kicked the mob out of Cuba—-a very recent occurrence and especially clear in the mob's memory just four short years later in 1963.

As a Marxist dictator, Castro attempted to round up the mobsters and have them shot ala Joseph Stalin in the 1940's-1950's Soviet Union. As it was, the mob lost hundreds of millions of dollars from their casinos, the numbers racket, prostitution and other vices. Unlike many of us who lived during that time and have forgotten what the crime syndicate lost the mob remembered. Though, as noted earlier, they would make a bundle on arms shipments.

In my view the turning point came in the summer of '63, specifically when a whirlwind of events swirled across the country, converged and compressed into the short space of forty-eight hours during two days in June. The events of those two days forever changed America and would have a profound effect upon the future course of the country as well the future lives of the people involved in those events.

The first of those events occurred on June 10, 1963 when Kennedy delivered a speech at American University that he and his speechwriter, Ted Sorenson had prepared. Kennedy purposely kept the speech under wraps and did not send it to the State Department for their review in advance, which would have been the normal procedure.

As it turned out, some newspaper editorials hailed the speech as a great State Paper, though Americans by and large gave it very little notice. In spite of that fact, many people are familiar with at least one excerpt from that speech...

"In the final analysis, our most basic common link is that we all inhabit this small planet; we all breathe the same air; we all cherish our children's future; and we are all mortal."

Where the speech did receive considerable attention was in the Soviet Union where the Russians sat up and took notice of the olive branch extended from the American President during the height of the Cold War.

The Cuban Missile Crisis of October '62 had sobered the young president and he embarked upon a very thoughtful approach to his presidency. Behind the scenes, he made overtures to the Soviet Union about a Nuclear Test Ban Treaty via letters to Soviet Premier Khrushchev, letters that began during the Cuban Missile Crisis and continued afterwards.

With his speech at American University, Kennedy made his views public. He wished to usher in a new era with the Soviet Union. It was Kennedy and Khrushchev who, in effect, attempted to begin a détente between the United States and the Soviet Union in their private letters before the populations in either of their respective countries were ever aware of it.

After the American University speech, Kennedy sent an emissary to the Soviet Union to negotiate a Nuclear Test Ban Treaty, and he also sent along an array of sophisticated communication equipment of the time—-faxes, teletypes, and telephones.

During the Cuban Missile Crisis, it had become painfully evident to the American President that events were more likely to spin out of control without instantaneous communication with the Soviet Union. The communication equipment was installed and

America and the Soviet Union were henceforth connected with a hot line.

The American University Speech was the beginning of a thaw in the rhetoric of the Cold War, as were the letters between the two leaders that preceded the speech.

Kennedy's view of the world had changed markedly, and he was determined that we must never again approach the brink of a nuclear holocaust. That was a very laudable goal indeed, but it was another sentence in that same American University speech that filled a totally different group of people with a high degree anxiety.

"Let us reexamine our attitude toward the Soviet Union..."

An entire generation of Americans had been taught...to the point of being brainwashed...that the Soviet Union with its accompanying Communist system of government was evil and something to be feared, hated and opposed.

Now, an American President, one who had stood up to the Soviet Union over missiles in Cuba, effectually stated that America's role in the world need not necessarily be as the sworn enemy of the Soviet Union—-at least not to the point of a scorched death in the holocaust of a nuclear war.

It was truly a remarkable statement in the context of the times in which that speech was delivered. Kennedy, the wounded veteran of World War II, a Cold Warrior and a hero of the Cuban Missile Crisis had become a Statesman.

However, a very vicious group of people became deeply concerned about their business interests when this speech was delivered. Kennedy's words made a profound impression upon the American Mafia, as they also took notice but for very different reasons than did the Soviets.

The second of the events of those forty-eight hours in June occurred later that day.

On the evening of June 10th in Washington D.C...actually the next morning across the International Date Line in Saigon...a Buddhist monk sat in the lotus position, and, after soaking himself in gasoline, lit a match in an act of protest against the government of South Vietnam.

Instantaneously the monk burst into a ball of flame. As the flames engulfed him, the gruesome scene was captured in a photograph that was seen around the world via the Associated Press wire service.

Kennedy, along with hundreds of millions of other people across the country and around the world, saw the picture and it disgusted all who viewed it.

The monk's suicidal inferno added to Kennedy's skepticism of President Diem's leadership, which had long suppressed the majority population of Buddhists in South Vietnam.

The President knew the situation in Vietnam was deteriorating. He felt America could not afford to fight for a government that was not backed by the will of its own people. For Kennedy, that picture said it all and on the 10th of June 1963 it was the final straw.

Rumors had already circulated in Washington that Kennedy was preparing to withdraw an unspecified number of troops from Vietnam by the end of the year. Actually, it was Kennedy himself who had started the rumors when he said as much without specifying the exact number of troops to be withdrawn during a May 22nd press conference when asked...

"Mr. President, the brother of the President of South Viet-Nam has said that too many American troops are in South Viet-Nam. Could you comment on that, and give us some progress report on what is going on?"

"Yes, I hope we could," the President answered. "We would withdraw troops, any number of troops, any time the government of South Viet-Nam would suggest it. The day after it was suggested, we would have some troops on their way home. That is Number 1. Number 2 is we are hopeful that the situation in South Viet-Nam would permit some withdrawal in any case by the end of the year.... As of today, we would hope we could begin to perhaps do it at the end of the year, but we couldn't make any final judgment at all until we see the course of the struggle the next few months."

Kennedy believed he couldn't begin to withdraw anyone until the internal situation in South Vietnam was stabilized with the Buddhist population, and he was now very much leaning toward the possibility Diem had to go.

In a democratic society, the justification for a nation to wage war is limited to there being present at least one of three validations.

The first two are easily defined and quite easily understood. One is that a nation has been attacked; the second is that a nation is under threat of an imminent attack.

Simple, easily understood.

The third justification for war, however, is by far the most complex and the most encompassing—-that war is in the best interest of the country.

It is under the third rationale for war that European nations should have shed the shackles of restraint and appeasement and raised the rationale for war to stand up to Hitler when Germany invaded Czechoslovakia—-before Hitler began his stranglehold on the countries of central Europe.

The third validation for war can also encompass the moral imperative of intervening to stop genocide. Ironically, in a democratic society such as ours the moral argument of coming to the aid of the victims of genocidal slaughter has astonishingly rarely been invoked.

In the case of Vietnam, it was the third rationale that was called upon as part of the fight against the spread of Communism, though the rationale...the domino theory...was faulty.

Just as Thailand didn't fall after the collapse of South Vietnam, just as Malaysia didn't fall, or Indonesia, or Singapore, the domino theory was irrelevant. Indeed, when South Vietnam fell none of those countries were attacked.

Nowadays, it's quite popular to apply the pottery barn theory to the coup that overthrew Diem in South Vietnam in September, 1963—-*You break it; you own it*. But, like the domino theory in regards to Vietnam, the pottery barn theory was flawed. That theory did not apply to South Vietnam because the country was, in fact, already broken. Indeed, instead of breaking it, Kennedy believed if he could be reasonably certain of stabilization in the leadership of Vietnam, the country would be able to function with the support of its people and he could withdraw.

In the end, more than 58,000 young Americans would die in a civil war between the partitioned North and South Vietnam, while the political pundits in Washington time and time again with never ending bluster proclaimed America was fighting the expansion of Communism relative to the domino theory. History, much too late for those who fought and died there, would prove those political pundits wrong.

Kennedy, who wished to begin a détente with the Soviets, saw the situation more clearly than anyone, but in spite of his soaring popularity after the Cuban Missile Crisis, Kennedy hesitated on Vietnam just as he had hesitated for several years on Civil Rights. If he withdrew from South Vietnam before the '64 election, he was not confident of re-election, nor was he confident of being re-elected if he addressed Civil Rights during his first term.

Meanwhile, with events occurring at an ever-rapid pace, the third event of that fateful forty-eight-hour time span occurred the next day when Governor George Wallace of Alabama stood in a doorway at the University of Alabama on the afternoon of June 11th to prohibit the admission of two young Negroes to that institution.

Kennedy countered by federalizing the National Guard, the Governor stepped aside, and the two young Negroes registered as students to the University.

Kennedy overcame his reluctance to address the civil rights of American Negroes, as he finally felt obliged to address the American people. Kennedy quickly scribbled some notes for an impromptu speech, and on the evening of June 11th, the President addressed the nation on Civil Rights, while Vietnam was very much on his mind...

"Today, we are committed to a worldwide struggle to promote and protect the rights of all who wish to be free. And when Americans are sent to Vietnam...we do not ask for whites only. It ought to be possible therefore, for American students of any color to attend any public institution they select without having to be backed up by troops.

"We are confronted primarily with a moral issue. It is as old as the Scriptures and it is as clear as the American Constitution.

"If an American, because his skin is dark, cannot eat lunch in a restaurant open to the public, if he cannot send his children to the best public school available... if, in short, he cannot enjoy the full and free life which all of us want, then who among us would be content to have the color of his skin changed and stand in his place?"

On the heels of Kennedy's speech at American University delivered just twenty-four hours earlier, this too was a speech unprecedented for the times in which it was given. No president in American history had ever addressed such encompassing, gut-wrenching issues within such a brief span of twenty-four hours.

Like so many of the tragic heroes of history, Kennedy was truly and forlornly designated as a man ahead of this time.

Tragically, a fourth event occurred just hours after the President's speech of June 11th, when the secretary of the Mississippi NAACP, Medgar Evers, arrived home and was shot in the back, murdered by a cowardly assassin lying in wait under the cover of bushes. The assassin was destined to come to justice, but not before thirty years had elapsed since committing the heartless, brutal murder...a tale tragically and succinctly retold in *The Ghosts of Mississippi*.

Such were the rapid progression of events in the compression of forty-eight hours in June of 1963 that will forever be a watershed year in American History.

It was during that brief forty-eight-hour span that the fate of the thirty-fifth President of the United States was sealed. With the rumors of withdrawal in conjunction with the American University Speech, events converged rapidly in a rendezvous with destiny, and in 1963 the American Mafia was at the hub of those events.

The next morning a phone call was placed from Louisiana to Florida, though nothing specific was stated over the phone.

"We need to meet and talk about that speech."

"I don't give a shit about those nigger assholes."

"That's not the speech I'm referring to," retorted the voice on the other end of the phone.

Chapter 29

As for me, I did receive an assignment by the CIA that shipped me back to the States just as Pete Madison said I would. I was working in New Orleans as an analyst reviewing Spanish communications from Mexico and Latin America, mostly from Guatemala. That wasn't as mundane as it may sound because during the '60's the Kennedy administration paid a lot of attention to Latin America.

Mine was a 9 to 5 job but I found myself working a lot of overtime with all that was going on in Latin America. I didn't mind though. In fact, I welcomed the overtime, because I was no longer receiving those 'bonuses' to which I had become so accustomed when working with Pete Madison in Vietnam. After two months in New Orleans that was about to change.

One night I left the office at about seven o'clock and headed over to the French Quarter to get some dinner and take in one of the nude shows. Naturally, I planned to get a woman as well, but when I was about halfway through my dinner a guy approached and sat down uninvited opposite me.

I looked up in surprise. It was someone I'd never seen before. He was dressed in a dark suit and tie and he looked like a caricature of so many of those underling gangsters that you've seen in the movies. He was a heavyset fellow who for sure had eaten too much pasta and he had dark black hair that was slicked back. He pulled out a pack of cigarettes, lit one and proceeded to blow the smoke right in my face. He gave me a smirk that looked like he was just begging me to get up and start something with him. The guy appeared to outweigh me by more than a hundred and fifty pounds but that wasn't what concerned me the most. What made me uneasy was my assumption the guy was packing a piece. My assumption was soon confirmed as he grabbed his lapel and opened his jacket just far enough for me to see a holstered pistol inside his coat. He still hadn't spoken when he arose, squashed out his cigarette in my dinner plate and tilted his head towards the door in a gesture for me to follow him.

As I arose, I looked for the waiter so I could pay the bill.

"Don't worry about it. It's been taken care of," he spoke for the first time, as he walked on ahead of me.

I followed him out the door where a sedan awaited. He directed me into the back seat while he opened the front passenger's seat for himself. As I was about to get in, I saw a man seated in the back on the far side.

"Don't just stand there gawking, Narducci. Get in and close the door," he said, as he obviously knew who I was though I didn't recognize him at all.

I climbed into the back seat, and as the car pulled away the man in the back reached inside his coat, and I almost crapped in my pants. *Holy shit, here it comes,* I thought, but when his hand came out of his coat, he was holding a white envelope which he handed to me.

"We heard you did good work for us in Nam," he said without telling me his name. Since he knew who I was, I thought maybe I should ask him his name, but didn't, as I remembered what I'd been told at the Brown Derby about asking someone's name.

"Put that away for now," he nodded toward the envelope that I was holding. "You can open it later. We've got a job for you. You're going take a vacation...couple of days...fly to Houston. From there you're going to rent a car and head west," he said, as he proceeded to tell me the nature of the assignment.

Chapter 30

Sure enough, two days later I was standing with several other guys in the dead of night in the Sonoran Desert...a wasteland that stretched from Mexico up into Arizona.

I was in a location referred to as a pass-through point—-where the drugs from Southeast Asia via Mexico were unloaded and then sent to all points throughout the country.

As we were waiting for the flight to arrive, I wished I had brought along a heavier jacket, as I was wearing only a light windbreaker. I found out the hard way that the desert cools off considerably at night and I was literally shivering.

I was told that once the plane arrived, the drugs would be unloaded in a matter of minutes and placed in automobiles for transit to drops known only by the respective drivers.

The pilot was under orders to stay in the cockpit when he landed and to keep the engines running just in case the plane was discovered and he had to take off in a hurry. If they couldn't get the merchandise off the plane, an alternate prearranged landing area would be used. The mob always took that contingency into account to safeguard their shipments. I took some solace in the fact there were some other saps standing somewhere else in the desert shivering their balls off waiting for a flight that probably wouldn't arrive.

When the flight landed, it was dark, but I could see from the light in the cockpit that the pilot was my old acquaintance from Nam—-Pete Madison. He noticed me as well and opened his window.

"Hey, Anthony, how do you like being back in the States?"

"Oh, it's great! Getting some American pussy is refreshing after all those Asian whores. Hey, mind if I come up to say hello and warm up a bit?"

"Not at all, come on in. I'll open the cockpit door for you."

When I boarded and made my way to the front of the plane, Pete was standing in the cockpit doorway.

"You look good, Pete."

"I can't say the same for you, Narducci. You look a little tired."

"Yeah, well, I'm working two jobs, you know."

"Are those spooks in the CIA busting' your balls?"

"Not really but I'm working the Latin American scene now and it's really busy what with all that's going on down there."

"Well, take a seat," he motioned inside the cockpit and directed me to the unoccupied co-pilot's chair.

As I sat down, I noted the seats were comfortable and they swiveled so we could face one another. "Pretty nice," I said.

"Yeah, they try to make it comfortable for us with all the overseas flights you know. We have a few minutes at least to catch up while they're unloading. So, what the hell are you doing out here?"

"Actually, since I got back to the States, this is my first assignment in working for..."

Pete raised his hand to stop me. "Don't tell me anything. The less I know the better."

I nodded in understanding as I smiled. "You know, I don't think I ever thanked you, Pete."

"Thanked me for what?"

"For being my mentor, showing me the ropes, taking the time to tell me the rules."

"Oh," he chuckled, "you remember the rules, do you?"

"Oh, yeah, like rule number one, the first one you ever told me. 'You're told to do something—-you do it. You don't ask questions. People who ask questions make the bosses very suspicious, and, if they're suspicious of you, you might wind up dead.'"

Pete laughed. "Not bad, not bad at all, Kid."

"Yeah, I owe you."

"Nah," Pete dismissed my comment with a wave of his hand.

"No, really, you taught me a lot."

"Yeah, well, you were pretty green."

"There was one rule though that I don't think you mentioned."

"Oh?"

"Yeah," I replied, as I reached inside my jacket and pulled out a silencer-laden .22 caliber pistol from an easily concealed pancake holster. When I leveled the gun at Pete, his eyes immediately widened in fearful disbelief.

"You didn't tell me about rule number six, Pete."

He swallowed hard...his fearful stare unabated.

"Don't ever cheat the mob by skimming merchandise and going into business for yourself. Anyone who does that is dead."

I lowered my aim as a muted metallic thump sounded when the pistol discharged one bullet that ripped through Pete's kneecap. He immediately emitted a howling, gut-wrenching scream, as he instinctively reached toward his shattered knee writhing in pain.

I kept the gun leveled at Pete as several guys boarded the plane and ran up the aisle when they heard Pete scream. His screams were their signal. When they got to the cockpit one of them frisked Pete and removed a pistol from inside his flight jacket. Pete was still wincing in excruciating pain when they grabbed him from his pilot's chair and dragged him down the aisle.

Another guy came up the aisle and sat down in Pete's chair...the replacement pilot no doubt. He was an odd-looking man who wore an obvious toupee and his unusual peculiar appearance was enhanced because he had no eyebrows. If I had to describe him, I would liken him to a rodent.

My instructions had been to disable Pete Madison, not to kill him.

I lingered there in the cockpit for a couple of minutes seated in the co-pilot's chair as I thought about the assignment I had just carried out. I must have been in a bit of a trance because that replacement pilot turned to me, and said, "You can put that gun away now."

I hadn't realized I still had the gun in my hand. I slid it back into my holster, and, as I got up and walked back down the aisle and disembarked the plane, I could hear Pete's shrieks of pain in the distance.

The fate of those the mob deems to have committed unpardonable sins is not a quick death. Skimming merchandise for the purpose of going into business for oneself is one of those unforgivable sins, and Pete Madison's fate was slow and excruciatingly painful.

Since then, even though years have elapsed, on some nights when the temperature is just right, and the air is crisp and cool against my face as it was that night, I can still hear in my mind's ears the echoes of Pete Madison's shrill screams of agony as if once again I was standing in the cool, night air of the Sonoran Desert.

Chapter 31

As the summer progressed and moved toward autumn, Kennedy stopped the rumors by making it official—-1,000 U.S. troops would be withdrawn from South Vietnam by Christmas of 1963.

Kennedy also made another decision.

In order to stabilize Vietnam and prepare for American withdrawal, President Diem as well as his brother, Nhu had to go. A military coup would occur. Ambassador Henry Cabot Lodge was in on the plan, the CIA, the American Military, as well as several, though not all, of Kennedy's advisors were informed.

Those units and CIA operatives stationed in Saigon, however, were under direct orders not to take any action...either overt or covert...to support the coup. That was not only for security reasons but again to ensure deniability—-like the Bay of Pigs—-a policy that was at the heart of the American spy agency's operations.

The man who would orchestrate the coup was the same man who would take over temporary leadership of South Vietnam, General Duong Van Minh, as the coup was to be handled solely by the South Vietnamese military.

The Nhu brothers were to be extricated from the capitol and given safe passage, as the State Department was working on what country they would be sent to and where they would reside in comfort for the rest of their lives. However, as the brothers were placed in the back of a transport and awaited departure the door opened abruptly and they were machine-gunned.

Such is often the case in a coup when power changes hands.

When Kennedy was informed the Nhu brothers were exterminated, the naivety of the young President became evident as he walked to the bathroom off the Oval Office and got physically ill.

I spent the remainder of the summer in New Orleans resuming my duties of reviewing cable traffic to and from Guatemala. One day, the first week of September, I got called into my boss's office.

"You wanted to see me, Sir?"

"Yeah, have a seat, Narducci," he said, as he flipped through some papers in a manila folder, which I assumed was my personnel file.

"How do you like New Orleans now that you've been here...," he streamed through some of the file, "for...uh...how long now?"

"Nine months, Sir. Oh, I like it fine. No complaints."

"Well, you're about to have a change of scenery."

"Oh?"

"You're being transferred to Texas...to the Fort Worth office."

"In what capacity will I...,"

"Well, that'll be up to your case officer in Texas. You did a good job here and I'm sorry to be losing you."

That surprised me because since I hadn't been here a year yet, I hadn't received a review, so I didn't know what he thought about me until just now...which I took as bullshit.

"Thank you, Sir," I nodded with appreciation.

"You do as well in Fort Worth, and it could go a long way toward a promotion for you, because you've built a good record for yourself."

I doubted he knew anything about my record, but I nodded in acknowledgement, "Thank you."

"They'd like you to report as quickly as possible, so I'll let you head home today and start packing. Just let me know when you're ready to go and stop by to say so long."

"I'll certainly do that."

As I left my boss's office, I immediately began to wonder if someone else was behind the transfer pulling strings as was the case when I came back from Vietnam to take the position in New Orleans.

I was secure in the fact the CIA had no idea I had done some jobs for the mob, and I knew that the CIA via the mob was still actively trying to hit Castro.

Kennedy had resumed that covert activity after the Cuban Missile Crisis passed. In any event, I didn't worry about what I'd be doing in Texas. I packed my bags, and reported to the CIA office in Fort Worth before the start of the next week.

Chapter 32

During the last week of September, well after my arrival in Fort Worth, I was visiting a club enjoying drinks and dinner when another anonymous figure sat down opposite me in an almost identical fashion as had happened in the Big Easy. Though he was a different person, he reminded me of that guy because he was just as big and he moaned slightly as he sat down, as if it were a difficult task.

He stared at me for what must have been half a minute. I think he was challenging me to say something like...who the fuck are you...or some such thing but I'd been through this before, so I played him by remaining silent and returning his stare.

"You're Narducci?" he finally asked.

"Yeah," I nodded without surprise with a self-satisfied smirk on my face.

"Someone would like to talk to you," he said, as he arose from his chair with another moan.

I knew the drill so I got up and followed him out the door. Once again, a dark sedan was awaiting us, and, as before, I climbed into the back seat.

When I saw the man seated in the back, I immediately recognized him as the same guy from the back seat of that car in New Orleans. As the automobile pulled away from the curb my surprise must have shown on my face.

"Why so fuckin' surprised, Kid? You think we only operate in New Orleans? We've got our flags planted all over the southwest," he laughed, as he reached inside his coat, though this time I didn't get nervous when he did so. He handed me another envelope, and, having learned from our last encounter, I immediately slid the envelope inside my coat pocket without opening it.

"You did a good job for us down in the desert and we need you to assist a few of our collectors. It'll be night work, so it won't interfere with your other daytime duties. Here's how it'll go. You'll be driving a collector around from spot to spot while they make their rounds, and you're to watch his back," he said, as he handed me a sheet of paper. "Be at this address tomorrow evening at 7 p.m. with your car to pick one of them up. He knows the make and model of your auto, so just sit tight in the car until he shows. He'll tell you where he needs to go. When he makes a collection, wait for him and he'll direct you to the next location."

I nodded in acknowledgement that I understood.

"By the way, your name has begun to circulate up to the big bosses. You're making a good reputation for yourself as an up and comer in the family...a standup guy. You play your cards right, keep doing a good job for us, and you'll be getting bigger assignments as time goes on."

"That's good to know," I replied, as I envisioned the money that would be coming my way, when the car came to a stop just a couple of blocks from the club.

"Okay, now beat it, and don't be late tomorrow night."

Chapter 33

It was just like the envelope man said it would be. The next night I drove a guy from location to location to make his collections, and I was very conscious of not asking any questions other than the address of our next stop.

It continued a couple of nights every week for two months until I was contacted to take a day of vacation from my CIA duties on an upcoming Friday.

I thought I might be going out of town for a three-day weekend assignment, but I learned it was merely a daytime job. It was the same basic instructions. I was to go to an address and wait in the car until someone arrived, who again had been given in advance the make, model and license plate of my car.

After a morning rain, it was a warm day and I had the driver's side window rolled down. I was having a cigarette while I waited for my passenger to show up at the pre-arranged time of 12:30 in the afternoon.

Suddenly, I heard what I thought was gunfire coming from behind me. I have never been in combat but I'd been to a firing range enough times to know rifle fire when I heard it...and it was close.

I saw some commotion in my rear-view mirror, but I couldn't see exactly what was happening. People were running, ducking, hitting the ground. Some of them were screaming. About ninety seconds later, a man came strolling casually up to the car and got in the back seat. He was a short guy of about five feet nine inches, slender of build with short hair and he was dressed in a light tan jacket and slacks. I could tell something was wrong about him. There was something out of sync; he was trying to be very nonchalant but he was sweating profusely.

He handed me a piece of paper with an address, and said, "Don't speed, and be sure to observe all the traffic signs, because I don't want us stopped for any reason."

I pulled away from the curb and out of habit flicked on the radio. A country-western song soon blared breaking the silence and I drove north toward the designated location. I had driven no more than five minutes when a bulletin came across the radio...

"Shots have been fired at President Kennedy's motorcade in Dallas. Details are sketchy at this point, but it is believed that the President was hit at least once. His condition at this time is unknown. He has been rushed to Parkland Hospital. Please stay tuned to this station for further bulletins."

I couldn't believe my ears, and when I glanced into the rear-view mirror, I saw the narrow stare of my passenger looking back at me...a sickly smirk planted firmly upon his face.

Chapter 34

As I drove through Dallas with my rider, I didn't dare look in the rear view-mirror again. It was as if...like a kid hiding under the covers...maybe not seeing the person in the back seat would mean there really wasn't anyone there.

When I approached an old, abandoned meatpacking plant on the outskirts of Dallas, my throat was so dry from nervous anxiety I could barely get the question out, as I asked, "Is this the place?"

"Yeah, I get out here," he said, and added, "and so do you."

I glanced over my shoulder and saw he had a gun leveled at me. I tell you I almost pissed my pants. I'd just heard the President of the United States had possibly been shot and I didn't have to be a genius to figure out the guy in the back seat had something to do with it. I didn't have any choice but to get out and go inside with him as he pointed his gun at me. I wasn't packing, as the only time I ever carried a piece was in the Sonoran corridor when I plugged Pete Madison in the kneecap. Part of my instructions that night was to get rid of the weapon so I buried it in a plastic bag a couple of feet deep in the desert sand. I never carried a piece since.

We got out of the car and my rider was behind me, instructing me as I walked in front of him.

"To the right," he said, as he directed me toward a door.

We entered and he directed me down a hallway and then through another door that led us into a large room where I saw four other guys inside. I knew immediately they were mobsters. One was squat, heavy set and wore a fedora. He looked somewhat familiar though I couldn't' place where I'd seen him. Two of the other three looked like enforcers. One was taller, hatless and more muscular. The other was skinnier and also hatless but had much more hair. The fourth guy had that authoritative look about him that told me he was in charge.

"Here he is," said my rider, as two of the men already had their weapons pulled before we entered the room and their pistols were trained on me.

I said a silent prayer believing these were my last moments on earth.

The bigger guy approached and frisked me to be sure I wasn't carrying.

"He's clean."

When my rider holstered his weapon, the short squat fellow in the fedora aimed his handgun at my rider and shot him at point blank range. My rider immediately fell to the ground grimacing in pain...a .38 caliber slug imbedded in his right leg.

I jumped, startled from the sudden loud clap of a gunshot that echoed off the walls of the large empty room. Because of our remote location no doubt, the shooter didn't bother to use a silencer.

My rider was frisked as he lay grimacing on the ground and his handgun was retrieved.

Then without any added fanfare, that fourth guy, the one who looked to be in charge casually pulled out a gun and shot my rider again...in his other leg. He immediately squealed a gut-wrenching scream.

From the sound of his high-pitched shrieking, I surmised the bullet must have shattered his tibia. I also surmised my rider must have committed an offense similar to that of Pete Madison. They wanted him to suffer or else they would simply have put a bullet in his head.

After the second shot was fired, a fifth man nonchalantly approached from the shadows and out into the open. It was the same man from the back seat of the sedan in New Orleans and Forth Worth...the envelope man who'd given me the cash and whose name I didn't know.

He viewed the man on the ground writhing in pain with initial indifference which slowly evolved into a pleasant smile. The envelope man turned to the squat man who'd taken the first shot, and said, "You did good Jack."

As it turned out, I would learn later there was a specific reason for the slow, torture of my rider. They kept me alive because they wanted me to witness the shooting and the disposing of the body. Sometimes the mob leaves the body out in the open for all to see because they want to send a message and they want others to see what gruesome things are done to a guy.

This was not one of those times. There would soon be no trace of the man I had picked up just outside of Dealey Plaza...it would be as if he never existed.

As the envelope man swung his glance around toward me, I swallowed back the lump in my throat. I knew the mob didn't leave loose ends, and I figured it would only be a matter of seconds before I joined my rider in a heap on the floor. I hoped it would be a quick death because I hadn't done anything to warrant a slow, torturous ending, but you could never tell with sadists. If they weren't in any hurry, my death could be slow and gruesome and they'd thoroughly enjoy doing it. They might torture me just for the fun of it.

My chest was heaving in dreadful anticipation of the inevitable and my hands were literally trembling. My shaking was so pronounced I doubt I could have even held the contents of a cup of coffee. They must have gotten quite a kick out of my extreme nervousness because they were all smirking at me and the envelope man stared at me as if he was looking right through me.

I was aware the more a person knows about what the mob has done, the more likely one's life could be quite abruptly and violently ended. I feared my end was very near.

I don't know if the envelope man was breaking one of the organization's cardinal rules, as he casually said, "He served his purpose." Then he snickered and flashed an evil grin.

He stared at me with a cold, inhuman stare, and said with astonishing understatement, "You look a little nervous, Narducci."

I swallowed deeply again and stared back at him with what I'm sure was the terrified look of a man who was spending his last moments on earth. The only reason I could fathom he was snickering at me was because he was a sadist and enjoyed inflicting pain. Or perhaps it was his way of boasting to show me how powerful he and his organization were.

I remained silent but I couldn't have spoken even if I'd wanted to. My mouth was as dry as cotton and I had no spit. Even though we'd arrived at this abandoned facility before any official word had been broadcast over the radio, I knew the mob had just taken out the President of the United States.

Then he smiled and broke the frightening silence by saying, "Hey, no need to be nervous. We're not going to harm you," he said, as he patted my face lightly with his left hand. "I told you that you've done good work and that you're an up and comer. Besides, you're our insurance, Narducci," he stated, as his smiled widened into a wide, satanic grin.

There was that word again so loved by the American Mafia.

"Can you imagine," he continued, "just for a moment, what the American people would say if they learned the man who was driving a getaway car is an active CIA agent?"

He let that sink in for a while before he shook his head in mock disbelief. "You could get down on your knees and swear on a stack of Bibles for a month you had nothing to do with it, but there's no way anyone would ever believe you knew nothing about what happened."

God! Talk about setting someone up. Of course! That's why the guy had broken the code and allowed me to witness the patsy getting shot. He wanted me to know more just in case I was ever found out or given up. I couldn't lie that I didn't know any details. I could only say I knew the details afterwards. Who would believe that?

I didn't know when they shot my rider that the idea was not to kill him. It was a similar situation when I was told to disable Pete Madison by shooting him in the kneecap and I was specifically instructed that under no circumstances was I to kill him.

The shot in the leg of my rider certainly worked as envisioned. He was disabled all right. The second shot he received was simply sadistic by that fourth man.

The envelope man continued. "Naturally, we're going to let the CIA know...discreetly of course...that you were there just around the corner from Dealey Plaza. We have pictures of you sitting in the car waiting for your rider to arrive, and pictures of him getting into the car. They aren't frontal pictures of you...only from the side and behind. It might take them a while but I think they'd be able to identify you," he chuckled, quite sure of himself.

I knew exactly what he meant. There'd be no need for authorities to make an ironclad I.D. on me. God, what a sap I was! I'd always used my own car when I drove on those assignments.

"We may not use the pictures," he continued, "and whether we mention your name or not to the CIA we haven't quite decided but don't worry," he laughed. "I think we can convince The Agency bosses to steer any possible investigation away from organized crime," he said, as he let out a chortle of louder laughter, as he added, "Hell, we don't ever have to kill you, Narducci, because you're already a walking dead man."

God, the mob had thought of everything!

"Just saying that a CIA agent was there," the envelope man continued, "should be enough insurance for us along with the fact the CIA enlisted us to bump off Castro," he laughed again, and continued. "You see the Agency still wouldn't want that Castro crap to get out. And we would protect your job too. The Agency is not going to do anything to you as long as we wish for you to do our bidding. Yeah, we should be home free, and for your sake, you should hope we are as well."

Indeed, some witnesses in Dealey Plaza that day reported seeing a man that resembled Oswald walking out of the Texas School Book Depository Building, head north on Houston and get into an awaiting automobile. But he had disappeared forever from the face of the earth—-compliments of the mob.

Through the years the snicker of the envelope man would remain in my mind...hauntingly so...and all that I learned about the Kennedy Assassination was confirmed by that one, sickly, evil smirk.

Someone within the mob, or controlled by the mob, suggested to who we later came to know as Lee Harvey Oswald that he should purchase a Mannlicher-Carcano rifle. It wasn't expensive and a fellow even loaned him the whole of twelve bucks to buy it, and Oswald used an assumed name as was suggested to him.

After delivery of the rifle Oswald and his friend went to a rifle range, had fun, shot some targets. That's how the mob got their hands on a slug from Oswald's rifle. They merely picked a slug that was slightly flattened for realism that would later be planted on stretcher in Parkland Hospital. So very, very simple—-a bullet from Oswald's rifle—-what could be easier?

Months prior to the assassination, on April 10th specifically, the rifle was taken from the garage where Oswald stowed it and a shot was fired through the window of the home of General Walker. The bullet missed him...barely...and unbeknownst to Oswald the rifle was returned to the garage. The incident however would further add credence to the lone nut theory after the assassination when the ballistics report was compared later to Oswald's rifle.

The day of the assassination, the same mob contact suggested that Oswald bring his rifle into work.

"I'll pick you up after your shift. We'll go shooting. But be sure you wrap up that rifle when you go to the Book Depository because they might get a little nervous if they see you bringing in a weapon," he laughed heartily.

"Yeah, that could certainly freak some people out."

My rider was the one who fired three shots at the motorcade. That was his lone assignment. The mob ensured he wouldn't fuck up and fire more than three because they only gave him three bullets and thus three cartridges were left behind. I don't know for sure but my educated guess is that the rifle was loaded with blanks or his instructions could have been to fire the rifle into the air, but I think the former is more likely.

My rider left the rifle behind as instructed. It of course was found at the scene and was easily traced back to Oswald. My rider wasn't a twin, but he had the same general build as the man who was *designated* as the assassin and it made my blood curdle when I thought of that unlucky schmuck being set up by the mob.

These guys were masters at setting someone up for a fall. I knew that better than anyone...at least better than anyone living anyway.

There's an unwritten rule in the mob—-well they're all unwritten actually—-but there is a rule that you never take out a hit man, because if you did, no one would ever carry out a hit. The guy they disposed of however was only playing a role. He wasn't supposed to hit the target. He was just another patsy; he was merely there to fire and plant the rifle, so technically speaking, the mob wasn't eliminating someone they'd hired to perform a hit. The mob couldn't very well have expected Oswald to shoot his own rifle and leave it behind to incriminate himself.

None of this was known to me that day in the meatpacking plant...only years later did I piece it all together.

What I learned in those subsequent years was there were others that day that actually carried out the hit—-teams of riflemen. How many teams, how many shooters exactly, and from which buildings they fired no one will ever know. All of them used the exploding dumdum bullets, hollow points that expand upon impact. I never learned specifically where those teams of riflemen were positioned around Dealey Plaza but from what I discerned in addition to having a team at another window in the Book Depository, there were other teams in adjacent buildings behind the motorcade. They were positioned in the Dal-Tex building and the County Records building. All three buildings are on the corners of Houston and Elm where the motorcade made that slow left turn. And I am one of those who believe there was a shooter on the Grassy Knoll.

The other teams were far less likely to be seen as attention would be drawn by the sound of the shots fired from the sixth-floor window of the Book Depository. That was a key—-the sound—-while the real shooters used silencers on their rifles.

To this day it still amazes me people are so obsessed with the number of shots heard that day in Dealey Plaza...one being that bogus story of the motorcycle cop with his microphone stuck in the open broadcast position. And, of course, when you have a hundred people in Dealey Plaza who heard shots you're going to get an array of how many shots they heard. I've always thought it strange that not a single law enforcement officer ever ventured a theory, at least none that I heard through the years, that silencers were used by the other shooters from other locations in all those conspiracy theories. It always made me shake my head in bewilderment at that piece of the puzzle never mentioned. It's kind of ironic when you think about it...no one uttered a sound about silencers.

Over the years, the American Mafia had grown very adept at setting people up and at covering their own tracks. These guys weren't the same ones who had open shootouts with Tommy Guns in the 20's and 30's. These guys were smart. They took organized crime to an entirely new level. When a mobster from the past would have taken me out for knowing too much, these guys actually fed me just enough information to ensure their plan would work.

The power organized crime wielded in this era was astonishing!

They had assassinated the most powerful man on the planet and got away with it by pinning it on someone else!

Chapter 35

That Friday afternoon in Dallas I was going to drive back home as I had the full day off, but under the circumstances, I decided it would be much more appropriate for me to go to my office in Fort Worth.

I thought it would look suspicious if a CIA employee remained on a vacation day after hearing the news that the President was assassinated despite the fact that I was a basket case after what happened in that abandoned meatpacking plant.

My instincts, which are generally correct, were faulty that day.

With the assassination of the President, I expected everyone would be on a status of increased readiness——the military, the FBI, my own CIA, even those in immigration along our borders—-all running around frantically. I expected all vacations and sick time would be cancelled in every federal law enforcement agency in the country.

Indeed, there was a rapidly growing fear permeating every aspect of the federal government that the Russians were behind the assassination of the President. That kind of concern would be understandable. After all, we were only a year removed from the Cuban Missile Crisis, but curiously none of the frenetic activity I envisioned occurred.

That's where my instincts were off.

There was no condition of high alert.

When I arrived at the office, I expected to see people rushing back and forth in an adrenaline surge of heightened concern, but my supervisor advised me the level of alert had not changed.

I went to the code room and checked the national defense status for myself and sure enough I found the alert level had indeed not changed. We were at DefCon 4.

DefCon is an acronym for Defense Condition. There are several DefCon designations used to measure the activation and readiness level of the armed forces. In all, there are five levels:

DefCon 5 is used to denote peacetime.

DefCon 4 is an increased level of readiness, which generally denotes a heightened sense of intelligence gathering and increased national security. Generally, DefCon 4 was the designation of the armed forces throughout the Cold War.

DefCon 3 denotes the switching of radio call signs used by the American military to those that are presently classified call signs and an increase in force readiness. Nearly forty years later, American Armed Forces would go to DefCon 3 during the September 11th attacks.

DefCon 2 refers to yet another step in heightened readiness. Since going to the designated DefCon levels, the only time that the American Armed forces attained the level of alert of DefCon 2 was during the Cuban Missile Crisis in October 1962, and the Strategic Air Command remained at DefCon 2 throughout the Cuban crisis all the way up to November 15, 1962.

DefCon 1 is the highest level of alert. It means that hostilities are imminent or that an attack has already begun. The United States has never gone to DefCon 1.

The President of the United States and the Joint Chiefs of Staff control the DefCon level. Thus, even with the assassination of a president, the Joint Chiefs could have changed the DefCon status. Additionally, since Lyndon Johnson had been sworn in as the new president just minutes after JFK's death, we immediately had a new president in place that could have changed the alert level.

I reviewed the cable traffic between the CIA's various offices back and forth traffic to and from the military. From what I read, the belief that the Russians were behind the assassination was growing.

I mention all of this because, curiously, the DefCon level never changed in the minutes and hours after the President Kennedy's assassination. I considered it very odd our level of alert didn't change if we were under the perception the Russians had assassinated our President.

Since our alert level hadn't changed, no one in the Fort Worth office had any sense of urgency to do anything. Why would they if no one in the government changed the alert status? Those of us in the CIA were stunned in a mode of disbelief like the rest of the country as we clustered around a small television in the lunchroom. We were simply watching for developments as was the rest of the nation.

My supervisor handed out some innocuous assignments but he was merely going through the motions. I was instructed to review the cable traffic in and out of Cuba for any correspondence on the assassination. The CIA wanted to know what the Cubans were saying because of their close connection to the Soviet Union.

Other agents were monitoring what the Russians were saying.

Reviewing the cable traffic in an out of Cuba was exhausting since I knew everything that I was doing was an exercise in futility. Neither the Cubans nor the Russians had anything to do with the assassination. There is something about the tedium of working on an absolutely useless project I knew wasn't going to lead anywhere that really wore me down and exhausted me.

I never told anyone about what I knew. I kept my mouth shut. If I had informed my immediate superior, I would have to reveal how it happened I was driving someone who only moments before had been on the sixth floor of the Texas School Book Depository Building.

Then, of course, I would have to tell them about his murder and the disposal of his corpse. I would have to tell them about my involvement with the mob—-beginning in Vietnam and then continuing in the United States upon my return. The likelihood anyone in The Agency would believe I had nothing to do with the assassination was absolutely nil in my mind.

The envelope man was certainly right about that.

Who would believe I was an innocent driver and had no knowledge of what had occurred? And if I did know what happened, who would believe the mob would allow me to live?

If I opened my mouth, I was screwed and I knew it. If I were to be arrested, the American people would scream for my blood that a CIA operative was involved with the murder of their President.

You think they'd believe I was an innocent dupe?

Yeah, the mob had done a real number on me all right.

Such is the fate of outsiders recruited by the American Mafia. One thinks it's an opportunity to make a lot of money but the mob recruits you for their purposes...not yours.

Sure enough, when I got a look at Oswald on television, I could see the physical similarity between him and the man I drove to the meat packing plant. Facially, they didn't match, but physically they were dead on in height, weight and structure. Even their hair was the same short cut, and that Friday in Dallas they were both wearing the same clothes.

On Sunday morning I was at home watching television just like most everyone else in the country that weren't in church. Like so many of us that day, I too saw on live TV Jack Ruby take out Oswald with a single shot from a revolver. And like so many others that day, it really freaked me out.

No one had ever witnessed a murder as it occurred on live television.

I knew immediately it was a mob hit to shut Oswald's mouth. I don't know what Oswald knew, but one thing was sure—-the longer he was alive the more questions would be asked.

The American Mafia doesn't like a lot of questions being asked. Whatever Oswald knew, the mob ensured no one else would learn it.

What did Oswald know? What could Oswald have said? Here are some of things I learned over the years...

Oswald purchased that rifle via mail order.

Someone gave him the money to buy the rifle. He could have said who.

He purchased the rifle under a false name. Someone told him to do that. He could have said who.

Someone arranged for Oswald to get a job at the Book Depository. He could have said who.

Someone told Oswald to bring the rifle to work but not let anyone see it. He could have said who.

Someone told Oswald to wait at a specified time in the Book Depository lunch room and not be late. He could have said who.

Oswald wasn't even in the sniper's perch.

If Oswald hadn't left the building, I'm convinced he'd have been killed in the Book Depository.

Someone told Oswald if anything went wrong, he was to go to a theatre in Dallas and wait there to be contacted. He could have said who.

I've heard the arguments since that day in Dallas that the mob couldn't have pulled off the assassination. Oh, you can bet your life they could...and did.

I've heard the skeptics say Jack Ruby couldn't have been sent in by the mob to silence Oswald, because then the mob would have to send someone in to silence Ruby.

No, they wouldn't.

I know firsthand the fear instilled in Jack Ruby to get him to walk into a Dallas Police station in broad daylight and shoot Oswald in the gut with no hope of Ruby ever escaping. I know the fear infused so deeply in Jack Ruby that he could feel the terror deep in his bones. I know the fear that permeated within Jack Ruby's being so completely it would keep him silent while he rotted in prison.

The mob knows full well how to terrorize a man so thoroughly that he'll do anything whenever he's told to do it.

You see, I recognized Jack Ruby when they showed his picture on television. He was in the abandoned meat packing plant that day with me. That's why the mob had us there—-to witness what they did to my rider. They wanted to terrorize both of us.

Jack Ruby was the first one who shot my rider in the leg. And Jack Ruby watched...as I did...when they dragged my rider screaming and threw him into a fiery incinerator very much alive and conscious.

Chapter 36

There were a goodly number of people in the government that believed nuclear missiles were going to be falling on American cities within minutes of the assassination. On the other side of the world, the Soviets were just as paranoid. They were scared shitless because they thought they'd be blamed and American missiles would be streaking toward their cities.

So, maybe Johnson was pretty astute after all in not raising the DefCon level, because if he had, it might have sent a signal to the Soviets who would have become all the more nervous, and nervous people are prone to mistakes—-like hitting a button perhaps they might not otherwise have pressed.

Slowly, those concerns waned both in America and within the Kremlin as both countries were able to take a deep breath and exhaled a bit easier and America's paranoia about the Soviet Union began to fade when there was no attack.

On November 29th, a week to the day after the assassination, President Lyndon Johnson appointed the Warren Commission to investigate the assassination of John F. Kennedy.

I was stunned when I saw one of the appointees to the commission was Allen Dulles, former head of the CIA whom Kennedy had fired after the Bay of Pigs fiasco.

Did Johnson appoint Dulles solely on his own instincts? Who knows?

Did some politician under the influence of the mob suggest to Johnson that he appoint Dulles to steer the Commission in particular direction? Who knows?

Did Dulles wiggle his own way onto the Commission because he had something on Johnson? Who knows?

Whatever the case, it came to pass Allen Dulles was named to the Warren Commission, and that insured the other Warren

Commission members would never learn of the CIA enlistment of the Mafia to hit Castro. If that information had seen the light of day during an investigation of the President's murder, the American public would have freaked out.

Whenever I have considered the JFK assassination, I've separated it into two distinct categories—-conspiracy and cover-up—-for there were two distinct phases.

The government cover-up as it relates to the JFK assassination wasn't some monolithic giant or huge multi-departmental cover-up whose tentacles reaching out in fingering involvement of various branches of the government, the intelligence community or the Armed Forces. Hell no! It was nothing like that. There was no grandiose cover-up along the designs of Oliver Stone's paranoia. It was a couple of guys. That's all it took to bury some of the evidence that would have been very embarrassing and would have sent some individuals to prison for a very long time. All that was needed was to steer the Commission away from some very sensitive information and point them in the wrong direction. The U.S. government quite simply is composed of men and that's all a couple of them did—-simply steer the ship of state away from the iceberg of sensitive, classified information.

There was a conspiracy all right, but it wasn't governmental.

The Warren Commission didn't locate the actual perpetrators because the Commission didn't look beneath the right rock. Had the Commission known about the partnership of the CIA and the mob to hit Castro their investigation would have taken a decidedly different turn, a turn toward the actual conspirators.

Even thirty years after the assassination when Stone made his movie the mob is given nothing more than a casual discarded mention.

Back in the 40's when I attended grade school, one of the things they taught was civics, but the teacher of my civics class never told us the American Mafia bought and paid for American politicians who in turn would grant favors to organized crime.

They don't teach civics anymore in American schools.

For all the conspiracy theorists through all the years that claimed a government cover-up, that was the extent of it, and it had nothing to do with who hit Kennedy.

It was peripheral.

Men were out to save their reputations and the government...of men and by men...was out to save its ass.

Except for Allen Dulles—-who expertly covered up and withheld information from the Commission about the CIA's involvement with the mob—-every other member of the Warren Commission years later could have lamented one of the sad, tragic lessons of history—-*Ah, if only we knew then, what we learned later.*

Chapter 37

Incredibly within days of Kennedy's assassination, the CIA began to allow for some time off as everything was operating pretty much normally. In a democratic constitutional republic such as ours, normalcy occurs quickly when power changes hands.

I was one of those who took some time off. I just couldn't stay in my apartment any longer. I needed to take a deep breath and get some fresh air, to get away, to clear my mind. Though everyone else was operating normally, I feared the mob might not need me any longer as a form of insurance since the crisis had passed. That thought made me very nervous.

Other than a day or two taken here and there, I had a lot of vacation coming I carried over through the years since I didn't have a wife and family to use it on. So, I arranged it with my supervisor to take a week off. I packed a bag, got into my car and started driving. I got on the road and headed east. Why east rather than west or north or south? I have no idea. I had no particular plan of any specific place to go or anyone to visit. I just wanted to get away. I was drained. So, I just drove.

It didn't matter several weeks had elapsed since that day in Dallas. I was still in a numbed trance because of what I had witnessed. Anyway, I headed through Texas and into Arkansas. I stopped for gas once and I must have driven well over six hundred miles before I stopped for some dinner at a truck stop. After all that time on the road and all those miles, I didn't recall one single foot of the journey. I truly don't remember anything about my journey. Looking back, I'm quite surprised I survived the trip without having an accident on the road.

I went to the counter and ordered the staple of every truck stop, a big thick greasy cheeseburger. Just as I was finishing the last bite of my burger, I suddenly became very frightened.

Shit!

The mob might think I was trying to run, to skip out on them.

How would they know that I was taking a simple vacation?

I started glancing around the truck stop.

I didn't know what to do. I couldn't get in touch with them. They always contacted me.

Damn!

I didn't even know anyone's name or where they hung out.

I was in a panic as I wiped some perspiration from my brow. I decided not to linger. I got back on the road, and continued heading east.

I was so scared!

Why I didn't turn around and head back to Fort Worth I don't know. I'm sure I wasn't thinking rationally at that point. As I drove, I began to wonder if the mob had really taken pictures of me that day showing me waiting in a car in Dallas as that Oswald lookalike approached and got in.

I wondered if the story of photographs was a ruse, a bluff, but I also wondered if they were going to use that other option of theirs—-to cash in their *insurance* policy—-and simply name me as being in Dallas that day. Even if there weren't any photographs, just naming me would be damaging enough. At best, I'd be questioned. At worst, I'd be arrested. Either way I'd be thrown out of the Agency on my ass. Or maybe the mob would simply eliminate me...be done with me once and for all. They'd already set me up. What would stop them from taking the next step? Nothing...absolutely nothing would stop them.

All of this was swirling in my brain as I crossed the Mississippi and continued driving east. I hoped somewhere along my journey my mind would be put at ease.

I entered a large city but in my state of mind I hadn't noticed any signs along the way as to which city it was. I pulled into at a motel and when I entered, I asked the desk clerk, "What town is this?"

He could have glanced at me with a strange kind of look on his face and put me down for that. You know the type...someone who takes advantage of every opportunity to bring you down when you're not quite yourself. They give you a look with an up turned eyebrow, accompanied by a facetious remark, and maybe a sarcastic chuckle. They were the ones in middle school or later in high school who were the bullies...not always physically but verbally. A lot of people get off on putting others down when presented with such an opportunity. I guess in some twisted way those looks they give you and their caustic comments make them feel superior. It's called leveling. They think if they do that, you'll be brought down and their self-esteem will rise and you'll both be on the same plane. Yeah, the desk clerk could have done that to me since I didn't know where I was.

"Nashville, sir, you're in Nashville, Tennessee," he said with a genuinely friendly smile.

I immediately thought he was an okay guy.

"Oh," I replied wearily, "I'm gonna shower up, but when I come back, do you have a bar? I'd like to have a couple of drinks before I hit the sack for the night."

"Oh, we don't have a bar, but there are several within walking distance, and if you're of a mind, we're only three blocks from the Grand Ole Opry. They always have great music there. Tickets are generally sparse, but I could call for you to see if any are available."

"Oh, no, I don't think so. Thanks, but I'm just going to have a couple of drinks and turn in for the night."

"How long will you be staying with us?"

"Just the night," I replied.

"Well, if there's anything you need, you just let me know. Checkout is at noon and here's your key, sir."

"Thanks," I responded, as I headed to my room.

The shower felt great after a full day on the road. It really woke me up and I was looking forward to swigging down a couple of bourbons—-or more.

After I got dressed, I headed down the street and sure enough, just a couple of blocks from the motel, I spotted a place called *Lou's*. When I entered, I saw it wasn't very crowded for a Friday night, and I headed immediately for a small table that I saw open rather than opting for a seat at the bar. A live band was playing country western songs to a room that was less than a third full.

A waitress approached and before she could ask me what I wanted I said, "I'm from out of town but it seems like a rather small crowd for a Friday night with a band playing."

"Yeah, well, it's pretty early yet and we're in close proximity to the Grand Ole Opry, but, when the show is over, it'll fill up here. So, enjoy the small crowd while you can, because it won't last long," she smiled. "What'll you have?"

"I'll have bourbon on the rocks, and make it a double."

She didn't bother to write it down, nodded and headed for the bar. She was back quickly with my drink which shouldn't have surprised me in the sparse crowd.

"My name's Karen. Just let me know if you'd like anything else."

"Thanks," I nodded, and immediately said, "Bring me another," as I grabbed for my drink. "Honest, I'm not joking. I'll down this real quick."

"No problem," she smiled and departed.

That first sip was pure delight as the liquid stung its way down my esophagus. The band was playing their rendition of *El Paso* and they actually sounded pretty good. I wondered if they ever made it to the Opry or just played in the bars around town.

The waitress brought my second drink and set it on the table. I looked up at her, and felt obligated to say, "I'm not driving tonight. I'm staying at a motel a couple of blocks away."

She shook her head as if no problem. "You just give me a wave if you'd like another or anything else."

I nodded.

After she walked away, I took another sip of my drink and for some reason Jimmy Davis entered my mind. I guess that's how it happens sometimes. You're not thinking about anything in particular and all of a sudden you find yourself thinking about a friend who's deceased without any idea of why that person entered your consciousness at that specific time. Maybe it was the President's death that triggered the memory of my deceased buddy. Well, in any event, I found myself wishing that Jimmy were here now so I could buy him a drink. We would have clanked our glasses, and I would have toasted, "Here's to old friends."

Yeah, I sure wished I could talk to Jimmy to tell him about my current situation. I wondered how he would have counseled me.

I chuckled.

I could envision him quoting me a verse from the Bible without the necessity of flipping through the pages to find the correct verse that might be of assistance in offering me some solace.

I chuckled again.

He'd probably be asking what brought me to Tennessee and I'd have to say, "Beats the hell out of me, I have no idea. I just started driving and ended up here."

Maybe that was why I thought of him…subconsciously remembering Jimmy was from Tennessee.

Yeah, if we sat down to talk, he'd ask, "When did you get back from Nam? Are you still with the CIA? Are you married? Are you going to check out the Grand Ole Opry while you're in Nashville? The Opry is really big down here, real popular."

I wondered long and hard if I'd have confided in Jimmy about what I did for the mob in Vietnam and what I did for them in New Orleans and Fort Worth. Wondered if I'd have told him how the mob used me in Dallas. I'm sure he'd have hung his head right there at the table. Oh, not because Jimmy would have been judgmental, but because he would have felt concerned for me. I'm sure we'd have talked about the assassination and about his feelings as a Southerner regarding JFK.

The band stopped playing and announced they would be taking a thirty-minute break, which I welcomed, so that Jimmy and I could talk without the necessity of shouting over the music. I mean...uh...if he'd been here.

I swigged down the last of my second drink and waved to the waitress to bring me another double as I held up my empty glass. She brought my third drink promptly and I stared into the contents of the glass for a minute or so. As I continued to gaze into brownish liquid, a crooked smile crossed my face, and I found myself asking out loud, "What should I do, Jimmy?"

I'm sure he would have replied, "Well, I knew something was troubling you. You drive all the way from Fort Worth to Nashville for no apparent reason. No particular sites that you want to see; no particular people that you want to visit; sounds to me like you needed to get away from something."

I lowered my gaze and looked back into my bourbon on the rocks. After two doubles already and a long day I was feeling lightheaded.

I waved at the waitress for a menu and ordered the bone-in ribeye steak.

I took a sip of my third drink and I was pretty sure that I would have told Jim Davis everything. I think it might have helped me in the sense of just talking about it and getting it off my chest and unburdening myself.

From my time in Texas, I knew those Bible toting Texans in the Lone Star State could be full of a lot of hell-fire and brimstone, but I was positive Jimmy wouldn't have reacted that way toward me. I wouldn't have been surprised though if he had asked, "Did you ever kill anyone?"

I shook my head no.

I'd leave that one part of my story out when I was in the Arizona desert that night and shot Pete Madison. I wouldn't be lying by omitting that. Technically, it wasn't me who had killed Pete.

I think I pretty much know what Jimmy would have said. "Well, all I can tell you, Anthony, is that since you haven't taken a life, maybe it's not too late for you to make things right. Go to the authorities. Tell them what you've done and what you know. I know it won't be easy, but it is what you really need to do. Otherwise, if you don't, you'll never be at peace with yourself. You'll be looking over your shoulder for the rest of your life—-from possibly both the law and the mob closing in on you."

And I'm just as sure I would have answered, "The mob will never let me do what you're saying, Jimmy. I could never go to the authorities."

The waitress brought my steak and after I cut a piece and began to chew, I learned I was famished and I enjoyed that steak like no other in recent memory.

"The authorities have ways of protecting people, Anthony."

"What? Witness protection?"

Jimmy would nod.

"Yeah, well, maybe they can protect people. And maybe they can't."

"You can find courage through Christ, Anthony."

I'm sure I would have frowned at that. "Maybe He can give me courage, but can you assure me that He will also take a bullet from the mob that's meant for me?"

Perhaps Jimmy would have responded with something like, "He's already died for you once," he would chuckle. "You want him to give his life again?" he would smile. Jimmy could laugh at things like that. He wasn't one of those born-again Christians who didn't have a sense of humor about such things.

I gulped down the last of my drink and waved for the waitress to bring me a fourth.

Jimmy would look at the empty glass, and say, "That stuff is not going to help your situation, Anthony. It's not going to give you any comfort or any peace of mind."

"No, but it'll sure help in making me numb so when that bullet comes maybe it won't hurt so badly."

Whatever the case, whatever I might have confided in Jimmy, he would tell me what he thought and then he'd never mention it again unless I wanted to talk more about it sometime later. That's the way he was and I always appreciated that quality in him. Perhaps it was because he was a fellow southerner. What I mean by that is that Jimmy had good manners like many of his fellow southerners. That's why so many people from the south are referred to as *true country gentlemen*. It's their manners and good taste that set them apart from so many others. Yeah, Jimmy would say what he wanted to say, and he'd do it without lecturing or being condescending, and then he'd leave it to me to decide what to do.

The waitress brought my fourth double bourbon and I paid her for all the drinks and dinner and gave her a hefty tip. As she smiled a thank you and left, I raised my glass again, and without regard to anyone nearby who could hear me, I toasted, "Here's to happy endings, Jimmy."

As it turned out, I extended my stay in Nashville for a couple of days. I played some pool, took in a movie, had another great steak dinner at *Lou's*, and attended a show at the Grand Ole Opry so I could experience what that was all about. As a country western fan,

I've got to say that it was a great show. I was unaware until I attended the Opry that it wasn't just one performer, it was several. The night I attended, I heard Conway Twitty, Hank Williams, Jr., and a group called the Pecos Five. I actually liked them the best. I don't know why they never made it nationally, but they were damn good. Maybe one or two of those in the band experienced what occurred to so many others later in the mid-sixties. Maybe they simply broke up because one or more of them got drafted. In any event, all of the performances were great and the audience roared their approval, me included.

Chapter 38

When I left Nashville, I headed west, back toward Fort Worth. While I was on the highway, I kept thinking about what Jimmy would have said that night at the bar if he had been alive. God, I wished he was still around so I could have bought him a drink or two.

One phrase in particular from that night with Jimmy stayed with me.

'Maybe it's not too late for you to make things right'.

When I saw a sign for the turn off that would take me toward New Orleans, a thought suddenly struck me. I took the road south because I had an idea of how I would make things right though it wouldn't be in the way that Jimmy would have suggested.

Several hours later I arrived in New Orleans and checked into a motel. I got a good night's sleep secure in the fact that I'd come up with what I believed to be a very good idea.

The next day I visited an Army surplus store. I found what I was looking for, a metal detector. I also purchased a shovel and headed west out of New Orleans toward the Sonoran Desert in Arizona.

The gun I had used on Pete Madison in Arizona had a silencer and when I buried it, I had placed it in a plastic bag. If I could find it again, I was pretty confident the elements would not have gotten to it and done it any damage.

I was also fairly confident I could find the approximate location again. In fact, if the cactus I had seen that night beside the road was still there, I knew I could find the location of the buried handgun. I was not an expert on desert cacti, but the one I saw had a very odd, unique shape. The fact is when I saw it that night, I thought it was some kind of mutant cactus. It had a double trunk as if it were two separate cacti that joined a foot above the ground. From there it was even odder, as it grew into four separate offshoots...out and then upward like a menorah...except that there were only four places for candles.

It was midafternoon on the second day after I left New Orleans when I motored into the Sonoran corridor. That's actually an area of thousands of squares miles but I knew I was close. I hadn't checked the odometer when I left, but I was pretty sure I traveled close to fourteen hundred miles from New Orleans. Oddly, as the only driver, I wasn't exhausted in the least. In fact, I was invigorated. A rush of adrenaline surged through me because I was in pursuit of something that could assist me in making my idea a reality.

I slowed to twenty-five miles per hour, because one thing I had forgotten was on which side of the road that cactus appeared. For more than twenty miles I crept slowly along in the desert heat searching for the odd shaped cactus, my head swiveling from one side of the road to the other. I knew that the cactus was so unique the only way I would miss it was if it was no longer there or if I was going too fast and sped by it. I didn't know the life span of a cactus, but I hoped that one of nature's windstorms hadn't knocked it down or that it hadn't fallen victim to man—-an automobile swerving off the road.

When I spotted it, I was overjoyed and let out a loud whoop.

Yeah, it was still there! That had to be the one I was searching for! There couldn't possibly be another like it. No way!

I pulled off the road and slowed to a stop. I grabbed the metal detector and shovel from the back seat and paced off as best I could remember the approximate distance from the road.

I needed to draw in my mind some kind of quadrants so if I didn't find it immediately, I could move onto another section without going over the same ground.

I scanned the area and referenced the surrounding cacti and tumbleweed as my markings and began my search by swinging the metal detector slowly from side to side.

"Howdy."

I jumped suddenly from a voice behind me and quickly spun around.

"Oh, I didn't me to startle you," said a man in a highway patrolman's uniform with a Stetson atop his head. "I saw your car pulled off the road and you out here in the desert and just thought I'd stop and see if you were in any trouble."

"Oh, no trouble, I'm fine."

I knew I'd said that awkwardly, so I added, "You...uh...you know...you came up behind me...,"

"Yeah, I could see I surprised you," he smiled, as he looked to examine the oblong mechanism in my hands, and as he eyed it, he pointed toward it. "Is that there one of those metal finders?"

"Yeah, that's right," I replied, and knew I had to come up with some kind of explanation so that he wouldn't get suspicious. "Did you know that this whole area used to be an ocean?"

"Yeah, so they say," he confirmed, as he took off his Stetson and ran his fingers through his hair and then placed the cowboy hat back on his head.

I knew almost immediately that what I'd said was really stupid.

"It was a long time ago this was an ocean," he pointed out. "It was hundreds of thousands of years ago if I understand correctly, long before anyone ever came up with the idea of making metal. No people on earth back when this was an ocean. So, I guess one could say you can't be lookin' for buried treasure from a ship," he said with a smile. It was the kind of smile that not so subtly told me he was suspicious.

He paused and eyed me with skepticism and the awkward silence was distinctly uncomfortable for me.

"So, what is it that you're hoping to find?" he asked.

His voice was friendly enough, but there was no mistaking the fact he wasn't' buying the explanation of why I was here in the middle of the desert with a metal detector.

"Well, I guess it was pretty lame of me that you were going to believe something like that."

He nodded in agreement as he continued to eye me.

"Truth is, there was a gang of outlaws back when, and the story is they buried a fortune in the Sonoran Desert on this side of the Mexican border. I just didn't want anyone to know that I was looking for it. No offense."

"None taken," he said with a smile. "Yeah, I figured it was something like that. If you got nothin' better to do, far be it from me to keep you from it."

I nodded my thanks to him.

"Be careful out here though. The desert can be pretty tricky at times. Besides the heat, a sand storm can come up on you with no warning, not to mention the rattlesnakes in these parts."

"I'll certainly be careful."

"You keep an eye out, and don't stay out here too long," he said, as he raised his hand and tipped the brim of his Stetson.

"I certainly won't, and thanks for stoppin' and checkin' on me."

"You have a good day," he said, as he headed back to his squad car.

I breathed a sigh of relief and after he pulled away, I quickly got back to my search. After several hours I walked back to my car and took a break. I opened my water jug and took a very long drink of its contents and I quickly realized I was starving. Happy that I took the time to stop earlier at a grocery store, I made myself a couple of sandwiches of peanut butter and jelly. That may not sound so great but those sandwiches sure hit the spot.

By the time I finished, the sun had gone down and I glanced upward to see thousands of tiny pin lights dotting the evening sky.

Being a good distance away from any town and its accompanying light pollution, the desert stars are a spectacular sight. Miniaturized by the distance of so many light years, the tiny stars punctuated the darkness overhead but could cast no glow upon my endeavor far below on the desert sand.

Furthermore, there was no moon. If I did happen upon one of those rattlesnakes, I'd never see it, and it would be too late once I heard the ominous rattle. One of the reasons cowboy boots are the length they are is to protect against snake bites but I wasn't wearing a pair.

In the darkness, I resumed my search and accelerated my pace. It had cooled considerably now, but I was sweating profusely because of my rush to find that .22 caliber pistol.

Finally, the metal detector sounded.

I honed in on the metal object and when I thought I had the right spot I hurriedly began to dig. When I hit something, I bent over the hole I'd made in the sand, reached in and grabbed what felt like the plastic bag. I pulled the bag up out of the hole and brushed it off.

I had it!

I didn't linger nor did I bother to fill in the hole. There wasn't any reason to do so. I grabbed my shovel and metal detector and rushed toward the car. I slid the bag with the handgun and silencer under the front seat and placed the metal detector in the back along with the shovel.

In a moment I was back on the road.

Of course, as an agent with the CIA, I had my own firearms as well having access to any number of additional weapons should I ever want them. But the reason I had come so far for the gun now resting under my front seat wasn't only because it was equipped with a silencer. It was because it could never be traced to me—-compliments of the mob.

Chapter 39

I wasn't a field agent for the most part; those guys in covert operations had access to all kinds of untraceable weapons but that wasn't the case with me so that sidearm with the silencer was something I could really use. Yes, as a CIA agent, I could have requisitioned a number of various weapons but that would have been noticed and I didn't want to bring any attention to myself.

When I was back at my desk in the Fort Worth office the following Monday, one of my CIA colleagues approached. He leaned in so that no one would over hear him, "Hey, Narducci."

I looked up and saw he had a smirk on his face. He had the kind of look plastered across his face that he knew something that I didn't know, and he wanted so badly to tell me.

"What's up?" I asked, not the least bit curious as to what he wanted to say.

"You might find yourself heading back to Nam, Narducci."

"What?"

"In fact, a lot more of us might be going over there."

I stared at him with a quizzical look. "I don't get what you're saying," I said truly stumped.

"What you didn't watch any news while you were on vacation? Didn't you hear what Johnson did?"

"No. What?"

"He signed an Executive Order rescinding Kennedy's instruction to withdraw a thousand troops from Nam by Christmas. Happy New Year! It's really going to heat up now, buddy."

All I could manage to do was to stare into space at hearing that bit of news, and asked, "Do you think he's going to send more troops?"

"I'd put money on it and I only bet on sure things, Narducci. Yep, Vietnam is going to be for real now. I'll tell you one thing," he continued, "I sure don't want to be assigned to that hellhole. Don't say I didn't tell you."

He started to walk away and then stopped. A grin appeared on his face, as he leaned back in and whispered, "On the other hand, don't say you heard it from me either," he chuckled, as he turned away and headed down the corridor toward his desk.

Even after learning of Johnson's Executive Order, it wasn't Vietnam I was worried about. Each time my supervisor called me into his office, my heart jumped because I feared my boss had been informed by the mob that I had been in Dallas that fateful day in November. I was afraid the mob would cash in on their insurance and reveal I had worked for them in both Vietnam and the States. As each day passed without incidence, however, I became more relaxed and the flow of my overactive adrenaline glands began to ebb.

The days turned into weeks, then months.

Before I knew it, the calendar had moved into late summer of 1964.

It was a warm sultry August evening in Ft. Worth and for want of anything better to do I was watching the Democratic Convention on television the night Robert Kennedy made an appearance before the convention. He was there to introduce a film honoring President Kennedy.

When Bobby stepped up onto the stage the delegates went wild. He approached the microphone but each time he attempted to speak, the convention erupted in a deafening crescendo of applause, hoots and hollers. They weren't shouting him down; they were drowning him out amidst a tumult of thunderous applause...a tribute not only to his late brother but to Robert Kennedy as well. The delegates were at this moment anointing Robert F. Kennedy as the heir apparent to continue his brother's legacy...and he couldn't begin his speech because they wouldn't let him. For fully 20 minutes

Robert Kennedy stood on the podium repeatedly attempting to begin with the words, "Mr. Chairman..."

The delegates' enthusiastic, unrestrained cheers would not allow him to speak.

I didn't care much for political parties, conventions or political speeches and I was only 29 years old at the time so I hadn't been around that long, but that night was the most incredible scene of a politician addressing members of his political party that I ever witnessed...before or since.

That scene confirmed for me what I was already thinking when I went to the Sonoran Desert...my life now had meaning, a purpose. I would wreak vengeance upon organized crime wherever I found it and on whomever I could and I would do so for the rest of my life.

I knew what I had in mind would be an enormous task for one man and would take monumental planning, but I decided right then and there to get on with it.

Chapter 40

Those men from the abandoned meat packing plant were seared into my memory. I had gotten a very good look at each of them, not to mention the envelope man who I'd seen three times. I was confident that if I ever saw them again, I would recognize each of them immediately. I had no doubt about that.

The key was to figure out where I might find them. After all, I hadn't seen any of them since that day in November. Obviously, the places I frequented for dinner or drinks were not the establishments where they hung out.

I began to do some homework. I gathered all the information I could get my hands on regarding the mob in Ft. Worth, and Dallas. I also learned all I could about the New Orleans operation where I first encountered the envelope man.

Of course, I didn't have to waste time searching for Jack Ruby as he was in jail, but I figured I would have to hang out in clubs in Dallas if I was going to be successful in locating the other four.

Normally, gathering intelligence on anyone would not be difficult for a CIA agent, but I didn't want anyone to know what I was doing so it took longer than it would have otherwise. I didn't do it the easy way by flashing my badge which would have opened a lot of doors of information. I did it all covertly. I worked overtime, weekends, nights and remember this was long before the easy access to computer databases that we all enjoy now.

Sure, I could have made it a lot easier on myself and simply asked the local police for information on the mob hangouts but that would leave a trail that a CIA agent named Narducci was asking questions about the mob.

There was a second risk as well—-that someone in the Dallas Police Department would alert the mob that questions were being asked.

We knew Jack Ruby shouldn't have been in the basement of Dallas Police Headquarters Sunday morning when the accused presidential assassin Oswald was being transferred to the county jail. And it wasn't a fluke that he was at the scene.

Thirty-six hours beforehand, the very night of the assassination, District Attorney Henry Wade was briefing the press, when he said, "Lee Oswald was a member of the Pro-Castro Free Cuba Committee."

"That's the Fair Play for Cuba Committee," a voice among the reporters corrected him immediately. That was Jack Ruby's voice. Ruby had been roaming the hallways at Dallas Police Headquarters and attended that briefing.

I wouldn't trust the Dallas Police Department with something I needed to keep quiet from the mob. No way!

On the other side of the equation, if I was going to look for these men, I didn't want to walk casually into some club one night and risk them recognizing me so I grew a mustache, let my hair grow longer, and picked up a pair of eyeglasses, which had just plain glass for lenses. It didn't matter if the guys in my office saw me growing my hair longer or wearing a mustache but I didn't put the glasses on unless I was out and about. I figured the combination of those three things would be sufficient not to be recognized since those men had only seen me for a couple of minutes, and I made nowhere near the impression on them that they made on me that gruesome day. Of course, I hoped they hadn't paid any particular attention to my features but if they had, I was comfortable with the anonymity I created with my disguise.

By day, I worked in the CIA office as I continued to review cable traffic in and out of Latin America.

By night, I did my homework. I gathered all the information I could on the Dallas restaurants...skipping all the most exclusive ones, as I figured only the top mob boss would eat at those. The guys I sought were down the chain. Rating the restaurants on a scale from 1 to 5 stars, I visited all the 3's.

By night, I'd drive up to Dallas and stop at one of the bars associated with a 3-star restaurant. I'd stay an hour sipping one drink while I scanned the patrons for any of the men that I encountered that fateful day. Then I'd go to another of the 3-star restaurants and repeat the process. Finally, I'd visit a third restaurant at which I'd have dinner and a glass of wine as I read a book, while every few pages I would subtly check the crowd.

I repeated that process every night.

Three restaurants—-two drinks and a glass of wine—-in a time span of several hours so I'd always keep a clear head.

I left my weapon in the car under the front seat because I had no intention of using it when I recognized any of them...not on the spot. That would come later. The first priority was to find them.

I knew the odds of spotting any of them sometime soon were against me, but I also knew it was only a matter of time...of being in the right bar or restaurant at the precise time...and I had plenty of time.

Yeah, every night, my adrenalin surged in anticipation but I didn't need to rush this. I had no family. There was nothing that would interfere with my scheduling three restaurants a night. A couple of drinks, a glass of wine and a dinner every night could get expensive, but I didn't have anyone to spend the money on and so I put a substantial amount away through the years what with my salary and those earlier assignments from the mob which I had saved. I chuckled at the irony—-the mob had in effect financed my expedition to find them.

The fact that searching for them took a long time was really a good thing for me because it taught me patience and perseverance. Of course, I had those two qualities to begin with or I never would have ever been able to begin such a project. But that was using those qualities in everyday life. Stalking killers was much different.

Chapter 41

1964 moved into 1965 and after fully eight months of searching, my strategy finally paid off one night.

I was seated at my second restaurant bar of the evening, when two men entered and were ushered to a table by the hostess. I recognized them immediately. No doubt about it. They were the two who threw the guy into the incinerator.

While they ate dinner, I ordered as well but this time I ate at the bar. I lingered while they dined slowly and I waited patiently for them to leave. Finally, when they finished and left, I followed them. They got into one car and one of them was dropped off at an apartment complex. At least now I knew in which building one of them resided, if not the exact apartment. When the driver pulled away, I followed him and eventually I saw where he lived as well...a single-family ranch dwelling in a downscale neighborhood of Dallas.

I didn't make a move on either of them that night because my hope was by continuing my surveillance of one or the other that I could find where they reported on a regular basis. I was betting they would lead me to others as well. Besides, I wasn't in any hurry. I wanted to learn where the bosses were located, at least a boss that was higher on the food chain than them. I made a note of the license plate and when I got back to the office the next morning, I ran a check on it. That I could do routinely without anyone raising an eyebrow as to what I was enquiring about and I got the driver's name.

It took me another three months before I learned the identity of the three men I saw in Dallas. The mobsters I followed were Johnny Pinto and Gus Tagliani. As I followed this duo around Dallas, I learned they were two of the underlings that carried out various assignments given to them from higher ups in the mob. They made collection calls and broke some limbs when payments were late.

I watched them at a safe distance with a pair of binoculars and saw them break one guy's ankles, dislocate another fellow's thumbs, break arms and legs on separate occasions. With one fellow, Tagliani took a spoon to his eye socket, dug it in and popped out one of his eyes. You think that guy didn't do everything he was told to do from that point forward to protect his lone, remaining eye?

I continued to follow them and gather more information while another New Year's Day came and went...patience, always patience.

Soon it was the spring 1966.

The more I followed these guys the more I learned about the comings and goings of the mob itself. In order to pick up the conversations, I used a directional antenna. Though they have to be pointed precisely, they are very powerful and that gave me the ability to listen from a distance and thus reduce the risk of being seen.

I learned neither Pinto nor Tagliani was given any reason as to why they were to stuff that guy into an incinerator at the meat packing plant. It's like Pete Madison told me. When you work for the mob, they tell you to do something and you do it. You don't ask questions and you don't hesitate. That's the way the mob operates—-with no explanations and with as much secrecy as possible.

About the only thing those guys probably knew was to stay alert and watch for a couple of fellows who were on their way to the meatpacking plant. Of course, one of them knew which one of us to shoot. My rider was thrown into that furnace because he could have talked. The old standard—-he knew too much.

Years later I would get a real kick out of that series—-*The Sopranos*. Talking to a psychiatrist? Never would have happened. As soon as one of the mob bosses learned that another of them was talking to a psychiatrist that guy would have been history...no hesitation and no questions asked...done deal. I had no doubt at all they'd kill the psychiatrist as well as any receptionist and all the files would be burned...probably in a gas explosion gutting the office.

At the meatpacking plant I seriously doubt Pinto or Tagliani had ever seen my rider before that day. They wouldn't have known who he was or what he'd done. They didn't need to be in the loop on that. That's the way of the mob. They keep moving the chess pieces around only there's no board for anyone to see all the pieces. One piece often has no idea what another piece is doing. That makes fewer who know something specific about the operation, and thus the less chance for the bosses to be ratted out.

Though that day there was another underlying message to be sent in the way my rider was killed that I wouldn't understand until later. An example was being set for someone's benefit.

The third man from the abandoned meat packing plant was Saul Meyer. He was the sadistic one who had put that extra bullet in my rider shattering his shin bone. Well, I say sadistic because my rider was already on the floor but who knows, maybe this Saul Meyer was under orders as well to pump a second bullet into the guy.

Saul Meyer was higher in the echelon than the other two. I could see that simply by the way he dressed. I never learned exactly how high on the food chain he was, but if I were to make an educated guess, he was one of the capos.

I believe Saul Meyer had a certain territory of responsibility. He would have paid the boss regularly from his monthly collections from loan sharks, numbers, gambling, prostitution and any businesses that were mob connected...or mob protected...in his area. That's how it works with the higher echelon of the mob. They receive a percentage on everything when it comes to their territory's operations, and they continue to receive the same amount in the monthly collections regardless of economic conditions. If there is a downturn in the number of people gambling, tough. It doesn't matter. It's up to the underlings to get more people playing, because those underlings have to pay the boss the same amount every month.

Saul Meyer is Jewish and it's a myth the American Mafia has been composed wholly of Sicilians. Though most of those who I encountered through the years were of Sicilian descent, up to forty percent of the mob was made up of Jews, Irishmen, and even some Russians who had immigrated to this country along with an assortment of other nationalities.

The fourth man, the one with whom I was most familiar, the envelope man, I finally learned was Tommy Maldanado. He's the one that had first contacted me in New Orleans. Him I would save for last.

Chapter 42

I started with the two underlings Tagliani and Pinto. I studied their movements, their routine and most especially I studied the lay of the land where each of them lived. Doing reconnaissance was a must. If after I eliminated one of them and had to go it on foot, I didn't want to run into some unfamiliar backyard and find if fully fenced off and be trapped. Being aware of your exit routes...multiple exit routes...is a key.

I also studied the roads if I were to be followed by an automobile. What would be the best roads on which to lose someone? Were their turnoffs which I could use to duck into and quickly hide? I was also very cognizant of any cul-de-sacs and possible dead ends so as not to be trapped in that manner.

Additionally, on those nights when the moon is full, the moonlight truly makes a difference, so I picked a night when there was no moon at all and wore dark clothing as added stealth. I took up a position in a clump of bushes at Gus Tagliani's suburban apartment complex...shrubbery that was not located on the main sidewalk and in a spot in which I was not likely to be seen late at night.

When the night had come for me to make my move, I hid in the bushes and waited for Tagliani to arrive. I soon realized however that I was perspiring profusely while simultaneously my throat became parched. Nervously, my heart raced so fast I could barely distinguish one beat from another. I must have checked my watch a hundred times before Gus Tagliani walked past me at two in the morning. I watched him walk up the steps and into the main entrance of the complex. I told myself that I allowed him to walk past because I was being patient, waiting for the right moment. The truth is, I was so frightened I froze like an ice statue. I knew once I made my move there would be no turning back and that thought kept rolling around in my mind. Regardless of the fact the mob wouldn't know in the beginning who pulled the trigger on one of their men, I would one day most assuredly be in the crosshairs. The thought of that consequence prevented me from pulling the trigger.

I returned to my apartment thoroughly disgusted with myself for chickening out and I went straight to my cabinet, poured a stiff drink and gulped it down quickly in the hope the burning liquid would calm me. To some extent, it did.

The next night would be the last night of darkness before a new moon would begin to illuminate the earth below. I knew it would be now or never and this time I would be better prepared mentally to carry out my self-imposed assignment.

I returned to the same shrubbery, settled in and waited. It was again after two o'clock in the morning when Johnny Pinto dropped Gus Tagliani at his apartment. I noted that at this late hour, there wasn't any foot traffic in the immediate vicinity. I was confident I wouldn't be seen.

From my perspective in the bushes, I watched as Tagliani came up the walk.

Johnny Pinto pulled the car away from the curb and drove away.

It was only me and Tagliani now.

He passed the bushes heading toward the entrance of his building and my nervous anxiety soared. I already had my gun out, holding it to my side, so as to be fully prepared upon the arrival of my target. At one point I noticed my hand shaking but I told myself it was the cold night air. I made my move and deftly came up behind Tagliani pressing the barrel of my gun firmly against his back.

He threw his hands into the air immediately and I whispered, "You don't have to put your hands up. This isn't going to take long."

"What do you want?' he asked agitated but with a gruff voice as if he could bully his way out of this.

"I want you to close your eyes," I answered, as I pushed harder against his back with my weapon, and repeated, "I said close 'em!"

"All right, all right," he relented, as I reached around and pulled his gun out of his shoulder holster. He may have had other weapons on him, perhaps an ankle holster, but it didn't matter because it would be over soon.

"Got those eyes closed nice and tight?" I asked.

He nodded, "Yeah, yeah."

"Good. Now I want you to remember back to November 23, 1963 to that meat packing plant with the incinerator," I told him, as I leveled my handgun at the back of his head. I paused for three seconds and then fired once...the silencer muffling the sound.

Tagliani dropped like a rock to the sidewalk face first...his face smashing violently against one of the cement steps. I could hear his teeth crunch as he hit the cement, but I'm sure he felt no pain because he was dead before he hit the sidewalk.

I quickly tucked my handgun into my coat and walked away...though not too fast...but as I departed the area I felt no remorse whatsoever as to what I'd just done.

This was one of two guys that had thrown a man into a burning incinerator, alive. I actually felt like I'd let him off easy. Most avengers would have made him suffer.

In my view it was imperative that I hit Tagliani and Pinto the same night before the higher-ups in the mob could react to the killings, so I went straight from Tagliani's place to Johnny Pinto's house.

During my research I learned Pinto wasn't married and there wasn't anyone else living in the house. That was important. I was after the mobsters, not their families, not their friends—-just them.

I drove but parked a good distance away from the Pinto house in a parking area among other cars. There wasn't a need for neighborhood parking stickers back then but I did have fake plates on my car.

I moved through the backyards of other homes, disturbing a dog on the way. That was a screw up on my part—-missing the fact of a dog in that particular yard. The best research can run amuck but despite the barking I figured the owners or neighbors would think it was a rabbit or a squirrel that had caught the dog's ire. Even if I had stood absolutely still, the dog would have continued barking at the intruder, so I continued on my way toward Pinto's house.

I knew he didn't have any pets but I did a thorough scan of the house when I arrived and assured myself there was no one else there.

As I stalked Johnny Pinto, I saw the lights were on in the kitchen and he was moving about inside back and forth from the kitchen counter to the refrigerator. He was making a sandwich.

I merely waited for an opportunity. I watched him through the windows knowing he couldn't see me in the darkness outside while the lights were on within the house, as long as I remained far enough away from the windows, and I was very careful to be extremely quiet.

Once his sandwich was made, Pinto didn't take it into the living room and sit down to watch TV while he enjoyed his evening snack. He merely took a bite of it right there as he stood at the kitchen counter. After he gobbled down that first bite of his sandwich, he reached for a bottle of whiskey, poured some into a small glass and drank it down.

I proceeded to move around to the front of the house where the light at the front door was not on. Every step I took, I looked to see if there was anything below my feet as I didn't want to make a sound by snapping any twigs lying about.

There wasn't a front porch, just a small, square slab in front. I moved quickly but carefully as I slowly opened the screen door, quietly jimmied the lock and gained access.

I stepped carefully from the hallway into the living room onto a rug atop the hardwood floor. Wood doesn't need oil, of course, but you would have thought so when I took my next step and the floor squeaked as hardwood floors so often do.

Johnny Pinto immediately stopped chewing with his mouth half full with a large bite of his sandwich. He listened carefully as he pulled his weapon from his shoulder holster. He had two ways he could exit the kitchen...through the door to the dining room and into the living room or down the hallway to the front door. He chose the latter.

I might never have become so proficient in my tasks over the years had Johnny Pinto taken the other route. Sometimes, no matter how capable one becomes in such matters as these, a little luck goes a long way.

In seconds, Johnny Pinto deftly walked down the hallway, checked the living room and then moved quickly to the front door. He swung the door open with his left hand while in his right he held his gun ready. As he scanned the front yard from his doorway, he reached back into the house and flicked on the light. Immediately it illuminated the vicinity around his front door while he continued to scan his front yard.

Satisfied it was nothing but a creaky old house, Pinto closed his front door, flicked off the light and slid the gun back into his holster. He returned to the kitchen, opened the refrigerator and this time grabbed a beer. He popped the top and took a big gulp as he moved to the kitchen counter to return to his sandwich only to find it was gone.

He made a quick move for his gun but the cold steel I pressed against his skull stopped him immediately. He too put his hands in the air as he realized I'd gotten the drop on him.

He didn't turn around, but asked, "Are you a burglar?"

I didn't answer.

The alcohol he'd consumed earlier in the evening may have dulled his senses allowing me to get the drop on him, squeaky floors notwithstanding, but he was alert enough to know not to make any sudden moves.

"You want money?"

I didn't answer.

"If you want money; I got money."

Again, I didn't make any comment.

"I got money in the back of the house. I stashed it away. I can give you money."

"Move," I told him, as I pressed my gun harder against the back of his head, "If you turnaround, you're dead," I cautioned him.

He nodded adamantly and repeatedly, as he moved slowly out of the kitchen and down the hallway to one of the bedrooms...my gun continually pressed against the back of his skull.

"It's behind the dresser," he told me, unable to disguise the fear in his voice.

"Show me...carefully," I warned him.

He grabbed hold of the dresser with both hands, swung it away from the wall and reached behind it.

"Uh, uh," I warned him, as I pressed my gun against the back of his head.

"No, no, no," he shouted, "I swear. It's the money!" he yelled, as his hand came slowly back from behind his dresser with an envelope full of bills.

He lifted his arm so I could take the envelope from his hand, which I did and immediately stuffed the envelope inside my coat.

"I gave you what you wanted; I haven't turned around; I can't identify you," he said frantically, as he rattled off all the reasons why I didn't have to kill him.

I pressed the pistol hard against his skull again and his body became rigid in terror, as I leaned in slightly, and whispered, "I'm not going to hurt you."

I pulled my gun away from his head and fired one shot. This time a crimson spray slapped my face.

Johnny Pinto dropped to the floor in a heap, and as I stood over him, I said, "You see, you never felt a thing, which is more than I can say for your victims."

Now there were two down with two to go.

Thus, it was 1966 when mobsters Gus Tagliani and Johnny Pinto became the first fatalities in my vengeance against organized crime.

Chapter 43

I knew Tagliani and Pinto both reported to the envelope man and oh, how I wished I could have been a fly on the wall when word got out two of Tommy Maldanado's men had been hit. Aware of the mob's penchant for paranoia, I knew Maldanado would absolutely freak out! Yeah, Maldanado must have crapped in his pants. He would think there was a contract out on him, starting with those in his operation. He might have thought the mob was cleaning up business on anyone who knew anything about Dallas that fateful day. I truly hoped that was the case because I knew it would scare him shitless and frightened individuals make mistakes because they are consumed by their fear and don't think as rationally as they normally would.

As I mentioned earlier, there's an old rule in the Mafia—-you never take out the hit men. But time had passed, and Maldanado knew as well as anyone that various higher echelon mobsters broke the rules from time to time, regardless of how sacrosanct those rules might be within their organization. All they needed was someone's okay, someone who was high enough to sanction the hit.

I wanted Maldanado to stew a while in his own pool of fear so my next target was Saul Meyer. I purposely didn't go after him for several months. One reason is simply because he would have been on the alert and much too cautious after the two hits on his colleagues in crime. I wanted some time to elapse before I attempted to make a move on him. It would also mess with the minds of both Maldanado and Meyer when no more hits had been forthcoming. They wouldn't know what the hell was going on.

I must admit though when I took down Johnny Pinto and Gus Tagliani, I wasn't fully conscious as to how long I would be performing this retribution. I found the virtue of patience would serve me well through the years in my endeavor to wreak havoc upon the blight of organized crime upon our society.

Of course, Saul Meyer and Tommy Maldanado didn't know they had been marked for death. After all, they wouldn't have heard through the crime syndicate grapevine of any contract out on them because there wasn't one. But both must have most certainly suspected it with the deaths of Pinto and Tagliani who were both hit in the classic Mafia method—-a shot to the back of the head execution style.

The mob is especially fond of a .22 caliber hits to the head for hits up close. A .22 caliber doesn't make a lot of noise but it also isn't powerful enough to make an exit wound, however, it's not because they wish to avoid making a mess that they use a .22. Sadists that most of them are, they delight in the fact a bullet is embedded in someone's brain—-until a coroner digs it out.

When I thought enough time elapsed, I began to keep tabs on Saul Meyer in the evenings. Naturally, I kept quite a distance between us so he wouldn't get suspicious of being followed. I lost him a couple of times because I was so far back, but that was okay.

One night he was having dinner in a small restaurant with one of the new replacements, and when he got up to take a leak I waited for a few seconds before I followed behind him. If the new guy followed, I would have just taken a leak and left, but, when he didn't follow Meyer into the restroom, I took advantage of the opportunity.

Naturally, I didn't know if anyone else was also using the restroom at the time, so I decided I would head straight to one of the stalls when I got there.

When I entered, Saul Meyer was standing at one of the urinals. He heard the door open and he instinctively turned to look. When he saw me moving toward one of the stalls, he turned back toward the urinal. Having noticed no one in the restroom when I entered, I did a cursory check of any feet showing below the doors of the other stalls.

There was no one there.

I opened one of the stall doors and entered just long enough to pull my weapon. I exited the stall quickly, approached Meyer, and placed my handgun up against the back of his head.

"I just want you to know something," I stated in a whisper, as he stood there helplessly holding his wand.

I pulled the gun back from against his skull, and added, "I'm not anti-Semitic."

Then the familiar muted metallic thump sounded as my pistol discharged one bullet.

As he collapsed backward, his penis continued to discharge piss as his head slammed and bounced against the tiled floor.

I immediately exited the washroom, departed the restaurant through the back door and escaped into the night.

Chapter 44

As I drove home, I thought about my fourth and final target of the quartet, Tommy Maldanado. I'd done my homework in extensive research following all four men and like the others I knew where Maldanado hung out and where he lived.

When I didn't' seen him at any of his haunts, I staked out his house from afar with the aid of my directional antenna once again but I got nothing. He had a wife but she was gone and there was no activity around the home.

I headed to the apartment of Maldanado's mistress and staked her out for several weeks but again I came up empty.

I began to think Maldanado got so nervous he might have relocated to another city...that he might have gone to his boss and requested a transfer. That happens more frequently than one might think. The mob didn't always simply kill one another. Sometimes they watched each other's back and if getting someone out of town was best for him, they would do it. They would send someone from Chicago to New Orleans for instance, and vice versa. That is, if doing so didn't jeopardize the organization in any way.

As it turned out, Maldanado had gone to his boss all right, but his boss saw a very nervous man...one who was scared shitless. Frightened, nervous people worry the mob higher-ups. Concerned his underling might talk to the wrong people in his agitated state, the boss could fix it so Tommy Maldanado wouldn't worry anymore as well as never be seen or heard from again.

Of course, when the mob doesn't wish to send a message, they are expert at getting rid of people without a trace. Didn't I know it! I just kept thinking about that poor son of a bitch in that incinerator. I thought maybe Tommy Maldanado suffered the same fate, but after months of searching I finally found him.

He was lying low and keeping out of sight. He had kept moving around. Every week he was in a different motel. The night I found him asleep after he had tied one on, he was groggy when I interrupted his slumber.

"JFK," I whispered into Maldanado's ear.

Receiving no response, I continued to whisper the initials until the sleeping mobster opened his eyes. Initially, he was languid before the reality of his situation with the nighttime intruder settled upon him.

Suddenly, he lurched—-attempting to reach for a semi-automatic he kept by his bedside. Only then did he realize his hands were bound to the bedposts.

Once he was fully awake, his eyes widened in the same frightened horror he had brought to so many others on his rise within criminal syndicate.

I whispered yet again, "For JFK and for all the other nameless bastards over the years."

Maldanado's terror was reflected as he wrenched frantically against his bonds, his dilated black pupils widening in the horror he knew was about to befall him.

Though he still couldn't see my face in the subdued light, his mind searched his memory banks for some recognition of the voice he heard as a whisper in the night. It was useless as he didn't recognize my voice.

"Who are you?"

I leaned in closely and in a final whisper, uttered, "I ask the questions...not you...and it is so much more satisfying to me when you don't know why this bit of justice is delivered."

Tommy Maldanado would never have to worry about being awakened in the middle of a deep sleep ever again.

Chapter 45

The next day the calendar showed January 4, 1967. This was the day I began to breathe a little easier and there were several reasons for my new-found relief.

That morning, I tucked one of my newspapers under my arm and took a stroll to a diner about a mile away to enjoy a leisurely breakfast. It was a cool morning in January to say the least and I sat down at the counter to enjoy a nice hot cup of coffee before I ordered. I opened my paper and a news item instantly caught my attention.

So surprised was I by the headline that I dropped my coffee cup and spilled half its contents onto the counter.

"Sorry, sorry," I blurted out, as I reached for several napkins to mop up the counter top.

The waitress moved over quickly, and said, "Don't worry about it, honey. I do it twice a day myself," she said, as she wiped a rag across the countertop with one hand, while she dexterously held a coffee pot in her other hand and refilled my cup.

When my composure returned, I returned my attention to the headline I'd just read and I immediately contemplated my particular situation, my own mortality.

First, I thought about the fact I had not been approached by any mobster for another job assignment. That was actually quite a relief because had they approached me, I would have been very worried I might have been set up for a hit.

Second, my superiors within the CIA never approached me about my connection with the mob. That too was a great relief because it meant the mob in all likelihood had not informed the CIA one of their own had not only done work for the mob, but had been in Dallas that day. I surmised the mob was saving that tidbit of information for a more opportune time when they needed to take advantage of it the most.

Lastly, I thought about the most important reason for my mental well-being and my safety, as I stared at the news headline in the paper...

JACK RUBY DEAD
SUCCUMBS TO CANCER

He had died in prison the day before and so, the last of the men who had seen me at that meatpacking plant in Dallas was gone now.

Chapter 46

The very next week I was transferred to Chicago. Whoa! Talk about shock! And I thought it was cold in Fort Worth in January! When that Arctic wind hit me in Chicago, I thought I was one of those unfortunate souls in Dante's ninth circle of hell...frozen amidst the cold and ice.

As I think of it now, it was probably a good thing I was transferred to the Second City. In effect, it moved me around the chess board so to speak. It was much less likely my extracurricular activities would be discovered by the mob if I was out of town.

In Chicago my assignment was to review the cable traffic in and out of Cuba as well as all the Latin American countries. I suppose performing that function in Chicago was just as good as anywhere else. I mean I wouldn't have any better handle on the cable traffic if I were farther south like in Miami or New Orleans or along the border with Mexico, though I did travel from time to time to interview a few apprehended aliens who crossed the Mexican border.

On January 26, 1967 a huge snowstorm hit Chicago and I got stuck in it like most everyone else. At first, there were accidents galore but it wasn't long before everything snarled to a halt. Absolutely nothing moved in the blizzard of '67. Man, you should have seen the expressways. They were full of abandon cars and semi-trailer trucks that were caught in the snow. My car ran out of gas while I was stuck in traffic as did so many others and all of us had to trudge through the snow and bitter cold to get back to our homes.

When I got home, I was so cold I got into a hot shower and stayed there for thirty minutes to warm myself. When I got out of the shower, I dressed quickly, poured myself some brandy and sat down to relax and read my daily newspapers.

I was reading my Chicago paper and an auto accident caught my attention which occurred the day before. An automobile had collided with a semi-trailer. Though no one was killed, it made the papers because the accident had tied up traffic for hours. The car was not drivable and had to be towed. Nothing unusual in that, but the paper reported the car had Arizona plates. I guess it was simply because I knew how the system worked with the mob, that without even realizing it, my first thought instinctively went to an auto transporting drugs up from the Sonoran corridor. I guess that's how most of us interpret events—-through the shaded lens of our own accumulated experiences. Anyway, I dismissed those thoughts as nothing more than my over imaginative and melodramatic subconscious running away with me.

The next day I trudged through the snow with a gas can. It was a five gallon can and by the time I got to my car, I was exhausted. Anyway, I was luckier than most as the next exit was only a couple of hundred yards ahead, and there was a narrow clearing which afforded me a path to escape that jumble of trucks and autos.

I stopped at a restaurant that was open, bought a newspaper and soon my thoughts returned to drug trafficking when I read the Fillmore family of three had been slain in northwest Chicago. By itself that wouldn't have triggered any suspicious thoughts on my part until I read Mr. Fillmore had automobiles stored on his property...ones that had to be towed. The police reported there was no apparent motive for the triple homicide.

A triple homicide with no apparent motive started the wheels turning in my mind once again and my thoughts returned to that of an automobile heading north from the Sonoran corridor. I decided to check it out and made some calls to the local authorities.

I always took extra care not to use my status as a CIA agent when gathering information related to my night activities so as to avoid suspicion. This time, however, since I didn't have any evening plans, I used my position. I knew I could obtain all the information I wanted from local authorities regarding an automobile accident without any problem at all.

It's true the FBI and the CIA often didn't share information over the years. That was because of Dulles and Hoover. They set the tone of non-cooperation from the very beginning and it carried over in the intelligence community culture and lasted for generations. If either agency knew something, no way would either voluntarily inform the other. If, however, either agency was asked a direct question, more likely than not the specific information would be provided. Thus, if one of us wanted to know something regarding an individual, the FBI would furnish the information...including his whereabouts if they knew. Of course, we would make up a reason for our inquiry. That's how each of the agencies operated when dealing with the other...we'd rarely divulge the real reason for the inquiry.

I pondered contacting the Bureau in this instance.

If the driver was involved with what my instincts told me he was, then he could very well become one of my targets some dark and cloudy night. His sudden demise would likely raise suspicions toward the individual who was most recently asking about him. Thus, I decided against contacting the Bureau for any information on the driver.

Instead, I decided to use one of my many fake business cards to assist me in gathering information. Years ago, I had dozens of different business cards made for numerous and varied occupations which I used from time if I needed to cover my true identity. This was one of those times. It is amazing how many doors are opened with a simple business card.

I pulled out my abundant collection, thumbed through them and grinned widely when I found those that fit the occasion perfectly...an independent automobile insurance claim adjuster. When the Eisenhower Expressway was cleared, I drove out to Elk Grove, a suburb northwest of Chicago.

I entered the Elk Grove Police station with the confidence of someone who was quite at ease in dealing with the police as I approached the front desk...business card in hand.

"Hey," I said nonchalantly to the officer, as I handed him my card, and said, "I need to see the accident report on a vehicle with Arizona plates but I'm afraid I don't have much more to go on than that."

"That's all you got?" the officer asked skeptically.

"Guy calls me. Says he drove up from Arizona and was in an accident and wants an independent adjuster to take a look at it so he doesn't get ripped off by his insurance company. He tells me the accident happened in Elk Grove and says he'll call me back tomorrow to see what I think. Then the rummy hangs up on me. I don't even know the guy's name, make or model of the car. Didn't even leave me his phone number to call him back. What an idiot!"

"Yeah, a lot of ignorant Joes out there."

"Accident occurred on the day before the storm if that helps at all," I informed him.

"Let me see...that would be the 25th. I've got a ton of accident reports here that haven't been processed," said the officer, as he thumbed through some papers. "Damn storm of the century put us way behind."

I nodded in acknowledgement but said nothing further opting instead to allow him to peruse the papers without interruption or distraction. No small talk. Once someone is doing what you want them to do, don't distract them...less is more.

"Ah, here it is. Arizona plates," he said, as he proceeded to give me the pertinent details of the make, model, vin number, "and your customer is a Ruben Skarbek...S-K-A-R-B-E-K."

As he rattled off the information, I wrote it down to play along with my ruse, and without looking up, I asked, "And where is the auto now?"

Upon hearing nothing, I looked up and the officer's mouth was agape.

"What? What is it? Oh, don't tell me the car is missing…,"

"No, no, nothing like that. After the accident the car was towed to a location which the next day was the site of a triple homicide."

"What?!"

"The owner of the lot, his wife and son," the officer stated.

"Wait a minute! I read about that in the newspaper."

"Yeah, murdered the day of storm." The officer nodded, as he informed me, "the Fillmore family. I doubt you'll be able to transfer the auto to a shop for repairs until the detectives are finished. I don't know if they've concluded the on-site investigation but it's a crime scene. Maybe they'll let you have a look at the auto to make your estimate."

I nodded as the officer gave me the address along with the name and number of the lead detective, and he finished with, "Oh, and here's the location of Skarbek. No phone number but he's at a Chicago address."

"Thanks for all your help. I appreciate it," I said, as I turned and exited the station satisfied that I now had the name and the location of the driver.

Chapter 47

Rather than going to the location of the automobile, I went to my office and ran a check on Mr. Skarbek and found he had a yellow sheet for some petty criminal charges in Arizona. The charges were numerous but all amounted to petty offenses. So, why would a petty criminal in Arizona drive to Chicago? The triple homicide confirmed what my instincts had told me and I had no doubts whatsoever.

Skarbek was staying at a rundown hotel in Chicago so I decided to pay him a visit.

When I got to my car, I reached under my seat and grabbed my handgun and holster. I didn't have to check my gun for ammunition because I always kept it fully loaded. The silencer was attached and I slipped on the holster and headed for the hotel.

When I arrived, I saw there wasn't any elevator.

I took the stairway up to the third floor, and, as I began to head down the hallway I saw two men exiting one of the rooms. Something immediately struck me as being odd. Though they were on their way out, they were removing their gloves and stuffing them into their pockets. On a January day in Chicago that made no sense; they should have been putting their gloves on as they headed out.

Their presence confirmed for me that I'd been correct in my assessment. I sensed who they were immediately because I'd been around their type enough through the years to recognize that look of cold, dark detachment in their eyes.

So as not to draw attention to themselves they weren't attempting to hide their faces and I got a good look at them. That's a little trick that mob hit men employ—-nonchalance—-because the less people look in their direction, the better for them in not being spotted and not being recognized if they were in a lineup later.

Evidently, I looked at them a little too closely, because just as we were passing me in the hallway in the opposite direction, I saw one of them casually reach inside his coat.

I grabbed for my own gun, spun around, and hit the deck just as one of them turned and leveled his gun at me. I fired twice and hit him in the chest, then fired twice at the second man who had reached for his gun as well. One of my shots missed him, but the other hit him in the arm causing him to drop his piece. He didn't attempt to pick it up, he ran.

I quickly approached the guy on the floor, kicked the gun away and checked him.

He was dead.

I pulled out a couple of plastic bags which I always carried in case I ever came across something I wanted to gather. I used the bags now because in the hallway shootout neither man had time to put his gloves back on. I figured I could get prints. I carefully picked up the dead man's handgun along with the weapon from the guy I had wounded and slid the guns into separate bags.

I then went down the hall to Skarbek's room where I found the door closed though it had obviously been kicked in earlier. I drew my weapon and entered cautiously.

I saw Skarbek gagged and lying on his back atop the bedding that was saturated in crimson. They'd gone up the ladder on him. Skarbek had bullet wounds in each kneecap, one in the groin, one in the abdomen, one in the belly, and one in each shoulder. From the look of the wounds, they used two different guns on him. The one they used to inflict the pain was a small caliber weapon. One of the guns I'd picked up in the hallway was .22. It's one of the mob's favorite weapons of choice when they want you to suffer, because unless the slugs are in the head, they're generally not lethal—-at least not immediately.

The pain Skarbek suffered must have been excruciating before two larger bullet holes from a higher caliber handgun had entered his forehead just above his left eyebrow and blowing off a portion of the top of his head. From the number of wounds, he no doubt would have begged them to finish him, if not for the gag in his mouth.

They made him suffer because of the old mob standby—-he had committed some unpardonable offense. It was probably that accident he was involved in while he had the mob's merchandise in the trunk. Skarbek had received the fate of those who screwed up when transporting drugs up from the Sonoran corridor. Even if the accident with that semi-trailer truck wasn't his fault, that wouldn't have mattered to the mob higher-ups. They probably told him to stay put in the hotel before he was to receive his next assignment. What a sap! He never knew they were coming for him. I guess he wasn't smart enough to know he would soon be the victim of a mob hit.

I didn't feel the least bit sorry for him though, because, if I had found him alive, I'd have put at least one slug into one of his kneecaps to get him to talk. I came here to find out if he had anything to do with the Fillmore murders. If he had been involved, I would have killed him...just not as slowly and painfully as they did.

My thought was the mob might have used Skarbek to assist in the Fillmore killings when they retrieved the drugs from the damaged automobile. I thought I might find a gun, so I searched his room. Sure enough, I found a .38 caliber revolver under the mattress and slipped that into another plastic bag.

I looked once again at Skarbek lying dead on the bloodstained bed and shook my head that he had been so foolish to keep his revolver under the mattress. That's not a good place to stow a weapon, because it cannot be easily retrieved if someone stormed into the room, as his killers had done.

I then got the hell out of there without pausing to call the police, as the body in the hallway would be discovered soon enough.

I exited by the back door into an alley being careful to keep an eye out for the one I had wounded in case he was hanging around and waiting for me to exit into the open but he was nowhere to be seen.

I went around the block and returned to my automobile and placed all three of the guns from the scene under the front seats and headed back toward my office taking a long, convoluted route just in case I was followed. I continually checked my rearview mirror and was relieved that I didn't see any following car.

I stopped along the way and removed my holster and piece and slipped them under the seat as well. The area beneath my front seats was now quite crowded with weapons, and I had this terrible vision of being stopped by the police for a traffic violation.

I quickly dismissed any problem with local authorities, however, since I was confident that my CIA identification would suffice in getting me out of any kind of jam.

When I got back to the office, I ordered ballistics on all the handguns—a .22 caliber from the stiff in the hallway, the 9-millimeter from the guy I had wounded, and, of course, Skarbek's .38 revolver.

When I got the results of the tests, I made some inquiries into the farmhouse homicides with the local authorities. Naturally, I didn't inform them of the weapons I had recovered from the Skarbek murder scene, but I did ask them to send over a copy of their ballistics report from the bullets recovered from the murders of the Fillmore family.

When I did a comparison, I found Skarbek's .38 was a definite match as one of the weapons used in the Fillmore murders. So, there you have it. Skarbek screwed up by getting in an automobile accident so he was sent over with another guy to the Fillmore place where the car was towed to get the stuff back. A petty criminal who was made to participate in the murders. Because of Skarbek's participation in those killings, I would have eliminated the asshole anyway. That wasn't all however, as the ballistics report showed the 9-millimeter from the guy I wounded had also been one of the weapons used in the triple homicide.

I went over to the Chicago FBI office and looked at some of the mug shots of those who were suspected of being members of organized crime in the city, and once again I felt invigorated studying the comings and goings of the mob, especially in Chicago, the home base of Stefano Bonafacio.

I soon spotted a picture of a swarthy looking guy with a round face and cold, dark eyes. It was the guy I had wounded in the hallway. I read below his mug shot he was born in 1945. Thus, he was twenty-two years old in 1967...a relative newcomer.

As I continued to read, I learned he was considered an up and comer in the Chicago Outfit, but in the mob, one has to carry out a hit to prove one's worth. By participating in the farmhouse killings and by eliminating Skarbek he would have been making his bones with the mob if he hadn't hit someone before those killings.

His name was Anthony Gardelli.

Though Gardelli was wounded and his partner killed in the hallway of a seedy Chicago hotel, I doubt Gardelli would have been considered a screw up, as the chances of getting wounded or killed goes with the territory when a hit is ordered in the middle of the day.

The mob would in fact consider Gardelli's wound a trophy of sorts, a badge of honor in the performance of carrying out his instructions.

Though the higher echelon mobsters do get pissed when they lose one of their own at the hand of a rival, it's not because the bosses get overly sentimental about the loss of life of one of their underlings. They don't give a damn about the individual. It's a matter of ego. They look upon the hit, not as an attack on the individual that worked for them, but as an assault upon their organization, which often times is exactly what it is.

That wasn't the case here though.

I wondered who Gardelli thought I was. I wondered if Gardelli thought me to be an off-duty policeman or a detective who had come to talk to Skarbek the day our paths crossed in that hotel hallway. Most of all, I wondered what he reported back to his bosses.

No doubt the Outfit would have him lay low for a while to see if anyone from law enforcement came looking for him. If not, he was home free, but if someone did start asking questions about him, the mob would most surely have Gardelli killed.

I would later learn that Anthony Gardelli was the breed of the modern young gangster who studied and learned from observing the habits and ways of old-time gangsters.

Gardelli was a smart, intelligent, cunning mobster who learned a great deal from his contemporaries as well as studying and learning the history of those who came before him.

I can't explain why but for some reason he thoroughly intrigued me. I was very curious to see if he would rise within the ranks of organized crime over the years.

I put my directional antenna to work again listening in on conversations and after several months I learned Gardelli indeed had pulled the trigger in the Skarbek murder and the man who ordered the hit was none other than Stefano Bonafacio...the brutal bastard atop the Chicago Outfit.

I never informed the local authorities what I knew and they would never solve the triple homicide of the Fillmore family, but I vowed Gardelli and Bonafacio would each be dealt with in due course.

I saved all the evidence I collected from the scene of the Skarbek murder but I would not be impatient and jump too soon. I would sit on what I knew; I would bide my time as I always did and I would strike at a time and place of my choosing.

Chapter 48

The years passed and Vietnam was for real all right...a hot war...but as it turned out, I didn't get reassigned to Nam as one of my fellow agents jokingly thought I might. I continued with my assignment in the Chicago office and during my time there I gathered all the information I could digest on the Chicago Outfit...and then some.

Previously, when I was in Fort Worth, I subscribed to three out of town newspapers...the *Chicago Tribune,* the *Miami Herald,* and the *New Orleans Post.* When I moved to Chicago, I merely transferred my subscriptions to a new address.

I received the out-of-town newspapers the day after they were printed, but I didn't care about that. It wasn't like I was getting them for their day-old sports pages. I merely wanted to stay abreast of particular news stories I might see reported in any of those cities.

Miami was the base of operations of crime boss, Salvatore D'Amato, New Orleans that of crime boss Carlo Marchetti, and Chicago that of Stefano Bonafacio.

By using the papers for information, I would steer clear of drawing on the intelligence apparatus of the U.S. government. Besides, for the subject matter in which I was interested, the local news organizations would likely report on the story before the CIA would. Additionally, by going outside the Agency I could avoid any questions about why I was looking into some anonymous person's death so far away.

Yeah, I was looking for stories on gangland style hits.

Though I didn't expect any crime syndicate secret revelations in any of those papers I did learn a few things along the way. In 1966, for example, while I was in Fort Worth, I saw a picture of someone in the *New Orleans Post.* I recognized the individual immediately. I would never forget those rodent-like facial characteristics of the replacement pilot I'd seen in the Sonoran Desert where Pete

Madison had paid the inevitable price for cheating the mob. I now learned the replacement pilot's name was David Ferrie and it was reported he committed suicide.

I paused for a minute to consider what I'd read.

Suicides of mob-connected individuals are quite rare actually. One suicide that does come to mind was that of Frank Nitti, Al Capone's right-hand man. He took his life by shooting himself in the head. That was a lot of years ago, of course. He killed himself because he learned there was a contract out on him. That's one of the reasons suicides of mob guys are so rare. Generally, the potential target never knows beforehand he is marked for a hit and selected for elimination.

It's a very horrifying experience to learn the mob has targeted you for death. The future victim is forever looking over their shoulder, around every corner, never feeling safe, not even in public places like a restaurant and never being able to sleep peacefully. It takes its toll.

Knowing your death is imminent but not being privy to when precisely adds to the horror. The fear increases with every second that passes until it morphs into paralyzing paranoia and evolves into sheer panic. The terror is overwhelming. And, of course, the targeted victim generally doesn't know if it's going to be a quick death...or slow and painful. It's really quite understandable some guys can't deal with that and end their lives by their own hand.

Whenever I hear of a suicide of a mob-connected individual, I think of the fear factor first as one of two possible reasons for the suicide. But like I said, it's really rare since most are unaware they are the target of a hit.

What is much more common, however, is that the individual was hit, and his death was made to look like a suicide. Through the years the mob really became quite sophisticated with hits and making them appear to be suicides. There were automobiles going over cliffs exploding into a ball of flame, victims seated in their cars inside their garage with the motor running who died of carbon monoxide poisoning, and, of course, one of the great standards of a mob hit—-one that looks so genuinely like a suicide—-a drug overdose. The trick was to do it without leaving any indication of a struggle...like bruises on the body.

The mob is quite fond of these types of hits for the simple reason that if the local authorities rule the deaths suicides, then there are no questions asked, no homicide investigation, nobody brought to police headquarters to be interrogated about where they were on a certain day at a certain time and whether or not someone can corroborate their story. That all becomes moot in the case of a suicide.

This wasn't the 1920's when mob hits took place in the street amid the rapid fire of a Thompson sub machinegun. These guys were much smarter and more sophisticated than their predecessors. The cunning, ruthless mobsters of my time had learned a great deal from the past mistakes of others.

Yeah, the mob got quite proficient at *suicides* over the years and in the modern world of organized crime, suicide is the quintessential murder.

Whether David Ferrie's suicide fell into this category I don't know, but it was reported that Mr. Ferrie was a pilot who over the years did some work for New Orleans crime boss, Carlo Marchetti. Of course, that was an item of news I already knew from that night in Arizona along the Sonoran corridor.

As I placed the paper on the table, I smiled both within myself and outwardly as I realized that yet another man who had seen me in connection with my mob activity was now gone.

Chapter 49

For me nothing much changed until 1969 when my supervisor called me into his office.

"Narducci, you're being transferred to Madison, Wisconsin," he came right to the point.

"What?" I asked dumbfounded.

"You have something against the Badgers?" he chuckled, referring to Madison being the home of the University of Wisconsin.

"I don't understand, sir."

"Madison is a hotbed of anti-war protests. The government wants a presence there," he said.

Though I didn't have a clue as to why the CIA, a foreign intelligence gathering operation, would be requested in Madison.

"Boss, that's the domestic side of things; that's the purview of the FBI," I pointed out.

"If that's where our boss wants the resources of the CIA then that's where we'll assign them. You won't be alone, Narducci. Several others are being transferred from the Chicago office as well as from other offices around the country...all within weeks of each other.

"Is this another Communist witch hunt, boss?"

"Well, since our Commander in Chief made his reputation hunting communists, I suppose you could say the hunt is on," my supervisor responded. "But make no mistake, Narducci, like it or not, you need to show results."

I grudgingly nodded in understanding.

It was the Nixon years and a lot of unusual things were happening regarding agents of the U.S. Government, whether it was the CIA, the FBI, Treasury, or any other kind of federal government employees.

As a matter of fact, there were a goodly number of agents that retired during this period. Yeah, a lot of my fellow agents lined up jobs in the private sector. They simply left the CIA and went into some other endeavor. They'd had enough. They cut their ties with the CIA completely. The rationalization of serving your country did little in easing one's conscience of destroying somebody's reputation and career. Looking back, I wished I'd have had either the balls or the foresight to leave the CIA, but I didn't and in 1969 I was thirty-four years of age and thus not vested in the retirement plan. I had to stay...or at least that's what I told myself.

I was too old to infiltrate the student body of a university, so the CIA set me up in an elaborate operation in the next best way they could, and it wasn't a bad gig at all. I was to teach languages at the University of Wisconsin. I was furnished with a false identity, references and a resume that would be envied by a Nobel Laureate. I must say that despite all of my criticism of the CIA it is an organization that is expert in establishing cover stories for their agents.

My assignment, as a faculty member, was to determine if any faculty members were communists. Yeah, it was still the Cold War, and it was Nixon who was in power now, a man who had developed a reputation in his early days as a communist fighter. Some have thought communist hunting was simply a fairy tale and the government pursued only the moviemakers of Hollywood. Not so, as evidenced by the arrest of Ethel and Julius Rosenberg in the early fifties for treason. Communist hunters were very serious people, and the Rosenbergs were tried for treason, found guilty and executed in the electric chair. Their executions set the tone that hunting communists was indeed very serious business.

As far as my assignment in Madison was concerned, I was to attend as many faculty functions as were held. I was instructed to get to know everyone, not necessarily become friends with everyone that I met because that would be a bit suspicious, but I was expected to at least become familiar enough with all of the faculty members so that

I could to speak to them on a one-on-one basis. I guess you might say I was to be sociably friendly.

Besides determining the politics of a faculty member, I had an additional assignment. I was to learn if any of the faculty was fermenting anti-war sentiment, whether it was throughout the student body or merely with one student. Just the previous year protestors wreaked havoc in Chicago's Grant Park, though that would later be ruled a Police riot. My job in Madison was to see if any of the faculty was encouraging open demonstrations against the Vietnam War.

At that time protesting against the war was a sure-fire way of getting one's name placed onto Richard Nixon's enemy's list and attempting to link someone to anti-war demonstrators became eighty percent of my job.

Those six years I was in Madison, from 1969 through the summer of 1974 were a very dark period in American History. Few really know how shadowy and sinister it really was. In many ways it was very much like the communist witch hunts of the fifties except that I was intimately involved in this period of history, and thus to me it therefore appeared to be much more menacing.

I'm sure that Richard Nixon didn't give direct orders for many of the abuses that ensued during his years in the Presidency, but he certainly set the tone, a tone that his minions heard loudly and clearly. They were like sprinters in the starting blocks awaiting the sound of the gun for the race to begin, and when they got their marching orders, they were off and running as fast as they could go—-out to destroy the lives and careers of all who stood in their way. And for so many of those who carried out those orders, well, it was like an ego trip. They actually enjoyed ruining peoples' lives. Sadism shows itself in many ways and it isn't restricted to America's enemies.

If a faculty member was merely suspected of being a communist or an anti-war agitator, I had my instructions on how to deal with such a person, and I must say I carried out my instructions to the letter. After all, it was my job and that's what I kept telling myself.

How did a faculty member become suspected? Generally, any suspicion of a faculty member being involved in the anti-war movement came from the task force of which yours truly was a member. To determine if there were any professors stirring up anti-war sentiment, my colleagues and I investigated them by inversion. We checked out the students first. Once the students were identified as anti-war agitators, we then listed their classes and the professors they had for each class. That in essence made a professor automatically suspect. The obvious flaw in the system was there were so many students involved with anti-war demonstrations in Madison all the professors had many students who participated in some anti-war rally or demonstration. That dichotomy between facts and association didn't matter. The professors were automatically placed on a list.

When one of those professors was in fact spotted at an anti-war protest, I received my instructions. My assignment was to destroy the professor's credibility—-by whatever means necessary.

I shall cite as an example one in particular, Professor Eric Milton. He was forty-two years old and had been a professor for fully fifteen years. He was married and the father of two boys and one girl. To discredit him, I used one of the oldest standbys known to man. I hired a call girl. I instructed her on what she was to do, and informed her that if she played her part perfectly she could expect that her normal fee would be tripled. There's that incentive of money again. She was only too glad to help upon hearing about the large bonus.

When I saw Professor Milton between classes one day, I asked as nonchalantly as I could, "Hey, Eric, are you going to the party tonight?"

"Yeah, I think I'll stop by."

"Will Mrs. Milton be able to make it?"

"No. I don't think she can attend this evening."

That was, of course, all I needed to hear and I 'invited' the call girl to the faculty function.

As I drove her to the function, I said, "I should describe Professor Milton for you."

"No need," she replied.

"What do you mean?"

"I'll find out on my own as I'm moving around the party and that'll make it all the more spontaneous when I meet him."

"Hmm," I muttered and concluded she was a real pro.

There was a doorman hired for the occasion and though we entered together we separated quickly so that I would not be introducing her to anyone and she was on her own to make her move on Professor Milton.

She played it coy in the beginning. She didn't seek him out or ask anyone about him, preferring to be noticed by him first. She was wearing a long dark blue dress, which was accented by a pearl necklace and small pearl earrings. At five feet ten, she was a tall woman with a remarkable figure and long, slender legs. She worked the party like the pro she was, going from one discussion to another. Her cover story was that she was in town for a job interview the next day for a position in the administration building, and, believe it or not, everyone there bought her story.

I was discreetly watching Professor Milton and I could see he was salivating as he eyed her from afar...oh, 'cross a crowded room...I chuckled to myself. Did I mention the reason I picked sex to discredit him? I did my homework and I knew he fooled around. That's how my getting to know the faculty members paid off. It's amazing how many men are so stupid that they go around bragging about their exploits to people who they hardly even know. Their own egos so foolishly set themselves up for a fall.

After about an hour the call girl casually made her way toward Professor Milton. She played Milton so well at the party I was beginning to get concerned he was going to get a hard-on right there.

"Hi. I don't think that we've met as yet," she said to him, as she extended her hand. "I'm Cynthia."

I think Eric's mouth fell open but he managed to struggle getting out a hello in reply and introduced himself. I meandered my way around the room until I got within earshot of the two of them.

She explained she was from out of town and here for a job interview in the morning.

"Well, good luck to you. Perhaps I'll be seeing you around then."

"Thank you," she smiled seductively. "I probably should get going. I want to make a good impression during my interview tomorrow, so I shouldn't make too late a night of this. Do you happen to know where the telephone is? I need to call a taxi."

"Where are you staying?"

"At the Hilton down on..."

"Oh, I know where it's at," he replied.

Indeed, he did, I thought to myself.

"I'd be pleased to drop you off," Milton offered. "I should probably get going now myself."

"Well, if it wouldn't be of any inconvenience to you," she said seductively.

"Not at all," he answered lustfully.

They left very soon thereafter, and when they arrived at the Hilton, Cynthia turned to him, and said, "Why don't you stop up for a nightcap...as a way for me to say thanks for the ride," she smiled seductively.

"Okay," Professor Milton replied, as he almost drooled on himself.

Once upstairs, Cynthia made a couple of drinks from the mini bar, and presented Eric with a gin and tonic.

"Here's to a successful job interview," he raised his glass, as gave her a lingering look up and down as he took a sip of his drink.

"And here's a nice thank you for a ride back to my hotel," Cynthia replied, as she sauntered closer to him and kissed him deeply on the lips.

Eric set his drink down, embraced her, and kissed her deeply in return.

The room had already been rigged with a concealed camera along with sound, as I wanted footage rather than still photographs. Cynthia knew where the camera was located so she wouldn't block the lens from a full view of Professor Milton.

Through the years as a government employee, I participated in electronic surveillance training that was offered and became quite capable at it, though I cunningly never let it be known that I was proficient at eavesdropping. By that I mean when it came to testing us—-we were tested to determine if we could be fully certified technicians—-I answered only enough questions correctly to move onto the next training course. They graded us on a scale of 1 to 5 with 5 being the highest. One had to attain an average score of 4.5 overall in the training courses to become fully certified. If that sounds like a high standard, it is and there's a good reason for it. One had to attain a high level of proficiency because electricity plays a large part in surveillance. One had to become quite knowledgeable in tapping into electrical sources such as telephone lines and electrical wires. The CIA didn't want their agents electrocuting themselves in the process of placing the surveillance equipment, but even more important to the Agency was they wanted the surveillance to be competently put in place. If the agent accidentally shocked himself, it could blow a fuse and the mission would be scrapped. Or if the agent was clumsy with any particular apparatus and did a poor installation the bug could be discovered. I was quite proud of the fact that my overall grade was a 3.5—-just enough to continue onto the next course but never enough to become fully certified. Thus, my supervisors, nor anyone else within the Agency, ever knew of my actual proficiency level.

Of course, I could have maintained the anonymity of my expertise simply by taking a private course, but there are many things available to the CIA in all kinds of illegal apparatus to which the everyday man would never have access. It would have actually looked more suspicious if I didn't partake of the training the CIA offered its employees. So, I enrolled in the training provided and I learned it all.

By not becoming certified, I thus never had to worry about ever being transferred into an area or another assignment that would require such an expertise. Also, by maintaining secrecy of my expertise, if the CIA by some remote chance discovered electronic surveillance equipment had been set up during my night work, they would never imagine it had been me who placed it there.

I must say it's not such an easy task keeping one's expertise under wraps, because it's human nature to brag about what one knows or to provide an answer off the cuff if someone is discussing such things and has a question. I was forever on my guard and had to practice humility and self-control during the years...not to offer an answer when someone had a question. Whenever I enjoyed a cup of coffee around a tabletop discussion with other personnel, I had to consciously refrain from letting my knowledge out of the bag. I just figured it was nobody's business what I knew and their ignorance of my expertise couldn't be anything but a benefit to me in my nightly endeavors.

As a matter of fact, I could very easily have installed all the electronics in that hotel room in Madison, Wisconsin when we set up Professor Milton to take a fall. But, when the technicians came in to set everything up, I acted like I wasn't familiar with most of their equipment. When they were installing the equipment, I made small talk by asking them some basic questions as to how some of their devices worked and performed. I played that part very well, because the technicians didn't have a clue that I knew all about it.

Boy, did we ever get our monies worth when we hired that call girl. Cynthia was worth every penny we paid her...and more.

At five feet, nine inches, Eric was an inch shorter than Cynthia. Thus, her clothes fit him—-remarkably well as a matter of fact. She really went all out in dressing him up in one of her black garter belts, black stockings and a sheer black negligee.

When she mounted him and started humping him, we got it all on film. Needless to say, once we got the film developed, we had plenty on Professor Milton to discredit him. He resigned and within the week he moved his family out of town in exchange for the film.

Such was the job of one CIA agent in Madison, Wisconsin. That's where your tax dollars went during the Nixon years in the hunt for communists and anti-war agitators, and that was merely one example. There were countless other such incidents as well.

I offer no feeble excuses by way of saying we all needed our paychecks, or that we were under orders and were simply doing our job, because any such statements would not make what we did any more acceptable. We did it, we were despicable in doing so, and we were wrong. We all realized we shouldn't be doing what our superiors gave us as assignments but we all continued to do such things until we moved onto another assignment which we hoped was a little less despicable.

After Carter won the White House in the '76 election, the dirty tricks stopped. Actually, all that shit stopped under Gerald Ford when he assumed the presidency after Nixon resigned, and the general atmosphere in the CIA changed markedly.

All of us breathed a sigh of relief we could finally get back to doing what we hired on to do, what we were actually trained to do as CIA agents instead of all that other crap.

Yeah, we were all quite relieved when we didn't have to perform those obnoxious assignments anymore. How many lives did we ruin? Nobody really knows. It simply cannot be quantified.

Chapter 50

The years passed and I was back in Chicago full time.

Though I had let my subscriptions to the *Miami Herald*, and the *New Orleans Post* lapse, I hadn't forgotten about the mob and the other career I had embarked upon by night. I continued doing my research because there was some unfinished business. I still had not rendered retribution upon the ones who ordered the hit in Dallas.

I knew about those I suspected. I knew their names, their haunts, and where they lived. What I lacked was proof or at least circumstantial evidence that was convincing enough for me to act.

The temporary transfer to Madison, Wisconsin had worked to my benefit as I needed to wait for the right time. Too many deaths in too short a time period would not be in my best interest.

By the mid-seventies the government was investigating happenings in the Caribbean during the early sixties. Senator Frank Church of Idaho was Chairman of the Senate Select Committee on Intelligence Activities. He and his committee were beginning to uncover a lot of shit about the Agency—-its connection with the mob to hit Castro for one thing. It was the very thing Allen Dulles steered the Warren Commission away from.

The Senate Committee was serious about its work, and it was only a matter of time before members of organized crime would be summoned to testify before the Committee.

Sure enough, I learned a subpoena was issued for Chicago mobster Stefano Bonafacio to testify before the Committee, when a thought struck me as sweet revenge.

I took a couple of days of vacation and rented a car so I wouldn't be driving my own. I switched the plates on the rental with some bogus plates I always kept so the rental couldn't be traced back to me. Then I drove to one of the well-established suburbs of Chicago, River Forest, where many of the well to do resided. The streets were lined on either side with mature, shady elm trees, and the homes were large and lavish with lawns that looked like golf courses while flower beds and rows of bushes were meticulously maintained.

I wanted to check things out at Bonafacio's address, get the lay of the land and have a look at his neighborhood. When I arrived at the address, I saw several cars parked in the street and three of them were occupied. No doubt the mobster was under surveillance, as he had recently been returned to the United States after living for quite some time in Panama. Though he had retired so to speak from the mob a few years earlier, he was brought back to testify before the Senate Select Committee in Washington D.C.

I made a note of the various license plates and drove back to the office to check them out.

As I entered the office, one of my colleagues said, "What are you doing here, Narducci? I thought you were taking a couple of days off."

"Oh, I'm just tying up a couple of loose ends and just came in to double check something," I gave as a pretext.

I proceeded to look up the license plates from the cars watching Bonafacio and sure enough, one of the autos was CIA. The Agency didn't always do everything covertly. The realm of the CIA was overseas but in these years the Agency wasn't noted for following the rules, and, evidently, the Agency didn't care if the mobster might learn the CIA was keeping tabs on him...probably even preferred that he knew so as to make him nervous.

I looked up the prefix code and made a call. The agent on the scene picked up immediately.

"Yeah?" he answered.

"This is Todd Gilbert," I said giving him a fictitious name followed by more lies. "I'm working with the Church Committee in Washington."

"What can I do for you?"

"We've got a government official coming by the house tomorrow in connection with Mr. Bonafacio's upcoming testimony in Washington."

"Yeah, we know he was subpoenaed by the Committee," he said, a bit irritated.

"Anyway, this governmental official will be there at lunch time tomorrow."

"Yeah, okay, we'll watch for him."

"Well, that's the thing," I explained. "The official wants to remain anonymous and not be seen."

"Is he one of the senators?" he asked.

"Like I said, he wants to remain anonymous. It's a very sensitive matter because of this man's connection to the committee. It's imperative to him that no one sees him coming and going from the house, not even us, and I understand there are several cars in the area."

"Yeah, there's us, an FBI fellow, I think treasury is here as well. You say the official is expected at lunch time?"

"Yeah," I answered.

There was silence on the other end of the line for a few moments, and then, "Ah, what the hell. We'll just all go to lunch at the same time. We usually stagger our lunch times so someone will be here but would an hour be enough? We could make it longer if you like?"

"No, an hour should be fine, or, uh, yeah, maybe a little longer I suppose to be on the safe side."

"Okay, no problem. I'll be sure the others get the word."

"Thanks, I do appreciate it," I concluded, as I disconnected and smiled within myself.

The next day at noon, the automobiles with the various agents were not on the scene when I arrived. It was no problem entering the house, because in my research I learned Bonafacio never bothered to lock his door, not once in a while, but he habitually left his door unlocked.

I entered very quietly and considered it very fortunate the old house didn't creak with each step I took. I stopped and listened for a sound...any sound of Bonafacio moving about in the house, a TV blaring, something, but I didn't hear anything.

As I moved from room to room through the house, I soon learned it wouldn't have mattered if I had broken in, shattered a window and stomped into the house with the deftness of an elephant. What I found surprised even a seasoned executioner such as myself.

I got out of there immediately lest the perpetrator was still inside.

Chapter 51

The next morning June 20, 1975 the body of Stefano Bonafacio was discovered murdered in his home. Yeah, talk about irony! I was in his home to take him out, but someone beat me to it—-and not by very much—-before I stumbled upon his prone body.

I made some discreet inquiries and learned he'd had his throat cut so deeply he was nearly decapitated. He was also shot in the mouth six times, and to be sure he was dead, he was shot another half dozen times in the head.

A .22 caliber was used and the shots to the mouth were a message that could not have been clearer. The mob thought he was a risk and shut him up.

But who was the mob? Specifically, who ordered the hit on Bonafacio? Even if it wasn't clear to anyone else, I knew I was getting closer to who ordered the hit on the President.

During my inquiries I was told that it appeared Bonafacio was having a drink with someone as there were a couple of glasses of whiskey on a table which led investigators to surmise that he knew the person who killed him. Further, there was no forced entry. It was believed that Bonafacio probably let the killer into his home. Of course, I knew there wouldn't have been any forced entry with unlocked doors.

Such is the way with the mob when a high-profile mobster is marked for death. The mob often uses someone the victim knows and trusts, or if he doesn't trust him at least it's someone for whom the victim let's their guard down.

It seemed to me it was just like when the mob sent me to get the drop on Pete Madison that night in the Sonoran corridor.

A news article in the *Chicago Tribune* about the gangland murder concluded that person or persons higher in the chain of command of the criminal syndicate ensured purported Chicago mob boss Stefano Bonafacio did not testify before the Church Senate Intelligence Committee. Once again, organized crime silenced one of their own.

Investigators believed Stefano Bonafacio was the one Johnny Pistelli had initially contacted on behalf of the CIA when the inspiration arose to use the mob for a hit on Castro.

Johnny Pistelli was the man I met at the Brown Derby in Los Angeles. He had testified in 1975 before Senator Frank Church's Committee and in 1976 that Senate Select Committee on Intelligence had decided to recall Mr. Pistelli for further testimony. The Committee learned additional facts about certain things and wanted to question Pistelli further about those matters.

I did some checking on my own and it wasn't long before I learned Mr. Hollywood was presently living in Florida, but I waited until the following summer before I decided to take a couple of weeks of vacation to reacquaint myself with Johnny Pistelli. I waited because in view of the Bonafacio hit I thought Pistelli might be under surveillance, so I gathered up my own electronic surveillance equipment I thought I might need and booked a flight for Miami in the summer of 1976.

One night when Johnny Pistelli was fast asleep, I rigged up his automobile with a small innocuous camera lens. The CIA had paid for development of this minute camera that looked like nothing more than a button. I placed it atop the back seat into the upholstery where it looked ornamental and it appeared as if it had been there all along from the auto manufacturer.

It was sweltering in Florida in July and my clothes were soaked with sweat by the time I finished, but it was worth it as through that small camera I could see between the two bucket seats in front. Below the rearview mirror and beyond I had an unobstructed view through the front windshield and thus could see exactly where the automobile was heading.

In the morning Pistelli came out of the house, put his golf clubs in the trunk and got behind the wheel. When he started the car, something blocked the camera's line of vision. I slapped my monitor as I first thought it was an equipment malfunction, but I soon learned from the listening device that my equipment was operating just fine.

"Head to the harbor," said a man from the back seat as he pressed a pistol against the back of the neck of Johnny Pistelli.

"Who are you?"

The man ignored the question.

"What do you want?" Pistelli asked, attempting to hide his fear.

"I just want you to drive to the harbor. It would be such a shame to waste a nice morning like this on a frustrating game of golf," he scowled.

"Why the harbor?"

The man's scowl evolved into a sickly grin, "We're gonna go sailing,"

By the time I arrived at the harbor two men had already escorted Mr. Pistelli onto a yacht and it was already moving away from the dock.

I quickly surveyed the area, spotted a rental and hired the guy on the spot.

"You see that yacht out ahead?"

"Yeah," the captain acknowledged. "You want me to keep him within sight but don't make it look obvious."

I must have done a double-take because the captain added, "Not everybody who hires me wants to go fishing," he smiled, as we departed the dock.

As we got underway the salty sea breeze slapped against my face as we gained speed and was a refreshingly welcome respite from the horrible humidity.

I moved to a spot where I wouldn't easily be detected and watched the yacht ahead of us through my high-powered binoculars. As it slowed, I asked the captain to stop the engine and allow our craft to drift with the current. I also asked him to set up a pole in the stern and feign that he was deep sea fishing while I watched the doings on the other boat.

I was too far away to see faces but I recognized Johnny Pistelli from what he was wearing. He was seated in the stern and appeared to have his arms secured to a chair. One of the men appeared to be holding a piece of rope as he moved around behind Pistelli and abruptly slipped the rope around his neck choking him.

Pistelli's legs kicked frantically, until his oxygen deprived body fell limp in the chair, as the other man watched dispassionately. The two guys then untied the ropes holding Pistelli in the chair and poured him into an empty drum they had placed nearby. There was a problem however. He didn't fit. They pushed and they twisted Pistelli's body but they couldn't get his body inside the drum, so they pulled him out. One of the men stepped away and returned a minute later with a saw. He went to work on one of Pistelli's legs above the knee.

Pistelli suddenly shrieked in pain as his blood spurted and sprayed into the air. He was still alive! As Pistelli's leg was being sawed, the excruciating pain raced through him and must have shocked his nervous system into consciousness. I could see the two men were totally taken by surprise. The garroting made him pass out and he was near death but it wasn't conducted long enough to kill him.

I saw one of the men tape a cloth over Pistelli's mouth and gestured for his partner to keep sawing.

Pistelli struggled while the man behind him held the cloth tightly over his mouth.

It appeared one of the men was angry...so pissed off that Pistelli awoke from death that he pulled out his pistol and shot him at point blank range finally killing him.

"Jesus!" the other man shouted, startled by the sudden gunshot. "Give me some kind of warning next time, will you?"

"Next time, be sure the guy is dead!" he yelled back at him angrily, as he pulled out a knife and stuck it deep into Pistelli's chest.

"He's dead all right," said the man with the knife as he dug deeper into Pistelli.

"What the hell are you doing? He's dead!"

"Yeah, but now I have to get that bullet back, as he knifed deeper into Pistelli.

They finished the job of cutting off Pistelli's legs, crammed the body into the drum and weighed it down with chains. They then dumped the drum overboard into the bay.

Only then did they seem to care about the yacht that was drifting harmlessly a good distance away from them. One of the guys picked up a pair of binoculars and checked us out. He saw a man seated in the stern of the ship fishing leisurely without a care and unaware of what happened to Johnny Pistelli. They didn't give us a secondary glance.

The next day on my return flight to Chicago I wondered if anyone would learn about the Pistelli hit. The mob has made so many people disappear without a trace.

Though the Church Committee recalled Johnny Pistelli, they never got the chance to hear any additional testimony from him...just like Bonafacio.

Two weeks elapsed and I was reading my copy of the *Miami Herald* when came across another news item. A 55-gallon drum pushed to the surface floating in Miami's Dumfoundling Bay. Inside the drum was the gruesome body of Johnny Pistelli. Crime scene investigators said the buildup of body gases pushed the drum and its contents to the surface.

That was a pretty ghastly hit, indeed but another piece of the puzzle had been eliminated. There was one less person who could have talked about the CIA/Mafia hits on Castro, and, now of course could no longer have spoken and shed any light on many other subjects. The American public barely noticed the death of Johnny Pistelli, known within the mob as Mr. Hollywood. It truly amazes me people didn't put one and one together.

Naturally, the killer or killers of Johnny Pistelli were never apprehended and his murder is still on the books as an unsolved homicide.

I'm sure Bonafacio never saw it coming and was unaware he'd been marked for elimination but I didn't feel that way about Pistelli. As a matter of my own speculation, I suspected Johnny Pistelli was the hit man in the Bonafacio murder. After all, he worked for Bonafacio in setting up the entertainment for the mob-controlled casinos in Vegas back in the 50's and 60's. The Chicago chieftain would certainly have sat down for a drink with Pistelli in his home and would have been one with whom Bonafacio would have felt comfortable.

After Bonafacio was eliminated, I figured Johnny Pistelli would be very nervous and that's why he got whacked; nervous hoodlums are walking dead men in the eyes of organized crime bosses. I wasn't surprised at all that Pistelli was hit.

I sometimes wondered how I survived and wasn't hit with so many of the others. I thought about that long and hard. The likelihood the mob wanted to keep me upright for insurance purposes was long since passed, since Senator Frank Church's Committee did indeed uncover the CIA/Mafia attempted hits on Castro. That revelation sent shock waves through Congress and the country alike, as Americans were appalled when they heard the news.

The conclusion I came to regarding my survival was actually rather simple. From my initial contact with a mobster at the Brown Derby about using the Mafia for hits on Castro, to those who knew about me like Stefano Bonafacio were dead. For my work with the mob in Vietnam in getting drugs out of Asia, Pete Madison was dead. The mobster who contacted me several times in New Orleans and Forth Worth was dead, as well as those other hoods that I had seen at the Dallas meat packing plant. I think the explanation of why I was still alive was that I merely got lost in the shuffle. I simply got lucky that no one I had been in contact with in the mob was around to tell anyone about me. I think it was as simple as that.

Chapter 52

One evening I was watching some television interview show. The guest was a local Chicagoan who had a reputation of sorts as a leading expert on organized crime as a writer and lecturer. His full name was Trevor Shadrach Dorsch. The commentator addressed him as Professor Dorsch because he had a PhD.

He had long, bony fingers and when he smiled—-even on television—-he looked like he was much in need of a trip to the dentist. I guessed him to be in his mid-fifties. His long, stringy hair fell several inches below his ears, and he hadn't shaved for the televised interview as evidenced by the salt and pepper bristle on his face which appeared to be a couple of days old. He was unkempt which I'm sure gave the audience the impression he didn't care whatsoever in his appearance and that Professor Dorsch was indeed an eccentric.

As Professor Dorsch was being interviewed, however, I became very interested in what he had on his mind, because he was saying things about the mob. From what he was saying, I was stunned he still remained in an upright position. The facts and details he cited mesmerized me to the point that I was sitting on the edge of my seat as I listened to him.

"I'd like for you to tell our audience whether or not something is true, or whether it has been profoundly magnified in legend and lost in myth," said the commentator, but before he could ask his specific question, the professor interjected.

"Oh, there are lots of myths when it comes to the mob. As a matter of fact, the mob encourages many of the legends, especially the brutal ones, because the more vicious the story, the more it instills fear in people. Fear is a key to the mob's success. It is part and parcel to their mystique and they would be severely limited without it. Fear is what makes witnesses not testify; fear makes jurors vote for acquittal; and make makes judges rule in their favor. Yeah, organized crime plays the fear card in every hand they deal."

"Yes, I certainly agree," said the commentator.

"I know about most of the legends and there's another good reason for promulgating the myths on the part of the mob. It throws the authorities off track as to what really happened, creates doubt. I can tell you which ones are based on fact and which ones are totally false, and which ones have an element of both. Like almost any myth, there is some truth behind them.

The commentator nodded as the professor continued. "There's a story about a mobster in Detroit who wanted to instill fear in a rival, and within his own fiefdom of crime, so he picks one of his own underlings at random. His employee hadn't done anything wrong mind you, but the boss made up a story of how the guy was siphoning off some funds for himself. None of the other guys in the organization doubt what the boss is saying...they have no reason to doubt him...and the boss has the guy tortured and at various stages in his torment he had his goons take pictures that later were circulated throughout the city's underground of organized crime as a lesson to others. Man, you talk about being coldhearted. That mobster wins the award for torturing and killing that poor sap just to make a point to rival mobsters."

The commentator nodded, and said, "There is a legend that has been growing of late..."

"You want to know about Lancer," the professor interjected with an all-knowing smirk on his face.

"Yes," the commentator confirmed. "Is Lancer a legend you can confirm or one you will debunk?"

"Well, to begin with, that it is not one I would debunk because I am the one who gave the man in question the name of Lancer."

"Go on," the commentator encouraged him.

"First of all, let me say that when I discuss mobsters publicly or those involved with the underworld of organized crime, I never speak about anyone unless they are deceased. That is why I am still walking around. Lancer is an exception to that rule because he is not actually a member of the organized crime family. The tale, the legend, the myth, or whatever label you wish to put on it is that Lancer has been performing a function of ridding society of organized criminals for decades."

"So, he's a vigilante?"

"In a sense he is but he targets individuals of organized crime only."

"And when you say he's been doing this for decades…"

"Nobody really knows exactly how long; the timeline is part of the legend. Some say it's been going on since the 1920's."

"That would make him…,"

"Yes, quite old, and that's a good example of how the myth has grown over the years, and he makes the killings look like a mob hit with a .22 caliber to the head and so many of the murders are mistaken as mob actions ordered against another mobster. The fact is Lancer began sometime in the sixties. It was in the sixties I first detected rumors which were later backed up with facts that some of the hits on mobsters were not ordered by anyone."

"It's actually quite a good cover," the commentator suggested, "because it's often the case no one in law enforcement ever learns who actually ordered a hit."

"Precisely," the professor concurred.

"Were there any murders attributed to Lancer that you know are not true?"

"Supposedly, one of his targets was Stefano Bonafacio."

"How do you know he wasn't killed by Lancer?"

"All of Lancer's killings are intentionally made to look like the work of organized crime...to a point...but somebody really screwed up if they were trying to link the Bonafacio hit to Lancer."

"How is that?"

"Well, it's true Bonafacio was killed with a .22 caliber and that's Lancer's weapon of choice but it was overkill and that is not the modus operandi of Lancer. Someone pumped several shots into the Bonafacio's mouth, but it was the head shots where the assassin screwed up, and I'm sure it was something the killer was not aware of."

"What is that?"

"The mob is very much into respect. Oh, it's a twisted and perverted form of respect to be sure, but it's there nevertheless."

"How do you mean?"

"Well, when a high echelon mobster such as Bonafacio is slated for a hit, it's very disrespectful to hit him from behind. You see he was shot in the back of the head. The mob would never have hit a man of Bonafacio's stature in that way. They would look upon that as totally disrespectful. In the mind of mobsters, he deserved to get it from the front—-to know it was coming—-not get hit from behind. Lancer knew the ways of the mob. If he had hit Bonafacio, he wouldn't have hit him in the back of the head and he wouldn't have shot him so many times. No sir...the Bonafacio killing was absolutely not a hit by Lancer or the mob."

"Who was it then?"

"It might have been the government, the CIA perhaps who did the hit to keep him from testifying before the Church Committee."

"And all those shots in the mouth?"

"Just the killer's way of trying to make it look like the mob did it with the obvious message that Bonafacio either talked too much or the mob feared that he would talk. I'm sure the killer thought it would be quite believable since he was slated to testify before the

Senate Committee looking into the CIA's attempted hits on Castro. But the intruder screwed up with those shots to the back of the head. It's obvious he wasn't familiar with the mob's code of respect. Probably saw too many Hollywood movies as well. Oh, speaking of Hollywood—-that hit on Mr. Hollywood, Johnny Pistelli, smacked of someone outside the mob as well."

"Why?"

Pistelli was garroted. The mob doesn't like to take people out that way."

"Why is that?"

"Well, for one thing, it takes a helluva lot longer than a bullet, and unless the mob is sending a message with prolonged pain, they don't like to take a lot of time in performing a hit. The more time they take, the better the chances are that they'll be seen or caught. Also, during the entire process the victim is struggling with his arms and legs flailing all around. With garroting, there's a chance the victim will struggle free. Besides, it can be very messy."

"Messy...how could it be messier than a bullet...or a knife?"

The professor's eyebrows rose in bemusement. "With garroting, you're right up against the victim. The mess is when the victim loses control of his bladder and pisses all over the place, including the garrotter."

"Oh," said the commentator somewhat embarrassed and attempting to cover his naiveté.

"Anyway, doing Pistelli is part of the myth that maybe it was the work of Lancer, but garroting isn't Lancer's style, and it's my guess in separating the facts from the myth that the Pistelli hit was not the work of Lancer. Of course, on the other hand, that could be part of Lancer's plan too—-to keep everyone guessing and not pigeonhole him into one solitary modus operandi."

"So, we're really back at square one," the commentator chuckled.

"Perhaps," said the professor, as he smiled revealing his yellowed teeth

"Even if Lancer wasn't responsible for these particular last two murders we have discussed, if Lancer is real, what do you think motivated Lancer to begin killing in the first place?"

"Ah, now that's a question that ranks right up there with the meaning of life," Professor Dorsch laughed, and continued to speak through his cackling, "or in this case the meaning of death. Why is Lancer doing it? If you subscribe to the legend, Lancer has been knocking off gangsters for decades, but the why of it, his reason for risking his life against the most vicious human beings this country has known is anybody's guess."

"Hmm," the commentator moaned under his breath.

"His motive, you see, is part of the myth. You might say the legend of his motive has grown over the years as well."

"Are there any theories?"

"Oh, indeed, there are a few out there. One of the theories is that he lost a loved one, a relative or a close friend, someone who was killed by a mobster, someone who maybe was a witness or perhaps an innocent bystander who was killed by mistake and that knocking off members of organized crime is Lancer's form of vengeance. Another theory goes that he's doing it to rid society of the cancer that preys upon innocent citizens, and that someone he cared about died of a drug overdose. But who the hell knows what his motive might be?"

"What about the Skarbek hit in that Chicago hotel room back '79?"

"What about it?"

"Was it the mob or Lancer?"

"Oh, the mob hit Skarbek. There's no question about that one. Yeah, they made him suffer. Yes, that was definitely the mob."

"Why so sure?"

"Of all the hits ever attributed to Lancer, there was never any torture involved. Generally, it was one shot to the head, sometimes two. Lancer isn't a sadist. He hasn't been doing what's been credited to him because he enjoys it, or wants to inflict pain. It's more like he feels it's his duty."

"Which goes back to the theory he's killing to eliminate an evil scourge from our society."

Trevor Dorsch nodded

"Has anyone ever been contacted by Lancer?"

The professor shook his head, "not anyone who has lived, but I might add..." he abruptly stopped speaking. The professor glanced rapidly around the room...his eyes darting back and forth reminiscent of a trapped animal looking for an escape route. His hands started to shake, and he reached for his glass of water but his hand shook so badly he dropped it...the glass shattering against the floor.

Some other side of the professor's personality had just taken over.

It was about twelve minutes into what was to be a twenty-minute interview and I got the distinct sense Professor Dorsch was more than a bit eccentric as he proceeded to spit at the guy conducting the interview. I watched curiously as right there on live television for everyone to see he spit at the interviewer. Unbelievable! I was sure he would gain some notoriety for doing that. The program ended abruptly and I was intrigued by this fellow. I wondered why he wasn't dead and I did some research.

Professor Dorsch was indeed an eccentric and a somewhat demented individual who spewed forth outlandish theories on various subjects, organized crime being the largest reservoir of his repertoire.

I learned very few believed in his ranting that sometimes bordered on lunacy, but like all theories there was some truth upon which he based his hypotheses. He was an older man. I'd say in his early sixties. As far as I could determine, he was never a teaching PhD. He was a lecturer which for him was nothing more than hustling and signing his latest hardback manuscript at bookstores that he proudly signed for each person who purchased a copy.

I learned all I could about the writings of Trevor Dorsch. I purchased those of his books which were still in print and two others I found at the local library.

When I finished my reading, I then researched and gathered all the personal information I could get on Professor Dorsch. I learned that during one of his other interviews he spit at the commentator, though he missed his target and his spittle whistled past the man's ear. I put that together with the way he acted in the interview I witnessed and deduced Trevor Dorsch was afflicted with a form of depression. I further concluded if he was on medication, he should have his dosage increased.

Nowadays, not all depression is the down in the dumps, I'm-so-sad type of a malady. Much of depression is anger. Additionally, the professor was afflicted with the condition of paranoia—-probably due to the mob being his area of expertise.

In explaining such anger as the professor possesses, psychiatrists would use the all-encompassing label of depression. As psychiatrists explain it, anger is the outward expression of depression while depression is inward. I'm of the opinion the medical community should not lump those two disorders together. Perhaps that's why so many angry people don't get treatment...they don't think they're suffering from depression.

When I saw the professor, it certainly looked to me like he possessed some of that anger categorized under the general description of depression. I decided that when I stalked him, that I wasn't going to take his capture for granted, regardless of his age.

Just like my other targets, I began to follow him. He didn't go out much but I learned the places he dined when he did eat out. Mostly, he walked to eateries close to where he lived and he also visited a nearby bookstore on occasion in the evenings where he relaxed with a cup of coffee and fingered the pages of a potential purchase.

As I watched his every move, several weeks elapsed. On one particularly warm spring evening in Chicago...weather-wise a lovely spring day being a rarity in the second city...the professor exited his apartment. The mild weather brought a lot of people out onto the sidewalks some of whom stopped to enjoy drinks and a snack at sidewalk cafés. The crowds made it quite easy for me to keep close to the professor without being detected, as he walked about three quarters of a mile to a restaurant for dinner.

I went inside and sat at the bar sipping a couple of Pepsi's while munching on an order of barbecued chicken nuggets. When the professor finished dinner, he retraced his steps as he took the same route back. On his way home, he paused to enter the local bookstore near his residence and that's when I made my move.

The bookstore was not particularly crowded, so I moved immediately to the middle of the magazine stand where dozens of periodicals were displayed in three separate aisles. I was in the middle row and I quickly picked up a copy of *Street and Smith's* annual baseball pre-season preview. I really liked the format of the magazine of the statistics and how it broke down the strengths and weaknesses of every team and predicted each teams' finish in the upcoming season. If I hadn't known this magazine so well, I would have picked out another one with which I was quite familiar. It's one of the things you do when you're undercover or following someone as such...be able to speak intelligently about what you're doing at that very moment. That magazine by the way was destined many years later to be bought out by *The Sporting News* who retained the format I liked so much while selling it under their name though eventually it ceased publishing it.

As I perused the magazine, I nonchalantly scanned the coffee area just beyond the magazine shelves and sure enough, there was Trevor Dorsch flipping through a bargain book with two more atop the table. All three of them were history books. From this distance I couldn't make out the names of the authors but I could read the large print of the titles and each of them dealt with European history.

I took the *Street & Smith* magazine, walked over to the counter and purchased a cup of coffee and I then took a seat at a table adjacent to Mr. Dorsch. As I scanned through my magazine and sipped my coffee, I deliberately looked at Mr. Dorsch with a lingering gaze. My purpose was that he would in fact notice me staring at him.

Finally, he did.

"What?" he snapped at me.

"Oh, I'm sorry for staring. It's just that you look very familiar," I commented, and while I had the opening, I made the most of it before he could answer. "I know where I saw you! You were on TV! I saw your interview some time ago about organized crime which is a subject that fascinates me."

"Oh? Well, that's nice he commented," as he looked back at his book.

"I was amazed by what you had to say about organized crime," I said in a bit louder voice.

I could see he was immediately uncomfortable as he glanced around the café, and replied, "I don't really think this is the place...,"

"You were mesmerizing that night, at least to me you were," I complemented him.

"Well, thank you, but...,"

"I'm a bit of a buff on the criminal syndicate myself," I said, as I reeled him in with some bait. "I was...," I began, as I then glanced around the bookstore to feign being worried about someone overhearing our conversation. "I was with the government. I knew twenty years ago what the Church Committee is only now beginning to learn."

"They're just scratching the surface," he replied with confidence and an all-knowing smirk.

"Well, professor...uh...do you mind if I call you professor?" I asked knowing it would flatter him.

"No, that's fine," he replied, as he appeared to be interested now.

I wanted to refer to him as the professor because he has a PHD and that would show due respect, but there is another reason why I wished to address him simply as the professor. It's because I could never bring myself to address him by his title...Doctor Dorsch. It just sounded so nerdy.

He didn't bother to ask me my name. Evidently, he thought me merely a fan but he was interested in what I knew of organized crime as I knew he would be.

"So...uh...what did you do with the government?" he asked, as he flipped through the pages of his book which I could see he wasn't actually reading.

I'm sure I smirked, as I replied, "You wouldn't believe me if I told you."

"Try me," he suggested.

"CIA," I responded without hesitation.

"Yeah, sure," he scoffed.

"Hey, look, I don't care if you believe me or not. You asked; I told you."

"I thought all you CIA guys were really secretive about your identity," he commented.

"Nah, I'm not on foreign soil. I just read and interpret cable traffic."

"In what language is your area of expertise?"

"Ah, very good," I commended him. "It sounds like you know more than just some facts about the mob."

"If one wants to hold himself up as an expert on the mob, nowadays one has to know more than simply the organized crime syndicate. There's overlap," he commented.

I raised my coffee cup as if in a toast, "Good point," I smiled, took a sip of my coffee, and continued.

"I told you who I work with but I'm not going to be able to tell you much more than that," I replied, as being hesitant is much more effective than being eager when setting a trap.

"Well, I won't pretend that I'm not going to try to pump you for information. After all, I am a writer on the crime syndicate."

"Be assured I will ask you some questions myself," I chuckled.

"We can share information; compare notes," he said, as his eyes widened in a silent smile at the idea of new source for his writing.

"Okay, you're on; let's get a real drink."

We walked to a bar down the street and it was then that I fed the professor some information he couldn't possibly have known...no matter what kind of secret contacts he may have developed within organized crime...past or present. I gave the professor something he could actually check out and just enough that would interest him in another conversation. He took the bait.

My reasons for doing so were that I didn't know what kind of contacts this man had within organized crime but he somehow had access and I thought I might be able to avail myself of his expertise one day.

We had another conversation two months later, and then we met again a month after that. Soon, we were meeting every couple of weeks and though I continued to feed him some information, he had long since confirmed in his own mind I was a legitimate source on historical specifics of the mob, though he had no idea who I was, as I never provided him my name.

Over time I provided the professor with names, the hierarchy in several cities, the hangouts of the lower echelon mobsters as well as the locations and methods of several hits. That information along with the professor's separate sources enabled him to make a comfortable living as an expert on organized crime.

Of course, there were subjects on which I did not provide the professor with any information, how I obtained the information and my moonlighting to name a couple, though he suspected something of the kind as it was Trevor Dorsch who christened me with the nickname of Lancer, the anonymous, vengeful killer of mobsters.

The professor and I were destined to meet many times over the next thirty years.

Chapter 53

My quest against mobsters had begun in the mid-sixties when I eliminated those men in Dallas. Without any pretense of false modesty, I must say I accomplished my mission deftly, quietly, and under the stealth of darkness. And perhaps most importantly I accomplished it while remaining anonymous. I was good; I was damn good; I had become an expert at eradicating the evil cancer of the American criminal syndicate. No, not entirely of course, but I made a dent in it.

Other than my experience with those two hoods in the hallway of a Chicago hotel in 1967 which was pure happenstance when I'd gone to visit Skarbek that day, I always limited my targets to a solitary individual. One at a time is a key. Once I settled on my next target, if I found him with someone, I waited until the target was alone.

I never ventured overseas in my endeavors but over those thirty years the cities I visited during my slaying spree read like a travelogue across the continental United States:

Boston
New York City
Newark
Philadelphia
Pittsburgh
Cleveland
Detroit
St. Louis
Kansas City, Missouri
Houston
Reno
Las Vegas

In many of the cities I've mentioned there were multiple executions...and all of them were deserving. You can check them out if you like. They will of course be unsolved homicides and nearly all of them were considered gangland hits by the local authorities.

As I'm sitting here leaning against the Vietnam Memorial recalling my travels and speaking into this tape recorder, I only regret I ran out of years and didn't make it to the West coast.

In addition to patience, persistence played a big role in my success. I did my homework. I studied, researched and visited the favorite restaurants and hangouts of mobsters. I learned their every move. I knew when the bosses in the northern cities became snow birds and ventured south for their winter home and when they returned in late spring.

Often, years would pass between my nighttime adventures and such was the case now as the calendar showed 1998. In what seemed an instant, I was gazing into the mirror at a middle-aged man. The faces in organized crime changed as well. New faces emerge generally every ten to twelve years at the summit of power in each city in America where the crime syndicate operates.

Anthony Gardelli at fifty-two years of age now had reached the pinnacle of power in Chicago and he dealt with Dante Biselli of Detroit and Sergio Rovella of Cleveland in a triumvirate of criminal power. Both Biselli and Rovella were senior in age to Gardelli but there is no regard to seniority when it comes to wielding power in organized crime. As is frequently the case in the history of the Mafia, who is thought of as the next in line is often killed by a younger man's organization.

One night in downtown Chicago, Gardelli entered a bar on East Chicago Avenue just off Michigan Avenue. He turned to his associate in crime, Dante Biselli, with whom he was conducting some business.

"I think you're going to like this place. It's one of my favorite eateries. Back in the old days it had a dress code——coat and tie. That kept the tourists from Michigan Avenue from streaming in here in their blue jeans. Even now it's not bad though."

Biselli gave the place a cursory look and nodded without comment.

"Let's have a seat at the bar, have a drink and relax before we eat," Gardelli suggested.

"Yeah, okay," the Detroit mobster replied, as he glanced around the modest room with a skeptical eye. Only five tables stood in the cramped bar area, of which two were occupied at the moment, while a mere ten barstools stood around the small alcove bar. The diminutive space seemed even smaller because of a low eight-foot ceiling with recessed lighting.

It might be cozy and intimate for the locals Biselli thought but it was a bit claustrophobic for him. It was obvious the owner attempted to make the space appear larger through the use of mirrors, several of which were placed strategically throughout the room.

To the right stood a piano where later in the evening Hal Roach would finger a wide variety of tunes with great skill. To the great pleasure of the thousands of the restaurant's patrons over the years, Hal Roach was destined to be at his regular seat behind the piano for fully thirty-seven years. It was still early now, however, and Mr. Roach and the dinner crowd had not yet arrived.

As Gardelli and Biselli took a seat at the bar, none of the other seats at the bar were occupied.

The bartender approached with a polite smile to greet them.

"Good evening, Mr. Gardelli. It's nice to see you again."

"Ah the curse of being in the service industry," Gardelli scowled, "you have no choice but to say that whether you mean it or not."

The bartender smiled. "Your usual, Mr. Gardelli?"

"Yeah, and I brought a friend along tonight."

The bartender nodded politely acknowledging the new customer, "And what would you like, sir?"

"Scotch rocks."

The bartender nodded again and went to his task of preparing the drinks.

Anthony Gardelli flashed a crooked smile, as he turned toward his guest and related the story of one particular paranoid mobster. "I move around so no one will think I'm a creature of habit and know my comings and goings. There was a colleague of ours in Pittsburgh some years back who was so cautious and fearful about being hit that when he went to a restaurant, he would change tables after eating his salad, and then again after he finished his entrée before dessert arrived. One night his fanatical paranoia actually paid off. A pair of gunmen had been tipped as to the mobster's exact location within the restaurant. Imagine their surprise when the gunmen burst through the door and leveled their guns at the designated table only to find it was empty."

"Yeah, that would give them a jolt alright," said Biselli.

"An even bigger shocker was his bodyguards opened up on the two gunmen and killed them on the spot. When the police conducted interviews with the eyewitnesses among the horrified restaurant patrons, they learned the two deceased gunmen had burst in with their guns drawn. The killings were quickly ruled self-defense; no arrests were made and no charges filed. The Pittsburg boss sat back down at yet another table, and ordered an after-dinner liqueur."

"So, his paranoia paid off," said Biselli.

"For about six months," Gardelli nodded, "until his competitors took up a position outside where he lived and gunned him down on his way out of the house."

"A man's home used to be sacrosanct."

"Yeah, there was a time, but there's no respect anymore," Gardelli lamented. "There are too many people outside the family getting involved in our interests and they don't show the same respect."

While each of the gangsters brought along one of their own personal bodyguards so they could dine in relative security, the bodyguards stood near the front entrance of the bar. Anyone entering would have to pass the two men who looked like oversized doormen. They looked closely at everyone entering and kept a trained eye on the nearby dining room as well.

Biselli noticed mirrored etchings of a large **'E'** on either side of the bar against the back wall, and asked, "What's that stand for?"

"This is 'Eli's...The Place for Steak'. It's noted for great food, the best steaks!"

"Good. I'm hungry tonight."

The bartender brought the drinks and set them down, while Anthony Gardelli flipped a hundred-dollar bill onto the counter and gestured the difference was for him.

"Thank you very much, Mr. Gardelli," he said, as he moved down the bar to the register where he remained to allow Mr. Gardelli some privacy.

Gardelli lifted his drink. "Here's to a very successful association."

"And a very lucrative one," Biselli added.

Gardelli laughed. "Is there any other kind?" he asked, as Gardelli offered Biselli one of his Cubans.

"Thanks, but I've got several of my own," he said, as he reached into his coat and pulled one out.

"Yeah, I guess you would have your own," said Gardelli, referring to his Cuban connections. "Isn't it amazing?" Gardelli asked rhetorically. "That communist Castro is still in power after all these years. It's too bad he went into a communist dictatorship for his life's work," Gardelli chuckled. "He would have been great in our business, and a helluva lot richer."

"What makes you think that he's not in our business?" Biselli asked.

"Well, you would know," Gardelli acknowledged Biselli's unique relationship with the Castro regime as the source providing Castro with small weapons.

Biselli expounded, "I learned a great deal from studying the ways of Salvatore D'Amato over the years, namely, how to grant Castro certain concessions, so I can operate and conduct business with the Cuban regime.

"It's a long way from Detroit," Gardelli commented.

"I have my men in Miami. So, how is our foreign investment doing?" the Detroit boss inquired.

"What? You don't know how rich you've become? How the hell do you think we're doing?" Gardelli asked rhetorically, as he exhaled a large puff of smoke from his stogie.

"The locals aren't troublesome?"

"No," Gardelli chortled. "They've been neutralized with bribes. I guess in your vernacular you could say they've been Castro-ized," he laughed heartily.

"Well, that's certainly good for us," Biselli agreed. "Can you imagine what the old guard like Luciano would think about us and our operation of today?"

"I think our profits are so high he would be overwhelmed and unable to fathom such sums of money," Gardelli replied with great pride.

Biselli nodded in agreement. "By the way, when is Sergio due in?" Biselli asked, referring to the third member of the organized crime triumvirate.

"Later tonight," Gardelli answered.

"Does he still have a lid on everything?"

"Are you kidding?" Gardelli laughed. "Whether it was Nam, Colombia, or Mexico the dumb asses have never caught onto the operation, and we keep it that way by continually changing our drop off and pass-through points."

"Yeah, keep moving them around like on a chess board," Biselli stated.

"You got it. That's one of the keys all right. I learned a lot from the pioneers in our business. I studied their operations. I became a student of their ways. After all, you've got to admire the ones who survived. Some of them lived a long life and made law enforcement look like a bunch of chumps. That's not simply happenstance. There's a reason they were successful. If you want to know how to operate, you study the masters," said Gardelli.

"A guy like Tony Accardo," suggested Biselli.

"Yeah, now there's a name. He was Bonafacio's boss behind the scenes. He retired just before the Apalachin Conference in the late 50's and so he was never tied to the mob. I think he saw that raid coming fairly soon."

"Some say he was the one who tipped police," Biselli noted.

"So the rumor goes. Maybe so, maybe not, but in any event he let the mouth, Bonafacio, be out front."

"That crude son of a bitch, Bonafacio, got what he deserved," commented Biselli. "He was always running his mouth. Arrogance is what did him in. Thought he could keep talking with no consequence."

"That Accardo though," Gardelli shook his head, "he was a genius. He stepped into the background at precisely the right time and became consigliere in 1957. He let Bonafacio make a fool of himself."

"How do you mean?"

"He let Bonafacio attend the Apalachin meeting in '57 in his stead and he was one of those arrested. He let Bonafacio be the guy who was visible to the Feds. The arrogant asshole, Bonafacio, thought he was immune from ever being touched by anyone. He mouthed off and talked too much about things he shouldn't. But rather than hit him, Accardo saw to it that Bonafacio retired. He sent him off to Latin America in the mid '60's. Bonafacio would probably still be alive limping around Latin America with arthritis and bad joints if the Feds hadn't brought him back to testify."

Biselli lifted his glass of brandy. "Here's to the old masters."

A crooked smile crossed Gardelli's face, as he lifted his glass in turn. He would share a toast with his counterpart but he never trusted him and vice versa.

As they finished their drinks, Gardelli asked, "You ready for a great steak dinner?"

"Indeed, I'm starving."

Gardelli signaled the maître d' they were ready and he immediately grabbed a couple of menus and escorted the duo to Mr. Gardelli's table.

"I hope everything will be to your liking this evening, Mr. Gardelli. Please let me know if there is anything you require."

Gardelli nodded and the maître d' returned to his station while each of them ordered another drink before perusing the menu.

When their drinks arrived, it was Gardelli who said, "You know, speaking of the old bosses, from them I learned how to sacrifice shipments for the good of the operation. That's why we give up so much. We have a bigger operation so we must make bigger sacrifices."

Again, Biselli nodded.

"The old timers used to sacrifice one out of every fifteen or twenty shipments so the Feds would think they were doing a good job in shutting down the drug trade. Now they think they're doing an even better job.

"That's why they go to work for the government," Biselli laughed. "They're too stupid to make it in the corporate world, not to mention the absence of balls they would need to make it in our world."

"Yeah, those old timers sure were smart...," Gardelli commented and stopped abruptly as if he were distracted.

Gardelli's eyes moved into an emotionless stare. It was a stare Biselli had never seen before from his colleague. It was the look of a man who had just discovered an underling had done something he shouldn't, something unforgivable.

"What is it?" Biselli asked.

"I was just thinking about Bonafacio" said Gardelli, as he stared at nothing in particular. "I was thinking the old man was able to avoid jail all those years and survive the Feds, only to be the victim of a hit."

Biselli did not mention the Bonafacio hit by accident. He wanted to see Biselli's reaction, but Biselli made no discernible response. He remained silent, as the two syndicate bosses reflected silently upon the old man's demise while their eyes were set upon each other and clearly showed their aversion to one another.

Chapter 54

When Gardelli and Biselli finished dinner at Eli's, they walked leisurely down Michigan Avenue while their bodyguards followed a couple of strides behind them. They walked to a nearby restaurant on Chestnut Avenue which featured a cigar bar upstairs. The two bodyguards sat at an adjacent table and sipped on nothing stronger than a coca cola. The bodyguards were not allowed to drink alcohol while on duty as the bosses wanted their minds sharp and they never dared break that rule. They were watching their bosses' backs, while simultaneously keeping their eyes on the stairway beyond.

That hadn't changed over the years, something the current heads of organized crime had in common with those who had preceded them. They were very cautious as they continued to rely on their paranoia to stay alive.

As Gardelli eyed them, he noted they were in place and sipping soda pop.

"What is it?" Biselli asked. "You look distracted."

"Yeah, I guess the old man is on my mind," said Gardelli, as he continued to stare at the bodyguards.

Finally, Gardelli turned to Biselli, and said, "It reminds me of something with old man Bonafacio a number of years ago. He took some of us out to eat for his birthday celebration. One of the bodyguards that night had a shot of whiskey while he was on duty watching the old man's back. Bonafacio learned of it and had some underlings pour the bodyguard's drink of choice...whiskey...down the guy's throat. They must have poured a gallon into that guy. Before the stuff has a chance to get into his system and kill the guy, the old man orders his men to cut the guy and when the 90-proof whiskey started to pour out, they lit him up. The guy's stomach blew right out of him in a ball of flame.

"I'm glad you didn't tell me that story over dinner," Biselli scoffed.

"What are you getting soft, Biselli?" Gardelli chuckled loudly.

"I'll tell you Bonafacio became more sadistic as he aged. He got what he deserved."

"Who got what they deserved...Bonafacio...or the bodyguard?" Biselli asked for clarification.

"Both of 'em did," Gardelli snarled.

"Hmm," Biselli muttered, as he lit a cigar seemingly unfazed.

"So, what's the topic you want to discuss tomorrow with me and Sergio?"

"Transportation," said Gardelli, seeing no need to be secretive about the upcoming topic.

"What part of it concerns you?"

"We're okay within the U.S. but I want to be sure we keep changing our methods of getting the stuff from overseas. We've got a lot invested in this operation and we need to constantly protect our interests."

"Well, I can certainly see why you didn't want to mention the subject matter over the phone. Any preliminaries you want to discuss now or some things you want me to think about before Sergio arrives?" Biselli asked.

"Now that you mention it, perhaps there is something. How many car dealerships do we have now?"

"Well, that would be...,"

"Just the foreign car dealerships," Gardelli specified, and added, "just those dealerships that import automobiles from overseas."

Biselli nodded in understanding, "I'd say thirty, maybe thirty-five across the country. I could have one of my men tell me for sure. Why?"

"What do you think about bringing the stuff in on those?"

"I'm not following you," Biselli said with a confused look.

"Nobody ever checks the autos we're importing. That's something you can think about...routing the stuff through European and Asian car manufacturers before getting it into the U.S...just the imports, not the autos that are manufactured here."

"Hmm, yeah, I see what you mean now," Biselli mused.

"Give it some thought overnight and you can tell me what you think tomorrow. The stuff wouldn't be brought in solely that way, but I want to have as many avenues available to us as possible."

Biselli nodded, "I get it."

"And while you're thinking about that, consider the logistics and any kind of problems you might foresee if we were to go that route."

"Right, I'll give it some serious consideration."

"Good, because we've got to keep changing our modes of transportation and have the stuff coming into the country in a number of different ways," said Gardelli, as he exhaled a large puff of smoke that swirled upward toward the ceiling where several vents whisked away the smoky cloud.

Chapter 55

Over the years I visited Professor Dorsch often at his home, so one morning at nine o'clock I made another visit. I rang the bell and when he came to door he looked annoyed at being awakened. He usually slept until eleven o'clock after late nights out, which occurred nearly every evening. He was his usual unkempt self...the white stubble on his face now appeared to be several days-worth of growth.

"Oh, it's you. It's been a while," he said through sleepy-eyes.

"Sorry, I thought you'd be up, professor."

"You know I'm semi-retired now. So, what brings you by?"

"I need your help," I replied without being specific.

"No doubt, no doubt," he said, as he swung the door open wider and waved me inside. "You've needed my assistance many times over the years."

As I entered, he directed me toward his modestly furnished living room which was surprisingly clean and dust free. I took a seat on the couch while the professor sat in an easy chair and repeatedly scratched his scalp.

"What time frame you interested in?"

"January 26, 1967."

Trevor's eyebrows arose in slight surprise. "Well, that's certainly specific," he shot back at me, "but do you really expect me to remember a date out of the blue?"

"I'm hoping so with your excellent memory."

Trevor didn't bite on the compliment, but retorted, "You know, I never liked you very much. I think you're obnoxious, so don't try to flatter me. That ain't gonna work."

I smiled weakly.

Trevor Dorsch arose. "Look, before we get started, let me get some coffee perking and fix myself some breakfast," he said, as he headed toward his kitchen.

"Sure, go ahead," I said, as I reflected on what it cost me to get information from the professor...nothing. He never took anything from me except drinks and a steak dinner every once in a while. It was always an ego trip for him. He was content merely to enhance his reputation as an expert on the crime syndicate throughout the U.S. When I asked for information, it stroked his ego...a reconfirmation he was the master of information regarding the mob. Of course, I fed him some information from time to time without charge as well and he never asked how I came by such information.

"You want some breakfast?" he shouted from the kitchen.

"No, thanks. I already ate," I yelled back.

One might think the professor, talking as an expert on organized crime, would have had a very short life span in light of the way the mob deals with people who talk. The professor, however, only spoke in detail about those who were deceased.

One of the things I observed over the years is the professor can get carried away and go more than a bit over the top when he's talking. I learned not to interrupt him when he gets on a roll, because that's when I would get the best information. I'd ask a few questions and once he got going, I'd rarely make any comments. I'd just let him ramble and while he was meandering through various unconnected thoughts there was usually something within his utterings that I could use. Eventually, he would stop on his own and only then would I ask a question if I needed a clarification on something.

The professor brought a plate of eggs and sausage links into the living room along with a pot of coffee. He set the pot and plate on the table, and then went to a china cabinet and pulled out a coffee cup. When he turned around, he saw I had plucked one of the sausage links from his plate and chomped down on it.

"Hey! That's my breakfast! I already asked ya. You said you ate! If I knew you wanted some, I'd have made more."

"I didn't have any meat this morning," I smirked, as I devoured the rest of the sausage link.

Trevor scowled as he sat down. "So, go ahead. What do you want to know?" he asked, as he stuffed large portion of scrambled eggs into his mouth. "Go on, go on," he exhorted, as some egg escaped his mouth, slipped down his chin and he scooped it back in with the palm of his hand.

"Stefano Bonafacio...,"

"That sadistic son of a bitch!" he screamed cutting me off before I could say anything else. "Don't get me started on that fuck! You want me to hurl my breakfast?" he yelled, as bits of eggs sprayed from his mouth which he didn't attempt to retrieve this time.

"You know, he didn't just have people killed. He prolonged their death. He had them tortured, not for hours but for days. He had his henchmen take pictures of his victims at various stages of the gruesome tortures. Yeah, yeah, and then he'd circulate those pictures so everyone would know not to mess with Stefano Bonafacio," yelled Trevor, as he took another bite of his eggs, and continued to speak with his mouth full.

"Bonafacio wasn't just a sadistic bastard...he was arrogant too. He thought he was untouchable; he thought nobody could lay a hand on him, because of his government connections, you know, the CIA, and earlier with his connection to old man Joe Kennedy, and thought he was especially insulated when Joe's kid became President. Bonafacio thought he was above it all, like nothin' could ever happen to him. Toward the end, it was his arrogant mouth that did him in. Just before he was summoned to appear before the Senate Committee on Intelligence, Bonafacio, was talking—-even bragging—-about how he and the CIA teamed up to put the daisies on Castro, and, you know, it's not like they were ever successful in any of their weak-assed attempts to whack Castro."

I didn't bother to interject that the mob hits on Castro were merely a ruse to have the U.S. intelligence community believe the mob was acting on the government's behalf, and I knew he was aware of that. This was one of those times when I let the professor speak without interruption.

"Bonafacio was bragging to anyone who'd listen. Hell, it wasn't even a legit murder attempt by the mob. They were using the Feds and the government was too dumb to know it. What an arrogant asshole he was! He was a fool thinkin' he could go around shooting his mouth off. That committee was nosing around into the CIA's assassination attempts on Castro. You know what they called that committee?"

I knew but I shrugged my shoulders.

"Here's a typical government mouthful for you. They called it The Senate Select Committee to Study Governmental Operations with Respect to Intelligence Activities. That's so typical of those bureaucratic politicians. They always keep running off at the mouth and God forbid they ever limit themselves to a title of a mere two or three words when they can use thirteen instead. Anyway, it came to be known as the Church Committee, because Senator Frank Church of Idaho was its chairman. Thank God the press shortened the name of the Committee."

"So, what happened?" I asked, though I was quite familiar with the committee's work.

"What happened? Where have you been...Mars?" Trevor shot back at me, as he grabbed his coffee cup and slurped some into his mouth.

"I'm stunned you're even asking. What happened? You live in this city; you're a government guy and you don't even know the history of...hell!" he yelled, as he picked up a sausage link with his fingers and shoved it into his mouth, and continued. "He was hit in

June, 1975 and never testified before the Church Committee. You know how he was hit?"

I shook my head feigning ignorance in an effort to prompt Trevor to continue.

The professor shook his head in disbelief as he chewed, gagged slightly, cleared his throat, and continued. "You are pathetic! I can't believe I've been getting any information from you all these years. Bonafacio was hit because of his mouth! You know he was shot six times in the head?" Trevor asked rhetorically. "Yeah, but that wasn't all. He was also shot half a dozen times in his mouth! Don't know which shots occurred first. Depends on how sadistic the shooter was, but do you know why? Do you know why he was shot in the mouth?" he asked, as he gulped down some black coffee, and proceeded to refill his cup.

I stared at Trevor Dorsch without comment, as I gave him a free reign to rave.

"That's the way of the mob. When they eliminate someone, they often send a message. There's a lot Bonafacio could have said to those boys on Capitol Hill and the mob was concerned he might shoot his mouth off. So that's exactly where they shot him—-in the mouth!"

Trevor slurped some more coffee and reached for a dishtowel that he used as a napkin to wipe some of the liquid that had dribbled onto his chin. Having bought Trevor dinner several times in the past I was familiar with the noise he made while eating and drinking. That didn't make it any less disgusting but it was a small price to pay if I could get some usable information.

"And then what happened?" I prodded him.

"What do you mean, then what happened?!" he shouted at the top of his lungs. "How long have you been in this city?" Trevor shook his head again. "What happened was the hit on Bonafacio created a void. Oh, the young Turks vied to fill that void. This one or that one would take over the leadership of the business, but no one lasted.

Hell! One guy who took over after the Bonafacio hit lasted only two months before his body was found in a Chicago garbage dumpster. The void created by Bonafacio's death lasted through 1978," he yelled, as he paused in his tirade to clear his throat again.

I found myself hoping the professor was getting close to the point in his story that I was interested in hearing.

Back in the mid-seventies they were creating lots of 'vacancies' you might say," the professor laughed, and continued, "You know, they hit Pistelli too."

"Yeah, I read that."

"See, Johnny Pistelli was the go-between that connected the CIA to the mob through Bonafacio and Salvatore D'Amato and Carlo Marchetti for the hits on Castro."

Trevor was unaware of the role I played for the CIA in speaking to Johnny Pistelli as I had never told him.

"D'Amato and Marchetti were the biggest players in Cuba. It was ugly what they did to Pistelli. They stuffed him into an oil drum not far from Miami, Florida. The thing of it was, after they garroted him, they couldn't quite fit Pistelli into that oil drum, so they cut off his legs," he said, as he looked coldly into my eyes.

"There are those who say that Pistelli didn't die from the garroting but merely passed out and that he was still alive when they started sawing off his legs before they stuffed his dismembered body into that oil drum. The word is he regained consciousness while they were sawing him into pieces," his face distorted into an ugly expression.

I smiled within myself that the professor didn't remember he obtained that tidbit of information from me.

"Hey! You're not lookin' to reopen the JFK hit, are you?"

I pursed my lips and rolled my eyes in a gesture to signal he was way off base. "Uh, no. I'm not."

"Well, let me tell ya, I know plenty about that! Did you know, for instance...?"

I broke my own rule and quickly interrupted him. "I want to know about drugs."

"Drugs?" the professor repeated in surprise.

"I want to know if drugs were brought into this country after the Bonafacio hit."

Trevor choked and coughed up that last chew of his sausage which spewed into the air, and bits of something escaped through his nose. This time I glanced away.

"After? Hell yeah, drugs were brought into this country after he was hit!" he yelled incredulously. "After! During! Before!" he yelled, "and all this time I thought you were halfway intelligent. When do you think the drugs came in? You think they just suddenly appeared from beneath some little girl's pillow one night, and were compliments of the drug fairy? Of course, drugs were brought in! You have any idea how profitable drugs are for the mob nationwide?"

Before I could feign to venture a guess, he continued, "The money's huge, absolutely enormous! You know the mob makes so much money on cocaine alone that even after all their expenses like payoffs, protection, payroll, and transportation, they could lose 20 out of 25 shipments and still make money! Yeah," he nodded, emphasizing his point. "The government could literally intercept 20 of 25 shipments and it would still be worthwhile for the mob to be in the cocaine business. That's the kind of money we're talkin' about here! Cocaine, heroin, morphine are all enormously profitable. That's why so many people are killed. The money is huge!"

"Whose operation was it back in '67?"

"Whose? It was all of them! Marchetti was responsible for bringing the drugs in. He operated in New Orleans but he owned the Texas-Arizona corridor. That's where it entered the country. He arranged for protection to get the drugs in through Panama and up through Central America. It was in Central America where the makeshift factories converted the stuff into heroin or cocaine depending upon whether they were bringing cocoa or poppies into the country. Then the drugs were transported up through Mexico, into Arizona or Texas through the Sonoran corridor, and on to New Orleans," as he paused to take a gulp of coffee.

"Salvatore D'Amato owned the Florida corridor," he continued. "From New Orleans and Miami, the drugs went overland in automobiles up the East Coast and on to everywhere in the country. Bonafacio was in charge of the Chicago operation which included the entire Midwest.

"Drug trafficking went big-time after we got involved in Vietnam. Yeah, all the way back in the 60's," he said, as he began laughing, "hell even before that, in the fifties, and they used Air America, the CIA's own airline to transport the drugs on flights into Central America. Can you believe it!? Our own CIA was used to transport drugs!"

I knew all of this but it went to the professor's credibility, and I asked, "Why would the CIA do that?"

"Why? Because the CIA was in the mob's pocket...or at least some of them were," he responded, as he gulped some more coffee, and added, "Don't you get it?" he shouted so loud that his face reddened and a vein in his neck protruded in purplish incredulity.

"It was because of the CIA's connection with the mob in trying to hit Castro. And let me tell you, the mob learned their lesson with Castro. They lost hundreds of millions of dollars from their gambling casinos, their prostitution trade, and the drug traffic when Castro took over and shut them down cold. He kicked organized crime out of Cuba. A change of government in Cuba and the mob was out! And let me tell you, they were pissed! You don't lose out on that kind of money without a lot of rage!"

"Hmm," I nodded in agreement to keep him going.

"The U.S. Government backed Castro against the Batista regime and old Uncle Sam didn't learn that Castro was a Marxist until after he took over. And while the government had egg on their face, the mob lost everything they'd developed, millions upon millions of dollars! The mob went absolutely ape shit! They would never make that mistake again. Next time, they'd protect their interests in reverse. Change the government—-keep their interests in tact—-only I'm not talkin' about Cuba. Perceptions! Perceptions! It's all about fuckin' perceptions!"

"What do you mean?" I asked needing a clarification.

"Come on, captain," Trevor chastised me. "You're old enough to remember this. You've certainly got to know the mob is made up of paranoid psychopaths. They have to be paranoid or they wouldn't survive as long as they do. They've got to keep lookin' over their shoulder to see who's making a move against them. Watch their back. Trust no one. You see if they *think* someone is moving in on their territory, they eliminate him. If they *think* someone is going to talk, they shut his mouth and take him out before he can talk. If they *think* someone is a risk or knows too much for their own good, they eliminate him. If they *think* someone is going to shut down their lucrative drug trade, they hit him, and it doesn't matter who the hell he is.

"What do you mean, it doesn't matter who he is?"

"Don't you see? It was all connected—-Cuba, the CIA, Castro, the drug trade of Vietnam. It's all about perceptions and the word was out. It was what the mob thought Kennedy was going to do; they believed they knew because of his pillow talk with that Conroy broad. It was all a set up. They arranged women for Kennedy through the Bonafacio connection. Hell, the Conroy bitch was Bonafacio's mistress! Do you have any idea how bizarre that was? The President of the United States was humping a mobster's mistress! And from her they could have gotten the perception Kennedy was going do something, something they didn't want him to do. Hell, it might not even have been her, because Kennedy himself announced a withdrawal of troops from South Vietnam by the end of 1963. The mob knew they had to act before the '64 elections, even before Christmas of '63, before the first allotment of troops was to come home, because once a withdrawal was put in motion, it would be next to impossible to have the policy reversed. The mob knew JFK couldn't withdraw everyone before the elections. It's hard for people to think of it now in such terms. We have all the knowledge of what happened. Knowing that, we lose the perceptions of the time, the perceptions of the era. It's difficult for people to block out all the history of what they know, hard to block that out of their mind and think back as to what it was like during the Cold War in 1963. A lot of anticommunist feelings back then, an enormous fear about communists and the H bomb. What people forget to take into account now is that if JFK had made a move to get out of Nam *before* the '64 election, then he'd have no chance of being re-elected. He knew that. They'd have said he was soft on communism—-even after his success during the Cuban Missile Crisis—-and he'd have risked losing the election."

The professor paused in his diatribe, as he grabbed the last sausage and gobbled it down quickly while he reached for his coffee cup again and slurped a gulp to wash the barely chewed sausage down his throat.

"But once the '64 election was over, then JFK would have a free hand to do what the mob feared—-pull out of Nam—-and that would have put an end to the mob's poppy supply from Southeast Asia. Castro screwed the mob by kicking them out of Cuba, and the fear of a communist takeover was looming again...of North Vietnam over running South Vietnam.

When you realize all of that, when it all finally sinks in, you see that the mob simply acted before Kennedy did. They weren't about to get screwed in Nam like they took it up the ass in Cuba. It was a thing of beauty really," he glowed, as if admiring what the mob had accomplished, or at least basking in the knowledge that he had figured it out...the reason JFK was assassinated.

The professor smiled widely but had worked himself into such a frenzy that perspiration streamed down the sides of his face and while his heart pounded he inhaled and exhaled several deep breaths.

Chapter 56

Once the professor regained his composure, he placed his coffee cup onto his plate, grabbed the coffee pot with his other hand, he asked, "You sure you don't want any coffee?"

"No, thanks. I'm good."

He nodded and headed for the kitchen and resumed talking as he went. "Hell, all this crap about the mob using Cubans for the hit on the president is just plain bullshit. The mob never would have entrusted a group of disgruntled Cuban exiles for a job of that magnitude. No way! They'd have hired their own guns. And no way in hell they'd have entrusted a total zero like Oswald to assassinate the president. But set him up? And how! They used him royally! He and his rifle were both plants."

I could hear the professor easily enough as the kitchen was in the adjacent room with no door between it and the living room where I was seated.

"An educated guess is each team had a shooter and a spotter. The spotter is really a lookout to be sure no one comes up behind the shooter while the trigger man is concentrating on the target. I have no idea how many teams there were in Dealey Plaza that day but my guess is there were two teams and that neither knew of the other team being there."

As I was listening to Professor Dorsch, my mind momentarily returned to November 22nd.

"Though the teams had separate orders, they were the same orders—-1) hold your fire until after the President's car turned left from Houston Street onto Elm, and 2) be ready to fire immediately when you hear the first shot," Trevor surmised.

My memory of that day was as clear now as it ever was of me sitting in my car in Dallas waiting for my rider to arrive.

"They used a high-powered rifle all right but with a suppressor and the guns were loaded with dumdums to explode upon impact. That's why the authorities never recovered anything from the limousine, just that lone, single round found on a stretcher at Parkland Hospital which was a plant. They were silencer-laden rifles in Dealey Plaza that day but the only shots anyone heard were the ones the mob wanted people to hear—-the three shots fired from a rifle in the Book Depository from Oswald's rifle. Hell, Oswald didn't even fire the damn thing. It was some other asshole that fired from that particular window!"

I remember hearing those shots while I sat in the car and recognizing them as rifle shots. I never told the professor that I knew very well it was another guy who fired the rifle from the Book Depository, nor did I mention that I witnessed the mob arranging for that fellow's demise.

The professor continued. "And none of the real shooters had their weapons sticking out of a window for all to see. They were recessed, inside the window, like all good assassins do when they fire from an open window. It was a setup from start to finish. Just fire the rifle. That's all that had to be done. The mob had already ensured the weapon would be traced to someone who wasn't connected to the mob, but to a patsy who worked in that very building."

From the kitchen I heard the clanking of dish and cup as the professor washed them and then put some items back into the refrigerator. He then resumed, "The Mafia knew the assassination would never be tied to the mob, at least not without also implicating the United States Government, notably the CIA, because then the attempted hits on Castro would have come out. Basically, the mob was free to do whatever they wanted, and so they did, and the government couldn't do Jack Shit about it, because they helped put that killing machine in place. Bonafacio, Pistelli, D'Amato, Marchetti! They were all fuckin' involved in some way shape or form! Pistelli was just a glorified go between but the other three...the commission that gave the go ahead on the hit? Whose idea was it?"

I interrupted here by shouting a question from the living room, "What do you mean, whose idea?"

The professor appeared in the archway to the living room, and explained, "Whenever someone wants something done, one of them presents the idea to the others...to the commission."

The professor then paused and I got the distinct feeling he wanted me to mull that over in my mind for a while. I eyed him silently waiting for him to continue on his own with no prodding from me.

He stared back at me as if he were looking right through me. I got the distinct impression that the professor knew exactly who I was. It was the first time in all these years that I felt that way. Maybe it was because of how he looked at me. His gaze was different somehow. Anyway, my thoughts were confirmed when he quoted out loud from one of his books. "In the brutal world of organized crime in America, there has emerged a tale of a mysterious figure known only as Lancer who has wreaked havoc upon the mob. No governmental official nor any law enforcement agency has given credence or recognition to this tale. Nevertheless, the legendary account of the enigmatic figure has grown steadily with each passing year. Mobsters, who by their very nature live in frightened paranoia in order to survive, have experienced first-hand knowledge when in the darkness they heard *Whispers in the Night* and learned too late the legend of Lancer was not a myth."

Chapter 57

The professor had not looked away for an instant as he continued to stare at me with knowing eyes, and said, "Lancer was the code name the secret service assigned to Kennedy when he was president."

I was taken aback by what he said as I returned his steady stare, but I was not wholly surprised. I don't know how many seconds passed as we continued to eye one another before I broke the silence by asking, "How long have you known?"

He avoided answering directly but asked in return, "How many conversations have we had over the decades?"

I sighed, as I estimated, "over a hundred probably."

"I had a suspicion," said the professor, "and I was about ninety percent sure after our first dozen conversations."

"That's quite astute of you."

"Yeah, well, I've been in this business a long time," he smirked, "but I didn't create the legend of Lancer, I merely christened him with that name and added a touch here and there to the myth."

I nodded my acknowledgment.

"But getting back to the subject at hand, there's an old saying," he continued with a glint in his eyes, "if you want to know who was involved in ordering a series of hits, that is who was on the commission that sanctioned them, and you want to know who presented the idea to the others...,"

"Yeah?" I asked with great anticipation.

"Look to see if any of those on the commission were eliminated. If so, it would be by orders of one of the others on the commission. Bonafacio was one of those who was hit! It wasn't that asshole Pistelli! Both were whacked to shut them up."

I nodded in agreement.

So, who's left?" he asked rhetorically. "Look for the last man standing!" he shouted, as if he were challenging me to name someone.

"All this crap about conspiracy theories of the U.S. military, the CIA, the FBI, the Russians, Castro, or the anti-Castro Cubans is just that—-crap! All these years anyone with any intelligence at all can see the evidence! It's in plain sight for everyone to see it! Fuck! It's all there! Why do you think they sealed so many records? Embarrassing for the public to learn their government was working with the mob to hit Castro. Yeah, Dulles on the Warren Commission certainly steered them away from that."

My line of sight momentarily looked away as I considered what he was saying. I turned back toward the professor as he said, "Come on, you know who did it!"

My face reflected a weak smile but I didn't answer and I guarded against my body language revealing anything. I think I had always known in my gut who was behind it...just never wanted to verbalize it.

"It's very simple," said the professor with a wide grin. "Investigate the cold cases of the Bonafacio and Pistelli hits. Solve those two cases and you learn who snuffed Kennedy. Of course, Oswald was a patsy. The rifle was nothing' but a plant to lead back to Oswald! The bullet left on a stretcher in Parkland Hospital was just to show a link to the rifle. It wasn't exactly a pristine bullet but it was intact. It was all a setup from start to finish. Three shots were heard from Oswald's rifle and no one heard any other shots. What a bunch of morons! Doesn't anyone have a brain? Hasn't anyone got the intelligence to figure rifles can also have silencers mounted on them just like handguns?"

I eyed the professor and nodded.

"And the Ruby hit on Oswald to shut him up! Oh, that was typical mob hit through and through! The mob knows very well how to get people like Ruby to do things for them they would not otherwise do, and that incentive involves a lot of pain."

I looked at the professor through knowing eyes having been there with Ruby as we both witnessed that gruesome death at the incinerator. Ruby was supposed to have hit Oswald the very night of the assassination at the Dallas Police Department but either he couldn't get close enough or he chickened out. I think it was the latter. The mob thought so as well and they picked Ruby up the next day, Saturday.

The day after the assassination I returned to that same abandoned meat packing plant and parked around the far side of the building. I was looking for something...anything in the way of proof of what occurred there the day before.

Shortly after I arrived, however, I heard a car and ducked out of sight behind some empty crates. Two men came in and stoked the incinerator.

It wasn't long before the incinerator was going at full blast that two other men escorted Jack Ruby. The mob boys didn't shoot Ruby in the manner that they wounded the Oswald look alike, but they gagged him, tied his hands and feet and three of them picked him up and walked him toward the fiery inferno.

Ruby knew what was in store for him. He struggled and even through the gag his screams sounded shrill, as the fourth man said, "Jack, you had your chance last night and you passed on it."

Just as they were ready to stuff Jack Ruby into the inferno alive amidst his muffled screams and his futile struggle, the three goons placed him on the floor, loosened his bindings and calmly walked away.

The message the mob was sending to Ruby was as clear as glass.

The professor eyed me with a stupefied look on his face, snarled and shook his head in disbelief. "Ruby did it to save Jackie from having to come back to Dallas to testify," he scoffed, as he mockingly rubbed his eyes as if weeping. "Give me a break! What a load of crap! And people bought that shit!"

I remained silent allowing him to continue uninterrupted.

"Bonafacio and Pistelli were saps!" he laughed, as he mentioned them. "Pistelli's job was to recruit the hit men. Where he got them or how many he recruited is unknown. The point is the shooters never knew who hired them, never knew who was behind the contracts. All they ever knew was they were recruited by Johnny Pistelli," the professor stated, as he eyed me with a cold, dark stare.

"So, Bonafacio and Pistelli were the only links between the shooters and those who put out the contract," I ventured.

The professor nodded solemnly. "Yeah," he whispered. "All that supposition over the decades, the theory the mob couldn't have done it because somebody would have talked, someone arrested over the years would have given up the contract in exchange for a reduced sentence...," he shook his head.

"They couldn't give anyone up. None of them ever knew," I finished his thought.

"And the go-betweens were safe...for a while...until that Senate Committee started investigating. Once they started asking questions, Pistelli and Bonafacio had to go. Yeah, the Kennedy hit was a characteristic mob hit. No mobster ever got caught! No sir! Nobody ever brought to trial for it, which was classic of the mob, no trace. Who hit Kennedy?! Who hit Kennedy?! Morons!"

Abruptly, Trevor Dorsch stopped talking. His eyes darted quickly from side to side like someone who had just realized he might have said too much. For someone who only spoke about the deceased, he was suddenly very anxious. He reached for his pack of cigarettes and put one in his mouth. Nervously, the professor lit a match and his hand shook visibly as he raised it to light his cigarette.

As the professor reflected upon his diatribe, the nicotine surged through his veins and seemingly calmed him as sure as if he'd taken a jolt of bourbon. He desperately searched his immediate memory to determine if he'd mentioned anyone who was still alive, and thus, possibly putting himself in jeopardy.

Finally, he spoke in a nervous, muted whisper, "Hey, I thought you said you weren't lookin' into the JFK hit?"

I stared intensely at Trevor Dorsch but didn't answer him, as he once again reached for his cigarette...his hand trembling markedly.

After all this time, I finally learned what I wanted to know.

Chapter 58

Over the years I learned to wait them out, the mobsters, wait until their guard was down. Wait until they believed they were safe. That was difficult of course due to the fact they were all such paranoid individuals and were very seldom off their guard. Two of them I never could get close enough to make a move against were Marchetti and D'Amato. They were too insulated. Maybe my patience betrayed me in their case but I was too late to be a factor in their demise. Though both died natural deaths, I'm not ashamed to say I took pleasure in their fate. Marchetti took it up the ass and died of colon cancer in 1989. I couldn't have picked anything more fitting for him, while D'Amato died of throat cancer in 1991 and I hope he really gagged on it.

The fact that I didn't get them all didn't bother me. When I began this endeavor, I never thought I could get all of the top dogs. I didn't let that make me rush into trying to get more of them. Patience would continue to be my hallmark.

By 1998, I was still working during the day for the CIA. I was sixty-three years old and being immodest for a moment was still in very good shape. I wasn't able to jump fences anymore because my knees were painful and aching horribly on a regular basis, but I could still move around well enough for my work at night.

No one ever had a clue about what I did during my off hours. Those in the CIA had come and gone over the years and those in charge now had practically no idea who I was. When new supervisors come into a department, they rarely know much about the employees they inherit.

Over the last forty-three years I'd had numerous assignments in several locations and my favorite was Chicago. It's a great city with its restaurants and museums and it's quite a good transportation hub.

It's very easy to get in and out of the Windy city with flights at all hours of the day to practically anywhere you want to go.

I had one more target before I was finished with my night work. It was the man I wounded in a hallway of a sleazy Chicago hotel in 1967, namely Anthony Gardelli. I wanted him; I wanted him badly.

I wondered if Gardelli had any aches and pains over the years due to that bullet I put in his arm in '67. I certainly hoped he at least had some scar tissue that maybe a tendon or ligament rubbed against, though I figured it would only be a minor discomfort. A twinge in the morning when he awoke would be the best I could hope for.

Gardelli was the top mob boss in Chicago. Getting to the top is often tricky and complex for a mobster. Staying there is downright difficult. I knew Gardelli would be formidable so I went to work on devising a plan that would include not only Anthony Gardelli but also his partners in crime—-Dante Biselli of Detroit and Sergio Rovella of Cleveland.

Through the years I purchased additional handguns and high-powered rifles. Most of them were acquired in the late 60's and early 70's. I also had a collection of weapons I *confiscated* over the years from my work by night. Yeah, I had myself quite an arsenal built up, and I took good care of those weapons cleaning them regularly and maintaining them in excellent working order. There was no sense in having any weapons if they weren't in working condition. Despite the fact I almost exclusively used a .22, I certainly didn't want any of the others to jam or misfire at an inopportune time if the occasion arose that I needed to use one of them.

The first thing I did concerning the Gardelli/Biselli/Rovella triumvirate in my next scheme was to drive by the local Telephone Company and take pictures of the company vans. I then purchased a van of the same color and took it to a place that did some work for the Agency from time to time. I told the manager I needed the van to look identical to the pictures I provided him. I could have obtained a work order from the Agency but that would have left a paper trail, so I paid for the work out of my own pocket. The manager didn't ask any questions once I showed him my CIA credentials.

When the van was ready, I took it to a spot I previously surveyed that would be perfectly suited for what I needed. I parked the van by the side of the road and proceeded to splice a dialing device into the telephone line. I opted for the electrical power source because I needed a steady source of power, as I wouldn't be around to recharge or replace batteries.

From that dialing device I ran a hidden line to a nearby tree where I placed a camouflaged non-directional antenna less than 500 meters from Anthony Gardelli's house atop a tree branch, which wasn't visible from the ground below. I had purposely decided against a directional antenna because, though they are more powerful in picking up sounds, they also have to be pointed precisely. Since I was mounting the antenna on a tree limb, I calculated even a slight breeze would throw a directional antenna off.

With the antenna now hooked up to an electrical power source, I created a telephone number that I could dial up at anytime from anywhere in the country. The antenna would always be receiving, and once I dialed the number, I would be able to listen into any conversation that occurred inside the house or on the grounds around the perimeter.

It would be as simple as listening on the phone, and the antenna I planted was capable of picking up as little as a whisper. Mind you, it wasn't a wiretap on his phone, but an antenna that could pick up voices from within the house, whether Gardelli was on the phone or not. It was absolutely irrelevant whether they were talking on the land line or a cellular phone or simply speaking to someone in the house.

When I was finished, I took my van back to the auto place to return it to its original appearance. I planned to drive it to Detroit to the Biselli residence and then on to Cleveland where Rovella lived to repeat the same procedures, as I didn't want to be driving my van on the Interstate Highways with it looking like a telephone company van as that might draw unwanted attention.

Additionally, after I had planted the listening devices, I followed the mob drivers and when they had retired for the night, I planted magnetic GPS locators on their autos.

That sounds simpler than it actually was because I had to re-do my work several times on different autos because the autos were often swept for listening devices. Of all the things I ever attempted in all of my endeavors, what tried my patience the most and proved to be the most frustrating was rigging more than twenty different cars in those three different cities over the years.

It took a couple of years to put things in place a little bit at a time but I finally got everything installed in Chicago, Detroit and Cleveland. I was just about to leave on vacation to pursue my endeavor against organized crime when the Twin Towers in New York were struck.

That was the day America went to DefCon 3. All radio call signs used by the American military were switched to classified call signs and an increase in force readiness occurred immediately. All vacations and leave were cancelled and in addition to the Armed Forces the CIA was immediately placed on high alert.

My plan for the mob bosses would have to wait.

Chapter 59

My job in the Chicago CIA office in the wake of 9/11 was to assist in taking precautionary measures with regards to Chicago's skyscrapers. That day, the Sears Tower, the Hancock Building, and along with the other Chicago high-rise structures were evacuated. By noon Chicago looked like a ghost town in the middle of a workday. It was really quite eerie. Most of what happened that fateful day is clear in everyone's memory, so I won't go into any further details about it.

Once we learned the attack was the work of terrorists, the Agency put the word out asking if anyone knew Arabic. I did not as that was not a language of my expertise.

When the invasion of Afghanistan commenced, I was not involved. Since I didn't speak the language, the higher-ups didn't think I could be of much assistance, but I think the overriding reason was my age. I was kind of bypassed to put it simply. Younger CIA agents were used even though they weren't any more familiar with the language than I was. I'm not referring to the ground operation inside Afghanistan where younger agents in a combat zone necessitates that they are youthful and energetic. I'm referring to every phase of the Afghan operation including command posts, logistics analysts, and all the way down to simple supply clerks filling orders for ammunition, food and water.

I was given no part in any phase of the Afghan operation and I regretted not being a part of it. After all, I am first and foremost an American, but there was a changing of the guard within the CIA.

With the arrival of 2002, I turned sixty-seven years old and was granted the vacation I so much wanted to take.

"So, where are you heading?" my supervisor asked me as he feigned interest the day before I was to leave.

"Oh, I'm flying into Los Angeles and then I'll head up the Coast Highway very slowly so I can enjoy the drive. I've never been on the road up the Pacific Coast and I've heard that it's one of the most breathtaking, scenic drives in America."

"Hmm, sounds good. Wish I was getting out of here for a month. You have a good trip, Narducci."

"Oh, I've been looking forward to it for quite a while," I smiled in my lie because I didn't want him or anyone else to know where I was really heading. I would be driving all right, but I'd actually be heading for Detroit.

I allotted two weeks in the Motor City before driving on to Cleveland for two weeks on the southern bank of Lake Erie. It was to be my last vacation with the Agency. I was going to announce my retirement upon my return. When I arrived back in Chicago, I would be in a position to devote full time to my final venture against organized crime.

Chapter 60

I was staying in a Detroit hotel when I pulled out my cell phone and dialed the number that I used outside Dante Biselli's home. The mechanism kicked on and I was listening when two of his underlings knocked on his office door. Since I only had audio, I surmised Biselli was seated at his desk when the knock at the door came.

Though he was expecting them, Biselli waited for several seconds before answering, as he allowed whoever was at his door to linger and wait for the okay to enter.

The *"I-am-in-charge"* syndrome was ever-present with the Detroit mobster, as it was with all the top bosses.

Biselli reached for one of his thick cigars, snipped off the end, pulled out his lighter and puffed repeatedly on the Cuban. When he was satisfied it was fully alit, he drew in a large waft of smoke and then blew it upward, as if he lit up a victory cigar after a major triumph. The smoke lingered in the air, and the grayish mist hovered over Biselli's head like a crown of malevolence. He took his time as he blew another puff of smoke upwards.

Finally, he responded curtly, "Enter."

His two men opened the door and approached the desk where Dante was seated.

Though I couldn't see them, I knew the underlings. One of the men was Joseph Altobelli. He'd been with the Biselli organization for more than six years carrying out various functions for his boss. The other man was Frank Castiglione. He'd been with Biselli for fully twelve years and had personally performed six killings in that time for the Detroit crime boss. He was one of Biselli's most trusted employees, though the word 'trust' is seldom used in the underworld of mobsters when they are not related by blood...many times not even then as family members can be very untrustworthy...and when they are trusted it is still with one eye always open.

The two men were expected after carrying out their latest assignment, and as usual the two underlings stood motionless in silence before their boss. They did not speak in his presence until they were specifically requested to do so.

Without saying anything to his subordinates, Biselli reached out with his left hand and gestured for one of them to give him something he had requested as part of their instructions. It was Joseph Altobelli who handed his boss several pictures.

Biselli took the pictures and studied the charred features of the victim of a cruel and prolonged torture.

"Blow torch?" Dante asked nonchalantly.

"Yeah," Altobelli answered.

"Did you start on his groin area as I instructed?"

"Yeah, boss. Burned it all off before we went higher, just like you said," Altobelli replied, being very careful to restate to his boss the exact instructions he had received.

"Looks like you did a good job on his face too," Dante observed.

"Yeah, when we got to his face, we started with his eyes."

Slowly he began to nod.

That nod would be the only indication he would offer to his men as approval of their performance. The victim's unpardonable offense that had warranted such a brutal torture was he had skimmed something for himself from the monthly collections.

"How long did he last?"

"We did it slowly, like you said, took him over ninety minutes to die."

Dante Biselli scowled. "That's all? Crap! I was counting on him suffering for hours," he objected. "Next time, maybe you'll be more proficient at prolonging it."

Biselli reached into this pocket, retrieved his lighter and ignited the pictures. As they caught fire, he dropped the shreds of them into his ashtray and watched the remnants of the photographs burn, the flames consuming any trace of evidence.

"That'll be all for now," he said, dismissing them, as he returned to the matter at hand before the interruption...reflecting upon his illicit drug operation.

Like most mobsters who attained a high position in organized crime over the years, Dante Biselli was devoid of any conscience when it came to ordering murders. If he thought it was the best course of action to protect his business interests, he ordered it without hesitation. He never felt remorse, but there was an emotion that crept into his consciousness now, as he sat alone in his study, deep within his own thoughts—-gratefulness.

Biselli smiled widely as he reflected on the events of 9/11 and how since that day nearly all of the government's law enforcement resources were diverted to foiling further terrorist attacks upon the U.S.A.

As a matter of fact, in that split second when one of the fully fueled planes hit one of the towers, some Americans thought they momentarily saw the outlines of the face of evil within the thick black smoke that billowed upward in a fireball. Dante Biselli was one of those who saw it, and, afterwards, as he reflected on the events of that day, he came to believe that Satan himself had reached out from the depths of perdition and granted the mob a free reign to peddle their poisonous, highly profitable drugs.

As the two underlings exited and closed the door, Joseph Altobelli turned to his colleague in crime, and said, "I could use a drink after what we did to that guy."

"What are you getting soft?" Castiglione asked.

Altobelli scoffed at the suggestion.

"I like to hear them scream," said Castiglione. "Their screaming reminds me of the squealing, high-pitched howls of an animal being tortured."

"You torture animals?"

Castiglione eyed his partner with a sickly smirk that evolved into a wide grin as he replied, "Not anymore."

Chapter 61

Later that evening, Joseph Altobelli was numbed from the intoxicating bourbon he swilled earlier in the night. He had dozed off and was sound asleep when he was abruptly awakened. Though groggy, he quickly realized he was in no position to resist as a cold cylinder was pressed against his skull.

He slowly raised his hands while he lay on his side.

Thinking that any sudden movement would be fatal, he lay perfectly still.

He made no attempt to turn and see the identity of the intruder, as he thought that too could prove to be fatal.

"What do you want?" Altobelli asked.

Silence ensued.

"You want money?"

Silence continued.

"Who are you?" Altobelli asked through the lump in his throat, though he didn't expect a truthful answer.

"To you, I'm nothing more than a whisper in the night," as the handgun moved slightly away from the man's temple before firing.

A muted metallic thump sounded as the pistol discharged a single bullet to the brain.

I didn't linger as I headed immediately to my next stop...the residence of Frank Castiglione.

Chapter 62

The next day, while I was heading south from Detroit, I was listening again when one of Biselli's bodyguards came running and knocked on his boss's bedroom door. I could hear the door open hurriedly and forgoing protocol of not entering before being recognized, the underling stormed into the room.

"What the hell!" Biselli uttered in a guttural agitation at the sudden intrusion as he rolled over in bed and quickly grabbed for the semi-automatic that he kept beneath his pillow. Instinctively, he leveled it at the intruder.

"Sorry, Mr. Biselli, but we've got trouble, boss, real trouble."

Biselli's eyes blazed angrily as he aimed his piece at his bodyguard.

"Altobelli and Castiglione were hit last night."

The head of the Detroit branch of organized crime lowered his piece, abruptly sat upright in bed, an evil scowl fixed securely upon his face, his eyes now aflame with anger.

"What the hell do you mean they were hit...how?"

"A .22 caliber up close, head shots to both of them," he specified.

"Where did this happen?"

"At each of their homes while they were asleep," he answered.

"Get the rest of the boys over here right now!" Biselli yelled, fearing his organization was under attack by another arm of organized crime.

"Right away, boss."

Biselli immediately got out of bed and dressed quickly.

"Use the downstairs phone, and don't leave the house," Biselli screamed after his assistant.

Biselli's adrenaline surged, his paranoia kicked in as he became fearful that he might be next on the list. He didn't give a thought to his two employees who'd been murdered.

Chapter 63

One week later in Cleveland Sergio Rovella was lunching alone at a restaurant. He was flanked by two of his bodyguards standing nearby. Suddenly, one of his employees hurriedly approached his table. No one was ever allowed to approach a boss in that manner without being challenged and Rovella's bodyguards on the ready reached inside their coats.

The intruder immediately raised his hands to show the bodyguards he was not a threat, as he shouted, "I've got bad news, boss."

"Put your hands down," Rovella directed him, "and keep your damn voice down."

The man immediately lowered his hands.

"What's the news?"

"Furillo and Reese have been hit!"

Rovella dropped his fork into his plate of eggplant parmesan at the news of losing two of his men.

"How? When?" he asked quickly.

"They were hit last night while they were at home. Both hits were up close...a single .22 caliber to the head to each of them."

Rovella scowled with a stare of utter contempt as though his hatred were directed at the man who brought the news.

"How the fuck do you know?"

"They were both late and didn't call. We called them and when there was no answer, we went to check on each of them."

Rovella heard there were a couple of hits carried out on the Biselli organization in Detroit a week before. Rovella's first impression had been that Biselli himself was just cleaning up some business in his own house in Detroit. Rovella, however, wasn't doing any house cleaning in Cleveland and now he had a couple of his men dead as well.

A series of thoughts raced through Rovella's mind. Did Biselli think Rovella was behind the hits in Detroit? Did Biselli order the two hits in Rovella's organization as payback for the killings in Detroit? Was Biselli making revenge hits in any other town? Or was it only in Cleveland? Rovella knew that a couple of hits in two different organizations were not a random occurrence.

Rovella quickly realized he hadn't heard of anything similar happening in Chicago in Anthony Gardelli's organization. Was Gardelli making a power move? If so, it would be unprecedented and wildly ambitious for Gardelli to think he could simultaneously take control of the operations in Detroit and Cleveland.

"Get in touch with Dante Biselli," he snarled at his underling. "Set up a meet. Tell him it's urgent."

His underling nodded, but as he was about to walk away, Rovella stopped him, "Wait!"

As his man turned back around, Rovella added, "Don't mention anything about what happened here and be sure he doesn't speak to anyone about our meeting. It's got to be absolutely confidential. No one is to know that we're meeting to discuss business and be sure that the place is at a neutral site."

"Uh...,"

"What?" Rovella snarled.

"He may not go along with a meet if he...,"

Rovella screamed, "Just get to it and get it done!"

The man nodded repeatedly without further comment as he hurried away.

Rovella arose from his chair and signaled his bodyguards with a nod of his head he was ready to leave the restaurant. "Make a call," he said to one of them. "Get more men over to my house. Something might be going down."

Chapter 64

After I carried out my mission, I disposed of the van and was back on the road headed to Chicago in a rental car.

I don't know how far I'd driven but the pangs in my stomach informed me it had been a long time since I'd eaten so I pulled into a truck stop on the interstate, went inside and took a seat at the counter. I grabbed a menu that was propped up behind the salt and peppershakers and perused it.

A waitress approached me, and said, "You certainly look happy."

"I do?"

She nodded. "Most folks who come in here are bone tired, dragging from monotonous hours on the road, but you look like the cat that just ate the canary."

I smiled widely as she said that, because just as I had hit two of Biselli's men in Detroit, Rovella in Cleveland wouldn't have learned what had happened in his organization until I was well out of town.

Cleveland isn't all that far from Chicago but I planned on taking a couple of days to drive home. I wasn't in any hurry and I was going to take my time. I'd done what I'd set out to do. Yeah, I was feeling really proud of myself, and I guess that must have showed on my face though I wasn't aware I was smiling when the waitress noticed.

"I guess I'm smiling because I made some plans in my life recently, and two thirds of those plans have worked perfectly."

"Two thirds?" she asked.

"Yeah, you know one step at a time," I replied.

"Oh," she muttered, as if she understood what I was saying.

"I'm heading for Chicago and when I arrive, I will be devoting my time to finishing the final third of my plan."

The waitress nodded though she didn't have a clue what I was referring to, and said, "Hmm, it sounds intriguing."

"Oh, not really, I'm just finishing up some loose ends before I retire completely."

"Oh? What line of work are you in?"

"I'm in the criminal justice system," I didn't mind telling her.

"Oh, that sounds interesting."

I smiled widely. "It's not interesting to those I bring to justice, I can assure you."

"So, what'll you have, happy fellow?"

I glanced back at the menu, and responded, "Well, the meat loaf and mashed potatoes caught my eye. I think I'll have that with a cup of coffee."

"Would you like soup or salad with that?"

"I think I'll have the house salad."

"And what kind of dressing would you like?"

"Make it French," I said, as I returned the menu to its place on the counter.

"I'll put the order in for you and be right back with your coffee."

"Thanks."

I smiled within myself as I continued to consider my final plan. Through the years Anthony Gardelli advanced one rung at a time up the ladder of organized crime and had attained the supreme position of power...the head of the Chicago crime empire. Of course, I didn't know he was ever going to advance that far up the organization, but now that he was at the pinnacle a much lengthier fall would make it even sweeter to me.

The waitress brought my coffee, and said, "Here you go. It was just made. Yours is the first cup out of the pot," she smiled.

"Oh, thank you," I replied, as I immediately reached for the cup and took a sip. She wasn't kidding. The coffee tasted great not only because it was fresh but because it was very welcomed after I had been driving. I don't know why but coffee really tasted great whenever I took a break from a long drive. As I took another sip I reflected upon my plan and decided when I arrived back in Chicago it would be the perfect time for me to use the ace card that I had saved all these years.

Chapter 65

With my surveillance device, I was listening all the way back from Cleveland but I didn't hear anything interesting until a couple of days after I returned to Chicago. Biselli and Rovella agreed to meet at a neutral site in a restaurant in Atlanta. They were to meet two nights hence to discuss the latest happenings in their respective organizations but conspicuously Anthony Gardelli was not included in the conversation or the upcoming meeting.

Something was up so by midafternoon that day I was on a flight to Atlanta.

When I arrived, I checked into a hotel and when I got to my room, I immediately opened my luggage. This time the job of surveillance would require the portability of a battery powered device. I pulled out an earpiece, which included both a built-in antenna and miniaturized battery. The battery would provide up to four hours of power, which would be ample, though I carried spare batteries just in case the dinner and the discussion went well into the night. When I placed the device into my ear, I went to the mirror and took a look. The device appeared to be exactly what it was supposed to look like—-nothing more than a simple hearing aid. At my age that would be very believable and I was betting my life it wouldn't be suspicious.

I then went back to my luggage and pulled out the directional finder. This would enable the antenna enclosed within the earpiece to rotate, which would allow me to hone in on a particular conversation without the necessity of turning my ear toward the desired conversation. I programmed the directional finder to a specific frequency and hooked it up to a small battery. Both the battery and the directional finder would easily fit into the pocket of my jacket without any noticeable bulge.

It was now time to test my apparatus, so I exited the hotel and took a taxi to the Italian restaurant in downtown Atlanta where the meet was scheduled. Though their meeting wasn't slated until the next evening, I wanted to see the layout, and learn how my device operated amidst the many inane conversations that would invariably ensue amongst the restaurant's patrons during the dinner hour. Italian restaurants are generally rather loud...a characteristic the mobsters most certainly understood and used to cover their conversations when they weren't in a private dining area.

When I arrived, I was greeted by the aromatic scent of fresh spices that were mild and not overbearing. That was the mark of a true Italian restaurant...the ingredients were used to enhance the flavor of the food, not overwhelm it.

I immediately noticed the décor, as the walls of the restaurant were covered with wallpaper straight out of an old, Italian villa that depicted weathered masonry worn away from wind and rain that intermittently exposed the red bricks below. The wallpaper also displayed the picturesque scene of wooden shutters swung open at windows with flower boxes arrayed in an assortment of colorful Italian flora.

Momentarily, my thoughts drifted to Italy where I planned to rest and relax as I recharged myself. If things worked out as I hoped, I would soon be strolling along the streets of the eternal city of Rome very soon. If the weather was warm, I would dine at outdoor at a ristorante and savor the exquisite, appetizing Italian cuisine while sampling an array of Italy's fine red wines.

I snapped myself out of my daydream and noticed it was still early, as only about half the tables were occupied. I headed for the large oval bar I determined would be an ideal place for me to sit where I could spot anyone as they entered.

I took a seat and ordered bourbon on the rocks. When my drink was served, I immediately reached into my jacket pocket and went straight to work on the directional finder honing in on several different conversations. The apparatus worked like a charm, as the device picked up very little of the adjoining conversations once I adjusted the directional finder to a specific table. I marveled at the technology.

As a matter of fact, I realized I would be able to listen to Biselli's and Rovella's conversation at the restaurant in my earpiece, and if Anthony Gardelli was at home in Chicago, I could also hold my cell phone to my other ear and listen to him simultaneously if I so desired.

As I looked up, I caught my reflection in the mirror beyond the bar. My face mingled with the bottles of many and varied liquors lined up like sentries ready and waiting to be called into service atop glass shelving. I saw myself grinning between the bottles of spirits...grinning at the remarkable surveillance I had put in place and I knew I'd be ready for tomorrow night.

Chapter 66

The next evening, I was seated at the bar when four bodyguards, a pair from each organization, accompanied the two bosses into the restaurant. One bodyguard from each mobster's organization sat at an adjacent table, while the other two remained at the door to keep watch. I quickly reached into my pocket and adjusted the directional finder toward the table where Biselli and Rovella were seated. I got lucky. They weren't dining in a private room as each of them no doubt thought the more visible they were amongst the public, the less likely a move would be made against them.

It was Sergio Rovella who began. "I heard about the two hits on your organization."

Biselli eyed his colleague across the table without comment.

"What you might not be aware of is two of my men were hit as well."

Dante Biselli looked at his colleague with blank, emotionless eyes. Whether the Detroit crime boss was feigning ignorance with his silence Rovella didn't know.

"Look, we're both protected here," said Rovella, as he gestured toward the bodyguards seated at the next table, "so I want to speak frankly."

Biselli gestured with a wave of his hand for Rovella to do so.

"When I heard about the hits in Detroit, my first thought was you...that you were merely doing some house cleaning, or that someone local was making a move on you. But then when it happened to my people, I'll admit my next thought was that you were behind the hits in my organization."

"Why the hell would I...,"

"I thought maybe you were thinking I was the one who ordered the hits in your organization and it was payback."

"Well, as long as we're speaking frankly," said Biselli, "yeah, I thought it was you."

"Well, it wasn't me and now that each of us has lost two of our men, we have to ask ourselves one question," said Rovella.

"That question being…,"

"Has the same thing happened to Gardelli's operation in Chicago?"

Biselli sat a bit more upright with that remark.

"Have you heard of any hits in the Gardelli organization in the last few days?"

Biselli shook his head slowly in silence.

"Neither have I. Now, in view of what we've experienced, doesn't that seem odd to you?"

"Yeah, that does strike me as odd, but he'd be insane to think he could take over both Detroit and Cleveland simultaneously," Biselli snarled.

"There certainly has been plenty of crazies in our line of work over the decades who thought they could do something similar."

Biselli nodded in acknowledgment. "Yeah, power is like money," he smirked. "Once you've got it, you have an unquenchable thirst to get more of it…no matter how much you have."

"What we need to decide is whether we're going to bend over and take it up the ass or do something about it."

"You have something specific in mind?" Biselli asked.

"As a matter of fact, I do," said Rovella, as he began to outline his thoughts.

I listened intently through my earpiece while I dined on a ribeye steak at the bar, as Biselli and Rovella discussed their situation. When they concluded, I paid my bar bill and as I was exiting the restaurant, I realized I'd been so engrossed in their conversation I'd totally forgotten to dial up my Chicago listening device. I immediately placed the call and to my delight Gardelli was at home...and talking.

The swarthy Chicago boss was speaking with one of his lieutenants after he'd learned through organized crime's grapevine of the hits in Detroit and Cleveland.

"You think there is a war between them, Boss?"

"Maybe, but there is another possibility," thought Gardelli.

"What's that?" his lieutenant asked in anticipation of what his boss would say.

Gardelli, puffing on a thick cigar breathed out a large puff of smoke, and said, "Maybe those hits weren't from either of them," he speculated, as he pulled in another mouthful of smoke and slowly blew it into the out and away from himself.

"Who then?"

"Don't know," he shook his head. "It could be anyone outside their organizations, but if someone else is behind the hits then both Biselli and Rovella will suspect I ordered the hits."

"Why would they suspect you?"

"It goes with the territory—-always suspect the next most powerful man. And there's another reason to suspect me."

"What's that?"

"My organization hasn't been hit."

Gardelli's lieutenant nodded in acknowledgement, "Hmm," he mused, as he considered the situation, and commented, "If they do think you ordered the hits, you think they're going to come after you, Boss."

"Indeed, so I think we'll head them off."

"How do you mean?"

"We'll set up a meet...here in Chicago."

"Don't you think it would be better to meet in a neutral city, you know, they'd be more likely to agree if...,"

"Oh, they'll agree," Gardelli interjected. "Besides, if they do suspect me as being behind the hits, they won't be surprised I want to meet them here. I don't want any time to elapse before we meet. The less time they have to think about the situation the better, so set it up immediately...before the end of the week. Schedule the meet in one of our fine crowded Chicago restaurants to discuss the subject over dinner."

"Okay, you got it, Boss."

Chapter 67

Later that evening, Biselli and Rovella enjoyed an after-dinner drink.

"You mentioned you were concerned about the Afghanistan situation. What's the trouble? Is that advisor we're paying balking?" Biselli asked.

"No, he's still doing his thing as one of the Afghan political advisors bending the pretend president's ear to wean the Afghans off the poppy crop...,"

"And that weaning process is to be stretched out indefinitely if our guy does his advising properly," Biselli commented.

"Yeah, but it seems pressure is mounting from the Europeans to burn the poppy fields. It hasn't happened yet but I'm becoming increasingly more concerned about it. We're paying our advisor a ton of money to advise the Afghan president not to pull the plug on such a financially lucrative enterprise in a poverty-stricken country, because the people wouldn't stand for it," said Rovella."

"Yeah," Biselli bellowed, "and that shit is so easy to cultivate. It thrives with very little water and when people are in poverty, it sure beats the hell out of growing grains!"

"Hell, they've got grandmothers in the field cultivating the stuff because it's so much more profitable than growing crops, and they only get paid a fraction of what it's worth," Rovella noted.

Biselli laughed heartily.

"What's so funny?"

"Just a picture flashing through my head of an old Afghan woman in her burka working on her poppy crop," Biselli chortled.

Rovella chuckled as well but corrected his cohort, "I don't know if they wear those things when they're working in the poppy fields but it is a funny image."

As the laughter subsided, Rovella added, "I've already got the word to our advisor that it's his job to ensure the Afghan president doesn't change his mind. On the off chance that should occur, something very unfortunate could happen to a member of the advisor's family."

Biselli nodded his approval of the intimidation tactic and of the necessity to carry it out if anything changed in Afghanistan.

When Rovella's phone rang, he grabbed it, looked at the caller, and said to Biselli, "It's Gardelli."

Rovella took the call, and put it on speaker. "Yeah," he said into the phone.

"I heard you and Dante were having a meet. I'd like to meet with both you in Chicago as soon as possible. How does tomorrow night sound."

Rovella looked toward Biselli who nodded his okay.

"Yeah, we can do that. When and where?"

"Dinner at seven o'clock at Franco's. It's on Chestnut Street. We'll be very visible dining amongst the people."

Biselli and Rovella eyed each other with skepticism at the thought of a public restaurant would make them feel safe.

"Would you like me to arrange for pickup at the airport?" Gardelli asked, though he knew what the answer would be.

"No, that won't necessary," Rovella smirked.

"We'll meet for dinner then. Franco's on Chestnut," Rovella repeated. "We'll be there at seven o'clock sharp," he said, as he hung up and looked toward his colleague.

Rovella suggested, "We can fly from here together if you like...you and your men, me and my men...all of us on a private plane."

"My pilot flew me down here in a private plane. I'll stay the night in Atlanta and fly directly to Chicago tomorrow."

"Sure, makes no difference to me," said Rovella.

Biselli raised his glass and toasted, "Here's to a successful trip to the Windy City."

As their glasses clinked, unbeknownst to the mobsters, Lancer had listened to every word.

Chapter 68

The next afternoon, a man dressed in coveralls and carrying a tool box reached the top of the stairs leading to the roof. He turned and glanced down the stairway to be sure no one was there. Seeing no one, he quickly proceeded to pick the lock and move through the doorway and onto the roof.

He hunched down and moved to the side of the building overlooking the entrance to Franco's restaurant. He opened his tool box and adeptly assembled his high-powered rifle screwing on the barrel and securing the telescopic site into place.

He was ready now, ready for the minutes to pass into hours until the moment the targets exited and appeared on the sidewalk where they would be exposed. He had no way of knowing how long it might be before the targets appeared. As he hunkered down and stayed out of sight, he reached into his tool box and grabbed his thermos of coffee and one of the sandwiches he'd prepared.

Chapter 69

Michigan Avenue was crowded with shoppers and tourists as were the arterial streets that led to many of the city's fine restaurants. There was abundance of people as over the last couple of days, Chicago's weather had warmed. The mid-March mercury rose into the sixties during the day and lingered in the upper fifties well after sundown. Spring is always a long time in coming to Chicago and everyone was hoping that winter was finally behind them.

When the traffic light at the corner of Michigan and Chestnut changed, a stream of people walked across Chestnut Street. One of them was an old man who was unnoticed within the anonymity of the crowd. He'd been waiting patiently across the street through several changes of the light, and now he moved slowly westward. The old man approached Franco's and entered. He went straight to the bar where he ordered a drink and waited patiently until the time was right for him to make his move.

An anonymous tip by yours truly alerted the authorities to an upcoming meet of three of the most notorious mobsters in America...Anthony Gardelli, Dante Biselli and Sergio Rovella. Not only were the authorities tipped on the meeting at Franco's restaurant, they were also informed the two out of town mobsters would be arriving at the Chicago Executive Airport, formerly known as Palwaukee airport.

The Chicago Executive Airport, located in Wheeling, Illinois became the airport of choice for thousands of flights for executives in their private jet aircraft. Why? Because on the night of March 31, 2003 Mayor Daley abruptly closed Meigs Field on Chicago's lakefront when he unceremoniously ordered private crews under the cloak of darkness to destroy large chunks of the Meigs Field runway.

Mayor Daley wanted the land for a park but he did it under the ruse of 'security' in the wake of the September 11th attacks...despite the fact it was fully a year and a half after those attacks. Thus, Palwaukee airport became the airport of choice for the well-to-do and was soon renamed.

FBI agents were in place and ready to tail Biselli and Rovella when they landed. Agent Evans and O'Donnell of the Chicago office were in one car while a backup team of agents were in another car.

Agent O'Donnell impatiently tapped his fingers, as he asked, "So, if they're meeting at Franco's, why are we sitting out here at the airport?"

"Because even if the tip is legit, plans sometimes change on the fly and we're going to stay with these guys every step of the way," Agent Evans replied.

Rovella's plane arrived first and he waited in his plane for Biselli to arrive. When Biselli arrived thirty minutes later, the two mob bosses exited their planes simultaneously each flanked by a couple of their men.

Agent Evans remarked, "So, the tip was on the money."

A short time later Agent Evans barked into his radio, "They are all in one limousine, two bosses and four of their underlings. Be ready to roll," Agent Evans cautioned.

Chapter 70

Thanks to the second part of the tip the FBI received, Agents Herges and Sanchez moved into place at the building across the street from Franco's restaurant while Agents Evans and O'Donnell tailed the mobsters on the Edens expressway.

Traffic was snarled and barely moving as usual on the Edens as Agent O'Donnell asked, "You ever come in contact with Gardelli over the years?"

Agent Evans nodded, "Yeah. I was in the office when he was brought in once. That must have been twelve, fifteen years ago. It was in connection with a shooting. He was arrested, printed and spent the night in jail before his lawyer got him out."

"What happened then?"

"Nothing. Charges were dropped soon thereafter and as far as I know that night in jail was the only time he's ever been in lockup. It wasn't my case but I was there and I remember the arrogant smirk on his face when they had to let him go. Gardelli knew no one could make anything stick, arrogant asshole. Anyway, I never saw him after that. They got his fingerprints on file, and believe me any time we got finger prints on a murder...even if it was a domestic argument gone lethal...the prints were checked against all those in the database...Gardelli's included. Maybe we'll get him on a gangland hit someday."

"Speaking of gangland hits, you think there's anything to that Lancer monogram?" Agent O'Donnell asked.

"You mean, do I think there really is a Lancer?"

"Well, yeah, I guess that's what I'm wondering."

"Heard a guy talking about him once; they call him the professor. He's supposedly quite knowledgeable regarding organized crime. Can't remember his name off hand but according to him it's been going on for forty years."

"You believe that?" O'Donnell asked.

"Some say it's been going on as long as eighty years."

"No way!"

"Legends and myths certainly do become enlarged as the years pass, but I believe forty years is possible."

"O'Donnell shook his head in disbelief.

"Anyway, this guy said it's upwards of a hundred gangland hits over the forty-year period that he attributes to Lancer."

"Yeah, yeah, and that body count will continue to increase with each passing year as well," O'Donnell scoffed.

"Nobody really knows. I certainly don't," Evans shook his head, "I'd believe a hundred hits in forty years is certainly possible though...if it were true, I mean."

Chapter 71

Across the street from the restaurant, Agents Herges and Sanchez scaled the final flight of stairs and approached the door leading to the rooftop; they found it ajar.

Agent Herges' voice came over the radio in a hushed tone, "We've got a jimmied lock here on the door leading to the rooftop."

"We have a team standing by. I'll contact them for backup," said Agent Evans. "Wait for them before you make a move."

"We'll sit tight."

"And go radio silent from this point forward."

"Copy that," said Herges, as he turned to his partner, "we hunker down here until backup arrives," as he gestured to turn off the radio and Agent Sanchez nodded his agreement.

A few minutes later the limo pulled up to Franco's restaurant while Agent Evans eased his car to the curb half a block behind.

Dante Biselli and Sergio Rovella exited the limo with their bodyguards, entered the restaurant and joined Anthony Gardelli at a table where two of his bodyguards flanked stood alertly on his flanks.

"Took you long enough," Gardelli snapped.

"Took us forty-five minutes to get here with that damn traffic," Rovella complained.

"Fuckin' roadwork," Biselli snarled.

Chapter 72

When the backup team of FBI agents arrived, they moved up the stairs quickly and joined Agents Herges and O'Donnell.

One of the agents said, "There is no fire escape; the elevator is one floor below us so the shooter has to use these stairs to exit."

"Okay, we're going in," Herges whispered, as he and his partner drew their Glocks and Herges cautiously opened the door. Luckily, it did not creak but as they moved onto the roof there wasn't anyone visible from the doorway as the cupola housing the building's ventilation obstructed their view.

Agent Herges silently pointed for Sanchez to head to his right while Herges motioned that he would move around to the left. Herges pumped his palm downward a couple of times to further caution his partner to stay low. Agent Sanchez nodded his confirmation.

Herges then gestured for the backup team to stay by the door.

At a table in Franco's, Gardelli arose, and stated flatly, "Change of plans."

Rovella and Biselli flashed an icy stare at their host.

"Hey, you've got nothing to worry about. You've got your bodyguards same as me. I just like to be on the safe side and keep moving."

"Where now?" Rovella asked.

"What does it matter?" Gardelli scoffed. "You don't know the city, so you wouldn't have a clue if I told you."

"We haven't even ordered a drink yet," said Biselli through his ever-present scowl.

"Don't worry. It's not far and then you can slug down as many drinks as you want," said Gardelli, as he signaled one of his men to contact the driver to bring his car and the limos out front. "The three of us can go in the same limo if it'll make you feel more at ease."

"And we each bring along one of our own men too...in the limo," Rovella specified.

"Yeah," Biselli agreed, "you and your men lead the way when we exit the restaurant, and ours will be behind us...watching our backs."

"Whatever makes you feel at ease," Gardelli smirked.

When Lancer saw the crime-bosses head toward the exit, he arose from his barstool. He paused momentarily as the final two bodyguards entered the revolving door.

Lancer approached the maître d' station where he flashed his CIA identification and said authoritatively, "Don't let anyone else exit. There could be trouble outside."

Chapter 73

The man on the roof peered through his rifle's scope toward Franco's front entrance...his trigger finger at the ready.

Gardelli's two bodyguards in the lead stepped through the revolving door and onto the sidewalk. They scanned the immediate area and motioned to their boss that all was secure.

Gardelli passed through the revolving door followed by Rovella and Biselli with their bodyguards bringing up the rear.

The rifleman inhaled and held his breath to steady his aim and gently squeezed the trigger.

When his rifle didn't fire, he was incredulous. "What the fuck!"

"FBI!" Agent Herges screamed. "Drop your weapon!" as he and Agent O'Donnell had flanked the would-be assassin.

With his rifle inoperative, the man hesitated. His eyes flashed from side to side. He was tempted to reach for his holstered handgun but seeing an agent on either side of him he realized he had no chance. He dropped his rifle and raised his hands.

When nothing occurred outside the restaurant, Rovella made the mistake of glancing upward toward the roof across the street.

Biselli saw him do so and screamed, "Trap!"

Gardelli's bodyguards went for their weapons, but the other bodyguards behind them had already drawn theirs and fired at point blank range dropping both of Gardelli's goons.

As the staccato of gunfire sounded, Agents Evans and O'Donnell ran toward the sound of the guns.

With the bullets flying, the three mob bosses dove to the ground, and the four bodyguards bringing up the rear didn't see the old man. He fired four quick shots that dropped each of the bodyguards to the pavement.

Lancer approached and eyed the three crime bosses coldly as they were sprawled on the pavement though unhurt. Lying on his stomach, Dante Biselli turned over and found he was staring into the barrel of the old man's Glock. A silencer muffled the sound of a projectile that knocked him backwards, the back of his head bouncing violently against the cement sidewalk.

Sergio Rovella had turned over by now and he too looked up with wide-eyed dismay at the old man with the gun. He quickly began to scan his memory in an effort to recognize the old man, but a bullet to his head quickly put an end to him.

Lancer then looked toward Anthony Gardelli, who was shaking with fear as he lay on the sidewalk, and he raised his hand in a gesture for the old man not to shoot him.

"I have something else in store for you, Gardelli," said Lancer, as he fired two final shots.

Gardelli screamed in excruciating pain.

Lancer slipped his weapon inside his coat and spun back through the revolving door.

He approached the maître d' and said, "Call the police."

Lancer then headed toward the rear of the restaurant, walked casually out the back door and into the night.

Agents Evans and O'Donnell holding their identification in one hand, their guns drawn in their other hand, arrived at the restaurant's entrance but no one was left standing.

Chapter 74

It was past midnight when Agent Evans entered the office of Special Agent in Charge of Chicago operations.

He immediately asked, "So, how did it go down?"

"The way we see it the three bosses wanted to meet to discuss the hits on the Rovella and Biselli organizations," said Agent Evans.

"Yeah, we thought there was going to be retaliation for those. I know we got a tip there would be a shooter on the rooftop across the street from Franco's."

"Yes, sir. We captured the sniper before he got a shot off. He's already told us he was hired by Rovella and his targets were Biselli and Gardelli."

His boss shook his head, "Two crime bosses dead and six of their men killed outside a Chicago restaurant. The mayor is going ape shit about this."

"None of them were shot by us," Agent Evans noted. "Someone from inside the restaurant came up behind them. After he was finished with the bodyguards, he eliminated Rovella and Biselli."

The Special Agent in charge shook his head in disgust at the carnage.

"The maître d' told us that prior to the shooting a man approached him with CIA identification and told him not to let anyone exit because there could be trouble outside."

"What man?"

"An old man he told us. Shortly after the shooting, our backup team rushed into the restaurant through the back door, and they said they passed an old man who seemed lost. He asked them where the washroom was as they raced past him."

"You're not saying the shooter was...,"

Evans nodded gravely, "We think so."

"Dammit!"

"Yeah, we were that close to him," Agent Evans lamented.

"I suppose it's too much to hope for that we got lucky and the maître d' saw the guy's name when he flashed his I.D."

"Indeed, he did…Anthony Narducci. We've learned he's CIA alright, recently retired, and we picked up a guy at O'Hare airport."

"Let me guess. He had a one-way plane ticket out of the country."

"Yeah. He was heading to Rio and his passport says his name is Anthony Narducci, but it's forged."

"So, Lancer is Anthony Narducci and he doesn't bother to cover up his real identity."

"Nope. The fellow we arrested said he was hired to take a one-way flight. He was told that when he arrived at his destination, he was free to purchase another one-way ticket back home from the stash of twenty grand he was paid."

"Otherwise, this guy is…?"

"We think he's simply an elderly gentleman on a fixed income that could really use the money."

"And the real Narducci?"

"He's in the wind."

"Well, he's retired so we can track him by where his pension payments go…whether by check or by wire."

Agent Evans shook his head, "He took a lump sum retirement and the account has already been emptied and closed."

"Dammit! Any leads on his whereabouts?"

"Not yet."

As the Special Agent in Charge reflected on the situation, he said, "You know, even if Rovella had lived, how the hell could that asshole have thought he could have gotten away with such a blatant public shootout?"

"Boggles the mind," Agent Evans agreed, "the rooftop shooter would have had to take out not only Gardelli and Biselli but their bodyguards as well."

"You're right and how he would have been able to distinguish Rovella's bodyguards from the others," the Special Agent in Charge shook his head.

"Yeah, but Rovella's biggest oversight was he didn't take Lancer into account," Agent Evans noted without any reservation referring to the mythical figure out loud.

Special Agent in Charge let the comment pass without a challenge, as he asked, "What's the status on Gardelli?"

"Lancer really put the hurt on him...kneecapped him, both knees. Painful as hell but he'll live. Don't know why he hobbled him instead of ending him like the others."

"I know why. It seems a handgun was dropped off anonymously at a police precinct. Their lab boys got finger prints belonging to none other than Anthony Gardelli. They ran ballistics and the bullet was a match to an old homicide case. Captain over there knows we've been after Gardelli for quite some time and he notified us."

"So Narducci, aka Lancer, let Gardelli live so he can be put away," Agent Evans surmised, and asked, "Has the press been briefed yet?"

"Not yet, but when we do, there won't be any mention of Lancer so be sure you and your agents keep that to yourself."

"Understood," Agent Evans nodded his agreement, and added, "Who'd believe it anyway?"

"Well, that'll be all for now. Good job Agent Evans by you and your men."

"Thank you, sir."

As Agent Evans arose to leave, he paused to ask, "Do you have any theory as to why Lancer would let his identity surface?"

"Not a clue," he shook his head, "except...maybe this was it."

"How do you mean?"

"Maybe Lancer is done with it all and whoever fills the void of the crime bosses won't have to worry about hearing whispers in the night...at least not from Lancer anyway.

Chapter 75

I proceeded to make the final entry on my tape recording at the base of the Vietnam Memorial. Finished with my life's story, I pressed the button on the tape recorder. I placed the recorder on the walkway at the base of the Memorial. I'd been speaking for nearly six hours. All in all, I'd filled four separate cassettes, both sides, which I placed atop the recorder. I arose, propped my crutches upside down against the Memorial and casually walked away.

I smiled within myself; confident I would not be apprehended at the airport. Something I learned from the mob through the years was when you're traveling or making reservations you never use your own name. I had an expertly forged passport that I obtained the year before from a skilled forger who I had used several times in the past. I also had several credit cards with my new identity.

Without my crutches I could walk in short spurts without any problem...like at Franco's restaurant. Since the Vietnam Memorial is on the northern side of the National Mall, I merely walked the short distance to Constitution Avenue and hailed a taxi.

I instructed the driver to cross the Potomac and wait for me in the visitor's parking garage as I had to make one last visit to Arlington National Cemetery. As I made the short trek to the eternal flame, I could not help but be moved by row after row of white crosses that covered the cemetery grounds.

When I arrived at JFK's gravesite, I stayed only long enough to say a short prayer. When I concluded, I brushed my hand against the stones of Cape Cod granite, and finished by saying, "Rest in peace, Mr. President."

I returned to the taxi and went immediately to my hotel where my bags were being held after I'd checked out earlier. Then it was onto the airport for a flight that would take me to Rome to begin my rejuvenation process.

The End

Epilogue

Early the next morning in Washington D.C. two workers gathered the various items left at the base of the Vietnam Memorial. It was a chore they performed on a daily basis as they moved slowly along the wall from one end to the other. They placed the items into their wheeled hopper gently and carefully with reverence out of respect for those remembered...and for those remembering.

One of them shook his head, as he said, "What some people leave behind in memory of a loved one."

"Yeah, you can say that again," said the other.

"Look at this. Somebody's left a perfectly good tape recorder, several cassettes and a pair of crutches."

"Well, collect it all for storage...after all, that's what we do."

"Yeah," he agreed. "Maybe someday someone will have time to listen to the cassettes and see if there's anything worthwhile on them."

Postscript

It was nine o'clock in the morning in Italy when I stepped off the plane in Rome. Despite an overnight flight, I felt invigorated, and I was aware that with each passing day my body would continue to revitalize. I planned on spending seven weeks in Italy and scheduled time in different sections of the country...seven days at each location before moving onto the next locale on my itinerary.

In Rome I hired a driver the first day, threw my bags in the trunk and he took me to various sites throughout the city. I asked him to wait and then he'd take me to the next site I wanted to see. With a driver I could manage without my crutches and my first stop was the Colosseum. Constructed nearly two thousand years before, it was crumbling, ravaged by time, wind, and weather as well as pillaged by man. As immense as it stood, less than one third of it survives today, though they have begun some face lifting on the outside of the structure.

When I visited the next site, however, I witnessed the other end of the spectrum...the Pantheon. Also built two thousand years ago but never destroyed by invading armies over the centuries, it awed me when I entered. Its picturesque pristine appearance seemed to me as if the Pantheon had been constructed just yesterday and could stand forever. As I peered upward at the exquisite dome, beams of light streamed through the oculus gently caressing my face as I moved my head slowly back and forth in the healing light.

It was my first day in Italy and I was already beginning to show signs of rejuvenation as the wrinkles upon my face began to fade ever so slightly in the balmy Italian sunshine. Oddly, I sensed eyes upon me...that someone was watching me. The Pantheon had a goodly number of visitors but as I turned and scanned the crowd, I didn't detect anyone watching me. I brushed it off as a bit of nerves after my risky undertaking in Chicago.

In the late afternoon, I said goodbye to my driver and checked into a room in Trastevere. It's a neighborhood located west of the Colosseum across the Tiber River. It's an ideal section of the city to stay because it's removed from the touristy spots. After a shower, I took a short walk and sat down for an evening meal at an elegant setting...the outdoor terrace of VII Coorte which specialized in Sicilian fish and seafood. I arrived before the rush but as more people entered, I noted that many of them were locals...a sure sign of a good ristorante. After a refreshing glass of Prosecco, I ordered dinner and indulged in two glasses of white Sicilian Grillo while enjoying kingfish on potato cream and pioppini mushrooms.

Later, as I enjoyed my desert, I was confident that no one in the neighborhood would observe the subtle changes occurring in me as long as I adhered to my plan of moving each week to another part of Italy.

My week in Rome passed quickly and so, after the seventh day, I hired another driver and headed north to the quaint towns of the Cinque Terra. Upon my arrival, my knees felt seven years younger than when I stepped off the plane in Rome. I continued to feel stiffness in my joints but I was pain free as I walked the craggy, hilly coastline of the Cinque Terra along the scenic shore of the Mediterranean. On the fourth day of my visit, I enjoyed a light lunch in Vernazza and then hiked up the hillside. As I reached the top, nearly seven hundred feet above, Vernazza stood miniaturized below. I was mesmerized by the breathtaking view of the Mediterranean and the old castle that once guarded the harbor. I inhaled deeply and felt the refreshing, salty sea breeze as it caressed my cheeks.

After a week of old town hospitality, tasty seafood dinners, and wonderful views of the coastline, I moved eastward with a different driver across half the width of northern Italy for seven days in and around Milan. Upon my arrival, my features had the appearance of being yet another seven years younger but only I would notice that.

While in Milan, I visited the museum housing Leonardo DaVinci's the *Last Supper* and was thoroughly enthralled by its artistry. It was there I had the sense of being watched once more but again I didn't spot anyone.

From Milan it was only an hour and a half by car with another driver to Lake Como where I rented a room. There I took leisurely morning walks along the lakeshore, sometimes taking a seat and listening to the breeze rustle through the trees. In the afternoons I went rowing on the lake and I could feel the difference in my shoulders from the strain of rowing. Previously, such exercise would have been too painful to experience, but now the steady rowing worked as a rejuvenating balm upon my once aching muscles and joints.

When the seventh day passed, I hired a new driver and continued my journey as I headed east the remaining distance across Italy. I was dropped at a ferry stop where I awaited transport to Venice. You know, when you go to a city such as London or Paris or New York, you visit all the different sites within the cities, but in the case of Venice—-Venice is the site. To say it is a gorgeous city is a woeful understatement.

On my first afternoon I enjoyed a relaxing gondola ride on a canal that passed beneath the famous Bridge of Sighs. Centuries ago, after sentencing, prisoners crossed over the canal on this bridge on their way to prison, and sighed as they experienced their last glimpse of the exquisite beauty of Venice before being locked away.

Later, I boarded a water taxi with no particular destination and simply relaxed cruising the Grand Canal while viewing the strikingly majestic mansions at water's edge. I exited at one of the stops and took a leisurely walk absorbing the atmosphere of Venice. I happened to come across Trattoria Misericordia when dinner time had neared and sat down at an outside table along one of the narrow canals. I dined on Lasagna with Bolognese while sipping a fine Barolo, which some consider the most esteemed Italian red.

My time in Venice passed much too quickly, and I vowed to return one day. As my transformation continued, I hired a different driver and departed the city along the Aegean Sea. I headed southwest for my next week of recuperation and explored the hill towns of Tuscany. I spent every night in a different town, and every evening I sampled a different wine when I dined. The taste of Tuscany was indeed a delight and I found that Tuscan dinners were to be savored and enjoyed ever so slowly. The week in Tuscany relaxed me mentally as well as the restorative aspect of my physical being.

After a week in Tuscany, I hired yet another driver to take me to Naples. After the laid-back relaxation of Tuscan hill towns, I actually welcomed the crowds and the hustle and bustle of Naples. The charm of Naples enchanted me where pastel homes nestled amidst the hills mingled with one another along the coast. It was in Naples where I enjoyed listening to the sounds of Italian musicians performing their melodic tones and it instilled a renewed appreciation for the music of my ancestors.

On several clear nights after sunset, I took a leisurely stroll to the Mediterranean shore and sat down. As I gazed upwards, it wasn't the first time on this journey that I enjoyed the starry magnificence overhead against the black backdrop of the universe.

From Naples I took day trips to scenically beautiful Capri, the island from which Roman Emperor, Tiberius ruled the last ten years of his reign. On one of my trips to Capri I took an excursion to the Blue Grotto where sunlight bounces off the waters and reflects a magnificent blueish hue within a limestone cavern creating an otherworldly surreal atmosphere.

When I returned to Naples in the evening to dine in the old city, that feeling returned to me of my anonymity being in jeopardy.

I could have sworn that I was being followed, but I eventually dismissed that insecurity as being claustrophobic walking amidst the crowded, narrow streets.

When my week in Naples concluded, I proceeded via train on the final leg of my trip—-a return to the Eternal City for my final seven days in Italy. I was now brimming with youthful energy when I stepped off the train for my second stay in Rome. As I exited the station and onto the sidewalk, I was greeted by a brisk wind and brushed my hand through a now full mane of thick brown hair. It was unlikely that I would encounter anyone that had seen me on the first leg of my visit to Rome before the final alterations of my appearance were achieved. If I did, I was confident they would not recognize me after all the changes. I took no chances, however, as I stayed in a different section of the city as I checked into the Hotel Torino just under two miles from the Borghese Gallery. My first night I dined on elevated Roman cuisine at Ai Fienaroli...a charming restaurant with an old-world setting of a brick-vault ceiling and white table cloths.

The remainder of my final week of rest, I dined at a different sidewalk ristorante each night. Every evening the waiters reflected the best of the Italian people. They were ever polite, friendly, and full of life. While I enjoyed a diverse assortment of varying plates of pasta and relished different wines, the final changes within me occurred and my metamorphosis was completed.

I was back where I began—-at twenty years of age fully revitalized, youthful, and ready for my next assignment to be performed during the duration of my next lifetime.

As one of only three entities on earth whose physical being never expired, I, Anthony Abednego Narducci accepted my assignments through the centuries without complaint. As was always the case in the past, a new cover story would be arranged for my early years as an infant and later as a teenager.

When my nearly two months of recuperation in Italy concluded, I would no doubt receive instructions as to my next destination where I would begin my next assignment and would dedicate fifty years of yet another lifetime.

As I was finishing my dinner, a young man suddenly appeared at my table. I looked up at a crooked smirk flashed across his face. He didn't say anything as he took a seat while he reached across the table, grabbed a bread stick and took a bite. The young man was thin with an oval face and his hair was cut short. As he devoured the bread stick, he remained silent with the same crooked smirk. Those long, bony fingers gave him away though they were now attached to youthful hands.

"Trevor Shadrach Dorsch," I spoke the man's name. "I had a feeling several times that I was being followed."

"Anthony Abednego Narducci," he stated my name back to me. "Actually, we are now simply Abednego and Shadrach."

"True enough," I replied.

As I had been rejuvenated, so too had Trevor Shadrach Dorsch. He was transformed back into a young man. Gone was the long stringy hair, now cut short. Gone too was the weathered look of an old man as he was now about the same youthful age as me. Trevor Dorsch, having experienced the same metamorphosis as I had, was also destined to spend yet another lifetime on earth.

"I'll buy you an after-dinner drink," Shadrach offered.

As a waiter approached, I eyed the rejuvenated Mr. Dorsch with a grin, and said, "Okay, but it'll cost you, as I turned my attention to the waiter. "I'll have a glass of Cockburn's Fine Tawny Porto...the twenty-year-old Tawny," and as the waiter nodded, I added, "I don't want it in one of those tiny dessert glasses in which Porto is usually served," I said, as I my grin evolved into a full smile. "Make it a full pour in a standard wine glass."

"Very good, sir," the waiter smiled.

"No wait!"

The waiter spun around, as I said, "On second thought, bring me a whole bottle of the twenty-year-old Tawny Porto...with two glasses...we're going to have a nice long visit to catch up," I smiled.

The waiter grinned, "Very good, sir."

After the waiter departed, a glint came to the eye of Trevor Shadrach Dorsch, as he said coolly, "I happened to be in Cleveland when Biselli and Rovella met there. At one point when Biselli had to use the washroom, Rovella placed a call and arranged a hit. I heard the man say, he'd been in Chicago many times and that he'd actually eaten at Franco's. He said there's a rooftop across the street that would be perfect...said it wasn't a tall building, maybe five floors."

I was quite impressed with what Trevor Shadrach Dorsch was telling me.

"I've known that hit man for several years," he said. "I even know where he lives. You see, you're not the only one with surveillance equipment. So, I went to his place...a bit down the street of course...and later when he got on the road I tailed him. When he stopped for dinner on the road...," the professor's voice trailed off as he flipped a firing pin onto the table.

As I eyed it, I nodded repeatedly, and grinned, "Yeah, I thought you may have had a hand in that."

Notes

From Chapter 7:

"I refuse to believe that I was denied the right to be president on the day I was baptized."

Quoted from several speeches to voters prior to May 10, 1960 West Virginia Democratic presidential primary by John F. Kennedy.

From Chapter 28:

"Let us reexamine our attitude toward the Soviet Union..."

"In the final analysis, our most basic common link is that we all inhabit this small planet; we all breathe the same air; we all cherish our children's future and we are all mortal."

Excerpts from John F. Kennedy's speech to students at American University on June 10, 1963.

From Chapter 28:

"Mr. President, the brother of the President of South Viet-Nam has said that too many American troops are in South Viet-Nam. Could you comment on that, and give us some progress report on what is going on?"

"Yes, I hope we could," the President answered. "We would withdraw troops, any number of troops, any time the government of South Viet-Nam would suggest it. The day after it was suggested, we would have some troops on their way home. That is Number 1. Number 2 is we are hopeful that the situation in South Viet-Nam would permit some withdrawal in any case by the end of the year.... As of today, we would hope we could begin to perhaps do it at the end of the year, but we couldn't make any final judgment at all until we see the course of the struggle the next few months."

Excerpt from Presidential Press conference May 22, 1963

From Chapter 28:

"Today, we are committed to a worldwide struggle to promote and protect the rights of all who wish to be free. And when Americans are sent to Vietnam...we do not ask for whites only. It ought to be possible therefore, for American students of any color to attend any public institution they select without having to be backed up by troops.

"We are confronted primarily with a moral issue. It is as old as the Scriptures and it is as clear as the American Constitution.

"If an American, because his skin is dark, cannot eat lunch in a restaurant open to the public, if he cannot send his children to the best public school available... if, in short, he cannot enjoy the full and free life which all of us want, then who among us would be content to have the color of his skin changed and stand in his place?"

Excerpt from John F. Kennedy's speech to the nation on Civil Rights from the Oval Office on June 11, 1963.

About the Author

In addition to *Whispers in the Night*, Bob has authored full-length novels *Pictures on the Wall*, his initial novel on political courage, and *The Game Begins* about an elusive serial killer. Additionally, he is the author of numerous short stories including the Adventures of Ben and Bob series...the exploits of two modern day knights as they crisscross the globe confronting intrigue and danger in their fight for justice.

Raised in Downers Grove, Illinois, Bob is a graduate of the University of Oklahoma and lives in Glenview, Illinois with his long-time companion, Mary Ellen Conway.